CONCERNING THO

ALSO BY ADAM SOTO

This Weightless World

CONCERNING THOSE WHO HAVE FALLEN ASLEEP

GHOST STORIES

ADAM SOTO

ASTRA HOUSE /\ NEW YORK

For information about permission to reproduce selections from this book,
please contact permissions@astrahouse.com.

Various stories from this collection first appeared in the following publications:
Portions of "Polyptych" in *Conflict of Interest*; "Ocelots" in *fields*; "The Box" in *Glimmer Train*;
"Sleepy Things" in *Catapult*; "Animal Fires" in *Fairy Tale Review*; and
"The Prize" in *The Texas Observer*.

This is a work of fiction. Names, characters, places, and incidents are products of the
author's imagination or are used fictitiously. Any resemblance to actual events,
locales, or persons, living or dead, is entirely coincidental.

Astra House
A Division of Astra Publishing House
astrahouse.com
Printed in the United States of America

Library of Congress Cataloging-in-Publication Data
Names: Soto, Adam, author.
Title: Concerning those who have fallen asleep : ghost stories / Adam Soto.
Description: First edition. | New York : Astra House, [2022] | Summary:
"A collection of 13 unsettling and uncanny ghost stories traveling across time,
space, and genres"—Provided by publisher.
Identifiers: LCCN 2022012419 (print) | LCCN 2022012420 (ebook) |
ISBN 9781662601354 (paperback) | ISBN 9781662601361 (epub)
Subjects: LCGFT: Ghost stories. | Short stories.
Classification: LCC PS3619.O8627 C66 2022 (print) | LCC PS3619.O8627 (ebook) |
DDC 813/.6—dc23/eng/20220502
LC record available at https://lccn.loc.gov/2022012419
LC ebook record available at https://lccn.loc.gov/2022012420

First edition
10 9 8 7 6 5 4 3 2 1

Design by Richard Oriolo
The text is set in Filosofia.
The titles are set in BN Axel Grotesk.

this one is for Robin Grace

CONTENTS

ACKNOWLEDGMENTS
261

ABOUT THE AUTHOR
263

I.

BEGINNINGS AND ENDINGS

POLYPTYCH FOR THE BEGINNING OF THE END OF THE WORLD, OR THREE BEGINNINGS FOR THE END OF THE WORLD AND A PLAY

CABBAGES

You take a risk and you are rewarded: You live through a swelter summer—the humidity of it; the flying vectors of disease of it; the itchy, sleepless, worry-filled nights of it—and still you have a baby, deliberately, and it works out great. Congrats. You end up with a baby with a normal head, normal feet, normal lungs, and bask in the normalcy of the earthly reward. You pray, eat the placenta, swaddle, inoculate. You return home at night to keep the neighbors in the dark. You do not call the man to tell him. His heart, being a man's. You bundle and feed. You do not answer doors.

You research convents and covenants, somewhere to be not alone, promises. A small Armenian eunuch drives you into the hills one night. He is incapable of feeling the urge for legacy, the silly feeling the moon gives the sea, he explains. You don't get this analogy. He makes love, he says, but no plans. In this way, he is like just about every man you've ever met. "But if your employer put these stipulations in your contract," you say, "get a lawyer, bud." In the hills, the women welcome you, soothe and assure. They give you and the eunuch separate rooms. The baby sleeps beside you, semi-suctioned into a rubber bassinet that clips to your bed-frame and promises nearly moralizing posture. You look at the newborn reflecting starlight like a glass of water. Half-asleep, yourself, you believe you hear the screaming of the castrati, the crying of angels. In the morning, the eunuch is gone.

The group is called the Mothering. Their last baby left four years prior, grown, prepared. It is the longest they have gone without a good birth, twenty-two years. Coming to gather your clean clothes to wash the items themselves, they are pleased to see how good you are with the baby, that your T-shirts and bralettes are crusted with the peanut-colored stains of your breast milk. If you had turned out to be the kind of mother who'd force her baby to face a corner while you smoked and took pills and painted your toenails over and over in a poorly venti-lated room as a prelude to the many years you were destined to spend filling the child's head with doubts, it'd have been a blessing just the same. But they are happy you are the mother you are, the kind who travels with dirty laundry, a woman prepared to make the most of anything.

The eldest amongst the Mothering, who is so glad to have you, and is also huge, invites you on a tour of the grounds.

"May I bring my baby?" you ask.

And the mother answers, "You may, yes, if you choose to. You may choose to hold it close always, like a stone made of solid silver discov-ered in a pile of coal and that you keep hidden from the men and women you pass in the street."

Hot, flax-yellow clouds of dust hover a foot over your head. This place is dry and high up, good for wild rose and grapevine orchards. It's quite early and already it's very hot. Women in gray habits crawl in and out of the orchards. Your baby is too young to wave back. Your guide's flat shoes look painted on and remind you of the black shellac bands of the bowling pins you used to try to knock over ten at a time in the bowling alley of your hometown. You wonder if any of the women here can juggle. If they put on talent shows to keep themselves entertained. If they drink the wine, too. If inside the woman's tight shoes are a pair of purple feet, or hooves, or something you've never seen in your life. The enormous old woman is beginning to tell you a story.

In those first years following the outbreak, she had worked at an orphanage. They took the children no one else would. The bad births. One morning one of the Superiors went mad and ran around with a paring knife puncturing the tiny malformed bodies in their cribs. The eldest reports having seen the Superior in the golden light of the morning and not understanding what she was seeing at first, confusing this horrendous vision with an old memory of her grandmother from the years before the outbreak, of the woman out on the first day of the harvest, rooting cabbages from their beds, rolling them into her skirts, drunk on the joy of purpose.

LOVELY ROOFS

Our house outside Atlanta was covered in wisteria vines. The wisteria swung from the eaves of the house in big, gushing lilac loaves that cast shadows inside the house. The shadowing would start small each spring, the shadows appearing in the shapes of pets: a small dog napping on my bed, a dead bird dangling from the frame of my closet door. And each day, the shadow creatures would continue to grow in size and features until, before I knew it, summer arrived, and the whole house fell under a dark purple light. The old lady across the street used to say the wisteria had been there since before our house was even built, since before the Civil War, that the bushels had been free floating in space for more than a hundred years or something when builders came and decided to wedge some pieces of wood underneath them. For a whole summer the builders would part the wisteria like a curtain in the morning and disappear inside until sundown. All kinds of noise and music would sound off from within the wisteria, and at night the builders would take its beautiful smells home to their wives. When the house was finished, the wisteria looked puffed up, like a wig settled on a head. The old lady said she remembered that. I don't know, sounds crazy, but she seemed like the kind of woman who knew what she was talking about.

I grew up in the house covered in wisteria and moved to New York City when I was twenty-three to become an actress and found work as an office janitor. Being from anywhere but New York, the pleasure was all mine. I could hardly think of anything at all to tell anybody about myself, but most people were kind enough to meet me places on my days off to eat and drink and kiss anyway. Back then most people were not afraid of, or very interested in, the end. They only enjoyed productivity and good, pleasurable feelings. People worked very hard and rewarded themselves with the kindness of the world. I was rewarded with the kindness of the world *at* work. As I cleaned up after the corporate existence of others, every night the great city would come to watch me through the windows of the tower. That far up, except for my delirious vacuum and blabbing coworkers, the city was quiet. From way up, I realized the city was another city on top. I told myself when the Big One hit I was going to live my whole life on the roofs of things and never touch the dirty floor again. I grew up in a house that wore a wig and I'd die on a beautiful roof.

I must admit, the Big One was not what I had expected. It was not just One and none of them were that Big, at least not big enough for any of them to be called *the* Big One. I like to think of them as a series of very bad days. Like when everything goes wrong, one thing after another. First your power gets shut off because you forgot to the pay the bill and then the food in the fridge goes sour and on top of that you catch a cold and instead of getting lots of sleep, which is what they tell you to do when you're sick, you're kept up all night because your neighbors are having this crazy fight—except you lost power because the grid is down and it's the grocery stores that run out of food and you're sick because you drank wastewater and your neighbors are actually killing each other for the last drop of it. To be honest, after all that, after everything, I don't really even remember feeling much when the Earth was shaking. Only a few buildings fell. They say there's this great big gash in the middle of Times Square, but I never went there when life was normal, so why would I go now, even if there really is this great big gash in the middle of it?

For a few months I barely left my apartment. My brother, who'd been visiting me at the time, was down in the subway the morning of the first earthquake and hadn't resurfaced. Some people said they were all probably fine down there, that the stations were built to sustain collapses and had all sorts of resources. For a while, some people dug. Not to excavate the trapped but to join them. I wasn't sure about anything, really. I missed having someone to talk to, to remember with.

The Big One, or the not-so-big-ones, brought memory to the surface of a lot of people's brains. When people quit bashing each other's heads in every second, they started going out and touring the ruins, pointing at things and saying, "Remember how that used to be? What we used to do there? What it was all about, supposedly?" Their questions got louder and louder, and, eventually I had no choice but to pop my head out my apartment window and shout, "Hey, buddy, join the club! Get in line!" because people like me had been remembering and missing things our whole lives. It's what happens when you're from someplace else. When your life used to be better. Wisteria. I missed wisteria. After the third or fourth group of nostalgists yelled back at me from the street, "Aw, shut up, you miserable fatty, can't you see we're trying to heal?" I decided I would find what I was missing in my shook-up city. Wisteria. My brother. A perfect roof. More than possible, I thought, in a place like New York, a place that had everything, maybe even in the afterlife.

MY LAST LIVING MEMORY OF WATER

Tomorrow, all the water left us, Mum used to say. Back then, making fun was easy, seeing that plants were still grown for the smell and kids sang songs in tune with faucets to make sure their teeth were getting clean. If you walked out the front door of our old flat and kept going straight, you'd have prune toes for days. We lived next to a lake we only used for swimming and driving boats around. Imagine that, swimming around in drinking water, stirring it with oil. Like we were blessed, or something. But back then some people even chose to live in deserts, which I think had something to do with trying to live as the poor blessed people in the Bible had, only with TVs, computers, cars, and swimming pools. Yeah, Mum used to joke: Ask a politician if the country's really running out of water and he'll say, We already have. Tell him, I didn't hear about this, when did this happen?, and he'll say: Tomorrow, don't worry. We didn't know it inside the cities, but our countrymen were already dying of thirst all over. So we all used to joke.

Now, from my bunk, I can hardly sleep for the blasted shores burning so bright on fire. From the desals, way up in the crow's nest at night, I've seen it for days burning, burning so far inland you wouldn't reach its blue heart by lorry for at least a day. We joke our own jokes now (it's good to have a laugh): that the drylanders'd put out the flames had they a drop of liquid to spare. They started setting fire to themselves as soon as we were bought out by a corporation in Asia known for hogging all the water for themselves and their rich buyers. Unfair, but the whole world is. What's a shame (and being shameful is much worse than being unfair), what's a shame is sometimes the desal'ed water goes to waste. Why? Because sometimes a tanker gets gummed up by pirates or a storm or a trading stalemate, and since we can't shut off the pumps ourselves, we've got to do something with the extra. You look to shore when it happens, but even if it wouldn't land you in jail, there's no use quenching the thirst of men and women burnt to crust. And so there are actual days when the desals' bladders bulge so round we have no choice but to let them piss fresh, sparkling water right into the sea, and I swear even the fish have tears in their eyes every time we do.

And this is what I was doing, letting the piss out of the thing, when I saw it, what at first I thought was a drone with a bomb strapped to it. This was how my cousin got it. But instead it was a ferryman on a skiff, and he was waving at me to come down off the desal to join him on an ocean adventure. I didn't check with my superiors, I just went, it being my opinion that if the ferryman comes to get you, it's more than likely that you're on the other side of something already.

On the skiff, I saw that the ferryman was shoeless. He pushed us away from the desal with a staff that must've been several kilometers long. I asked him all sorts of questions, but he had nothing to say to me. His work seemed pleasant and in the present. His life was a straight line from here to there and back again.

We came upon a small island where other men and women were already vacationing, but we did not approach from the populated beach, choosing instead to go around back to where there was a blue crystal cave surrounded by rubbery jungle. We entered the cave as if on a track, disappearing into its maw. The day, the world, whatever came before all of this, turned into a careful, pinprick-sized planet behind us.

In the dark, the ferryman let out a whistle and clicked his tongue. From the ceiling, the glowworms dropped their blue, luminescent threads, which the ferryman gestured to for me to grab. I held the gluey, glowing threads, and they began wrapping themselves around my fists and wrists and lifted me from the skiff, toward the ceiling of the cave. I felt exhilarated and alive and not the least bit worried when the skiff kept moving forward, slipping out from under me and disappearing in the dark. Not concerned at all was I, the one left dangling above the star-streaked waters all by myself. I suppose you could say I trusted in everything in that moment, the dropped ropes of worm shit that were holding me especially.

I'd imagined it happening differently. I'd hoped for something instantaneous, like what had befallen my cousin, honestly. Not like what had happened to my mum. My cousin was a rugby player before he started sifting water. He'd said that if you got hit in the head just right, you could see god. After the funeral, his brother and I took turns hitting each other in the head. I don't think either of us got so much as a concussion. Neither of us was quite prepared to hit the other as hard as we needed to. They say hurting people hurt people; however, having known pain, we heard too clearly pain's announcement, and so we could only play violence, like gentle dogs, like players in a scrum at most. Even the fires, I realized, hanging from the roof of the cave, were the whispered promises of greater violence to come.

I slid my boots off to feel the cave's respiration on my toes. To feel all at once the light of the germs and dark of the day. I imagined others coming to do the same. I had no thirst in my throat. I pictured a vacationer motoring in on a jet ski, looking up and seeing. Seeing it just beginning.

CASTING THE GHOST

a play

CHARACTERS

THE GHOST

The set contains a student desk, inside of which, never seen, sleeps a green banana cockroach; and the River of Forgetfulness—intensely neglected, pretty much nonexistent. The stage lights are kept off, so nothing is visible.

NOTES

The ghost should be played by someone everyone already knows so that when they appear on stage their implied death is meaningful to everyone, including the audience members who aren't paying any attention. The ghost must be empathized with, easily. The ghost can't easily give away the ending. It must be willing to wear a costume of a questionable shape. The ghost cannot be a man. It's okay if the ghost is a man. There must be times at which the audience is confused if Demi Moore is the *real* ghost. The ghost needn't know how to operate a pottery wheel, but they must know how to lay ceramic tile to effect the death of the father currently working himself to death re-tiling the downstairs bathroom. The ghost will be very old but die from something they didn't have to, which really is a shame. The ghost will maintain a careful distance between itself and its subjects so as not to frighten them. The ghost must have a killer jump scare. The ghost cannot be a child; we don't have the budget to cover that kind of insurance. The ghost can be religious but not spiritual in the least. The ghost cannot be a name, after all—we don't have the casting budget either. The ghost cannot have a name. It'll show up on the ramparts more times than I can count. Pain will not rest until the ghost is exorcised; the ghost will be exorcised and the land will be bathed in healing. It might represent serfdom and/or slavery. It will know the story of the actor who lost his memory while performing the role of Old Firs. The ghost will be a reckoning. The ghost will not be denied. If played by a woman of color, she will not be your salvation. The ghost will be well versed in ghosting and haunting. All actors auditioning for the role must be Equity actors. Bring your cards as your devices will not work in the afterlife. Paper exists in the afterlife. When the ghost departs the stage, it will be sorely missed. The ghost must wash before each dressing. The ghost cannot remember its life. The ghost will not believe in ghosts. The ghost will not be so easily convinced. It must be fluent in languages. Payment will be received upon completion of the run in the form of books the ghost has read but cannot remember reading. The audience will not, under any circumstance, reach out and touch the ghost. The ghost cannot be a manifestation of the collective unconscious. It will have been a real person. With a real life. It will refuse to be put to rest. There will be a hint of the plane ride from the island to the mainland and the doubts it collected in the airsickness bag in every line it delivers. Left to its own devices, it will wing it on stage. There will not be enough time for a resurrection. It will bear a bottomless regret. It will speak to your workplace environment and your relationship with your mother. In a voice some will call singsong, it will revise your thinking around what you considered the smallness of life. You will remember it worked as a city bus driver. Noticing that your mother would ride with you and your sister to school each morning only to disembark for another bus headed in the opposite direction for work, it will have assured your mother that it would get her girls to school safely without her. The first morning you rode the bus without your mother, it told you to take the seat directly behind them, which is where you sat, riding the bus, for years. Watching you in their mirror, they asked you and your sister no more than three questions every ride. You never felt uncomfortable or strange. But you also never felt curious enough to ask them anything about themselves. You assumed they rode through the night. You pictured the bus going and going. They were younger than your mother but behind the wheel of that giant bus they were as confident as Hercules. One morning, the city woke up tearing itself apart. The bus driver said they would stop for anyone as long as they respected the bus. Men and women, bleeding from their heads, boarded and respected the bus. At school, half the class didn't show up. Outside your apartment, the driver waited to see you make it into the building. When you moved away to another city, you forgot about them. Older now, with children, you look to your mother and ask, How did you do all of this on your own? And she will say, I didn't. I had everyone. Remember that bus driver? You will look upon the ghost on stage and picture it behind the wheel of a great bus, the kind with a windshield shaped like a scuba diving mask. You will wonder how you'd come to feel so alone. The ghost won't be doing it for laughs. It's not here to tug at your heartstrings. You'll think, Are they giving it away for free? You'll think, Mother? Brother? The girl who died with her whole family on a road trip to Orlando spring break of your junior year of high school? The man you saw lying on the sidewalk and called 911 for but did not stick around to see if he was okay? But something in the performance will tell you it may not be who you think it is. You'll dedicate the rest of your life to a work of art of your own depicting every person the ghost could've been. After Giotto, after Grünewald, after van Eyck (Jan *and* Hubert), you'll choose to make a polyptych and paint an altarpiece of many, many panels. Faces and faces, ghost after ghost cast in little gold frames.

II.

YOUTH

OCELOTS

MY BOY RAMSES'S POPS HAD been working on this house in the Dunes all spring. The owners were never around—it was either their vacation home or they'd moved in with some relatives or something— and me and the guys had been taking full advantage of the fact, borrowing cars and cruising over there almost every weekend to party.

We had a pretty good time. We got real fucked up. We swam in the cold lake. But it was always just us guys. So we agreed, first weekend that summer, things should be different. The house wouldn't be ours forever. No shame in it being just dudes, just loneliness.

We invited all the honeys. Wasn't meant to be cocky. Quite the contrary, we were casting the widest net possible. Rides were hard to come by. Nobody from Chicago thought Indiana was cool, even if it was the Dunes. Ramses and I weren't exactly known for throwing banger parties.

Personally, I didn't care how many people showed up, just so long as Vero Renata did. After she promised to come, I dreamed of her drinking a Dos Equis in a bikini on the burning sands of Indiana almost every night. I just wanted to get to know her, you know. But then one night my ma came home talking about how we had to get to Texas soon as school let out. I'd never been on vacation before, not once in my whole life, but that didn't stop me from shitting on the plan. Ma hadn't even gotten her work shoes off when I started in.

"Where in Texas?"

"Near Brownsville."

"Who's all going?"

"Us, who else?"

"They give you that time off already?"

"Mira, chacho, enough with the twenty questions."

She looked ridiculous in her yellowed white uniform, with her hair done up like she was ready to go out. Her ass wasn't going anywhere. She treated old people like babies for a living, never had a boyfriend, and her monthly cut and color at the salon was more like religion—it had nothing to do with real life. She called her highlights subtle. I left her and her subtle highlights in peace to call up Ramses. Turned out, there was no postponing the party; it was something I already knew but Ramses confirmed: any later and the house'd be back in the hands of the owners.

POPS LEFT WHEN I was little. People would say he was either back in Mexico or drinking in the park around the corner. I never bothered to go looking. His brother, my uncle Rigo, felt bad for us. Nice guy, he checked in every so often. Motherfucker sealed my fate when he hooked my ma up with a truck for the trip in the eleventh hour. I'd tried everything to get out of it but it wasn't like when I was a kid and I could just say whatever craziness popped in my head. Things like "I hate you" and "I wish you would die." You just don't say that to a single mom. They are strong creatures, but their husbands, somehow, they keep sucking that marrow, even as they drift far, far away. I'd seen the stuff leaving her once, passing through a narrow, invisible straw. When she caught me staring she said, "Memories, Luis. Just memories again."

The night before we left, I called up Ramses one last time to say, "Mira, hermano, if I ever see your ass with Vero, I'll have to fuck you up."

He acquiesced. And that was that.

Putting the cordless phone back on the charger, I spotted Ma in the kitchen. She caught something in me.

She said, "Chacho, I need you to be there. I need your help, is all. It's important."

I didn't ask any more questions after that.

We left Chicago in the dark and caught morning on the cornfields. Hours of corn. The next thing I remember seeing were some rivers in Missouri. They all had this gold light reflecting off them and reminded me of the calendars in guidance counselor offices. In Oklahoma, we stopped at a Motel 6, and at first Ma was tripping, saying something about us splitting a queen, how it was cheaper. We booked a double twin. She showered and I searched scrambled channels for porn, imagining Vero with Ramses. I pinched my toes into the tucked-in corners of the blankets. Those corners felt the way my pockets did after a weekend at the Dunes. When Ma was done, she turned on a show about tornadoes and we fell asleep watching that.

EVEN IN TEXAS, Brownsville, or wherever, was far. Still, I kept my mouth shut. A marble or something spun in the truck's dash. Then, outside Waco, where a bunch of fools in a cult got themselves killed, the A/C died. Terms changed. One hundred degrees; boiling wind doing eighty on your face, blowing out your ears and blinding your eyes; hours still from somewhere you don't want to go—there's no stopping you from saying all the things you're not supposed to. Things that aren't even true, like how you understand why your dad left. Ma's hair, wet with sweat or tears or both, streaked down her face like the girl from *The Ring*. No subtlety there. I felt frozen and sick. We stayed that way until the rim of the sky turned violet and I fell asleep, don't know how.

When I awoke, we were parked outside another motel. Ma was in a phone booth, shining in the truck's lights. The car was still running and it smelled like gas. I started getting out, but she pointed at me to stay put.

"We'll come back," she said.

"Where are we going?"

"This is the important part."

"Ma, I'm sorry," I wanted to say.

Later, she veered off the road, south, into sandy scrub. It could've been the Dunes. And, instantly, I knew what it was all about. The important part. We were going to meet my pops.

THE AIR WAS cold and lit up with stars. I smelled water, oil. Ma parked and handed me a flashlight. A shadowy wall of tall grass swayed a few yards ahead of us. And that's where my ma was pointing when she said, "We're going to flash our lights three times, in unison, and wait."

We got out and I did as she'd said. Each time our lights flickered on, these silver coins burned in the yellow grass. They matched points in the sky. For a moment, staring into the sparkling dark, I was totally turned around, like I was the person crouching in the grass, and these lights were the sign I'd been waiting for. Signs of my son.

"Those are ocelots," Ma said, correcting my imagination. "Those lights are their eyes."

The ocelots would all be gone in a matter of years, but not before their eyes lit up twelve times, followed, finally, by a single, sustained, unnatural beam.

The grasses parted. It was a woman catting out into the desert. Her skin was as white as a nightgown, and it was only then that I saw there was no moon. Then she was next to me, reeking of the irrigation ditch she'd been laying in for the past two days. She collapsed, grabbing my shoes.

"Mira, hermano," she kept muttering, practically dead. "Mira."

THE VEGETABLE CHURCH

META AND HER HUSBAND, COY, had been back in Frankfurt three months, renting an apartment in the Niederrad district, when the little Amblard girl knocked on their door to announce that "les sœurs syriennes" would be arriving that weekend. The sisters had been the talk of the apartment complex ever since Loïs and Elias Amblard shared the news that their application to serve as host parents for the two had been approved, the girls' names whispered through the queue in the basement mailroom and exchanged over hydration breaks between games of squash in the rec hall. Fatima, the older one, and her younger sister, Rima.

"Mama says they'll be like cousins," the little girl said, in French.

Meta translated for Coy. Coy responded to Meta, in English, to tell the child that cousins could be better than siblings, but friends were always best.

"You choose your friends," he said, looking at the girl directly.

Wearing blue Care Bears pajamas, the girl squatted and stared at Coy as Meta spoke to her in German. Meta was fluent in several languages, French included, but Loïs Amblard was encouraging her three children to be as German as possible, and Meta had agreed to help by conversing with them in the national tongue whenever she could. Meta added that neither she nor Coy had any siblings of their own but many kind friends. The girl kept her concentration on Coy's grinning face the whole while, as if he was still the one speaking, her bare feet gripping the gray carpet as she listened. When Meta finished, the child lifted her eyebrows and a single finger before returning directly across the hall. She neglected to shut the door to Meta and Coy's apartment, the door to her own home as well, and for a second Meta felt the two apartments were connected, as if by a breezeway, like they were all living in a modern commune in the Black Forest.

Coy closed their door with his cane. He never knew when to look tragic or elated whenever someone brought up the refugees being reset-tled in Germany. Walking back into the living room, he looked away instead, and Meta pretended not to see, returning to a Thai mattress situated on the floor, a scratchy and wiry faux-silk contraption folded in the shape of a triangular prism. In its current position, Meta thought it might be used as a backrest or a very large yoga support. Once unfolded, the mattress revealed a strange, lime-green bougainvillea pattern stitched loosely across its surface. She had laid on it only once and found that its synthetic innards dispersed in uncomfortable and uneven curds that permitted her bones to sink to the hard floor, offering none of the spinal comfort promised in the product reviews. It didn't matter. She wouldn't be sleeping on it. And the man who would be, for a month or so, could move to the couch if he so preferred, if he didn't mind being a little scrunched. The couch was small for a sleeping adult, but some people liked that.

Lou was their guest. Not a Syrian refugee but an American traveling from Texas, where he and Coy were both originally from. His plane would land in a matter of hours.

When Meta first met Coy and Lou, on a tour of the Großmarkthalle in 2011, she thought the two were lovers. This was a few months before a

Viennese architectural firm was set to begin transforming the old indoor market into the European Central Bank's new headquarters, and she'd gone to see the place as it had always been one last time. She'd practically grown up in the market; her father had run a butcher shop inside for most of his life. Coy was in a wheelchair at the time of tour, recovering from a traumatic IED injury suffered in Iraq. Lou, who had been running the kitchen at the Benjamin Franklin Village in Mannheim when Coy suddenly appeared in the military installation's infirmary with his legs destroyed, was wheeling his friend around. The men were simply looking for something to do. They made for an unlikely couple, but their quiet with each other had convinced her.

After, the three passed a year together. Meta making her dour city livable; the American servicemen, the US military likable. Then Lou left for a job at Fort Hood—BFV, after sixty-five years, was being handed over to Germany; shortly after, Meta and Coy followed suit, the Texas Democratic Party convincing Coy he could unseat an incumbent Republican in the Texas House. He didn't make it out of his primary, and, eventually, Frankfurt called everyone back. First the couple, since married, with a position for Meta at the European Central Bank's brand-new headquarters—she'd run risk analysis in an office overlooking the site of their first meeting—and now Lou.

It was the autumn of 2016, and the failing leaves in the park were the leaves of Meta's memories. But it was not the past Meta had imagined herself returning to.

Dressing the Thai mattress with an ill-fitting sheet, Meta tried to sing a song she could no longer remember. Maybe the feeling was bemusement. When Coy said he'd invited Lou to stay with them for a whole month, at first Meta thought she would run away. An image of herself passing through the door, disappearing somewhere on the other side of the Main, floated in front of everything she laid eyes on. They'd only just started their new life in Germany. Lou was a part of the past she'd meant to leave behind. She'd managed to avoid him in Texas. But then she'd told herself and Coy that she looked forward to the reunion. Work at the ECB would be mostly onboarding. Round-trip tickets from Austin were at least $1,000 in October, and two weeks didn't justify such an expense for someone with Lou's income. She'd said these things aloud. She meant them. And yet an image of herself carried on across the Main. Feelings don't blend like pigment or light, she was realizing, they form rafts out of themselves like ants in a flood and float in a ball all linked together, half-living, half-drowned, discrete but entangled and all necessary. To what end, she had no idea.

Then the song came to her. American, dance-y. It sounded more like old Euro club. One of those songs so entwined with its music video, it played a specific scene in your head every time you heard it. In the video, Rihanna—yes, it was Rihanna—threw up a scarf. In 2011, the year it came out, the year Meta had tried clubbing again, the year she'd met Coy and Lou, it was all they played in the dance clubs they attended. Two thousand eleven was the year she relived being seventeen. Drinking to sickness. MDMA. Settling for the blurry average of sex and love.

She placed a folded quilt on the mattress for Lou, sang the chorus of "We Found Love."

"*Yellow diamonds in the light*," Coy muttered along with her, smirking on the couch. "You're still game for this?"

Locating the song was no epiphany. The size of her life was small, Meta had already reasoned.

"Absolutely," she told Coy. "I'm excited."

Their neighbors, Loïs and Elias, had three children under the age of ten, managed to kayak the Main, vacationed in South Asia. They worked from home, programming, but wore fashionable clothing all day. Along with their children, in the various rooms of their sprawling apartment, so much bigger than Meta and Coy's, with Persian rugs but no carpeting to speak of, they kept succulents, a narrow cat, oblong wood and gold sculptural ornaments. Whenever she was over, Meta sensed pleasurable adult ideas living in these objects. That the objects coexisted with children filled her with seemingly impossible agendas and sent Coy hobbling all over the apartment, withdrawing delicate things from small hands. And somehow the Amblards were about to take on more—the Syrian sisters were coming. In light of this, Meta felt empty but free. This is what the Amblard child had come to deliver her. The reminder that to be undone by anything less was shameful but a privilege too.

Meta handed Coy a pillow and its white cotton case.

"That was sweet, what you said to her," she said.

She could see her husband in his wheelchair again, his legs salvaged but damaged irreversibly. His cane, leaning against him as he sat on the couch fitting the pillow neatly into the case, though entirely necessary, seemed an exaggeration, an object which made him less distinguished or recognizable than like a boy dressed up as an elderly person in a school play. This was how fate had drawn him. Somehow, the top-heavy men she'd encountered, in airports, mainly, sporting exposed titanium prosthetics under their camo shorts, seemed more natural. An engineer claimed people with prosthetics would soon outperform those who were whole in the Olympics.

"She's always playing by herself," he said. "What is her name again?"

"Véronique. The girls will be good for her," Meta said.

Coy's cane, a gift from his mother, had a Dodge Viper's stick shift for a handle, I remember.

I REMEMBER THIS detail because I was one of the Syrian sisters, Fatima, sixteen then and awaiting my delivery from a Berlin refugee center around the same time Meta Hesse was singing that Rihanna song. At least I think she was singing that song. She told me once, "The day I learned you were coming, I remembered the lyrics of a Rihanna song." Much of this story I learned from Meta herself. The rest is compulsion. I know it's presumptuous of me to say what everyone was thinking and feeling at the time, but what's the point if I don't? Meta's given me *her* permission. And every person is savagely made out to be a metaphor to someone else, eventually. Consider what large meanings we held while the world watched us flee our homeland.

Lou didn't arrive when he said he would, and at six, Meta sent Coy out in the Volvo. He stuck to the neighborhood. From the car, he saw the Main loosening its silt as if winter itself were being born from the river bottom. The world appeared filled with only three things: Germans in olive and camel parkas, refugees, and trees dropping leaves. Many of the people Coy mistook for refugees were German citizens; many, German-born. Alone, Meta worried for both Coy and Lou. Then, thirty minutes after Coy returned, alone, Lou buzzed to be let into the apartment complex. The building was like places in America, with shops and a yoga studio and a false sense of community amongst the two hundred units of varying square meterage, and Lou still needed directions. Meta had been lost in the labyrinth many times and let Coy tell Lou how to reach them.

"I don't know where I got off the bus," Lou said, setting a camo duffel and backpack on the couch. Under a long wool coat, he wore a black T-shirt with a cartoon of Benjamin Franklin in army fatigues, and faded jeans. He had put on weight since they'd seen him last, and Benjamin Franklin's egg-shaped head was stretched strangely across his abdomen. Lou's own head was shaved, showing a trapezoidal dent where his skull caved in. He wore round wire-frame glasses, like Ben Franklin himself, and a blond fuzz encircled his mouth.

"I thought I was on the other side of the river. Went as far as the Galopprennbahn. There was some sort of protest," he said.

Coy heated a pot of mulled wine, and Meta informed Lou that the crowd outside the Galopprennbahn was an animal-rights group concerned about the recent deaths of several horses at the track. The stable's veterinarians couldn't explain it, and the community suspected captivity alone had killed the animals. This story was sensational; it had managed to make its way to Berlin, where Rima and I worried for the horses ourselves.

"It's a baseless claim. The track horses enjoy as much space and time outdoors as the animals in the countryside," Meta said. "Those people should go back to rescuing chickens."

"Saw the ECB had some protest trouble itself last year," Lou said.

Meta couldn't be certain if Lou was trying to upset her or if this was just the way he'd been since the accident, blunt and unconcerned. But then she thought that maybe this was the way he'd always been, recalling how she had used to worry about taking him out in public when he was still living in Germany, so quick was he to make a scene or initiate an altercation with someone.

"I don't remember that making American news," Meta said. "It would be surprising to me, with everything that's been going on in Iraq, your election, if such a story found space in the news cycle."

Lou said, "Cars were set on fire. Greece and Spain crippled with austerity, the ECB goes and builds itself a 1.4-billion-euro headquarters, can't say I blame 'em. I read about it on Twitter."

"It's important to treat yourself to something nice from time to time," Meta said.

This news story, I do not recall.

Coy handed Meta and Lou each a mug of steaming wine. The dark liquid smelled of cloves and anise and honey and cinnamon, in addition to the peppery-sweet and mineral odors of the red wine itself. The beverage turned Lou's smile purple. He looked crazed and happy after one sip.

"Check it out," he said. "Amy Winemouth."

After taking a drink of his own wine, Coy said, "She died." It had suddenly occurred to him.

"I guess she did," Lou said, looking into his cup with one eye.

Meta and Lou had used to sneak Amy Winehouse's song "Rehab" onto Coy's physical therapy playlists when he was still recovering in Mannheim. The singer had died in the middle of the summer that same year.

.   .   .

BUT I'D BETTER explain about the Großmarkthalle. A building that, to me, was as quintessentially German as the profession of traffic engineering, though for different reasons entirely.

Meta told me her mother called it an architectural travesty, a structure better suited for East Germany. Cold and austere, she thought it was an enormous barge that had grounded itself alongside the river the first time she saw it. To young Meta, the market's grated glass and steel façade resembled the giant face of a charming classic car. Inside, helping her father manage his books and run the register behind his meat counter, she lost herself in the diverse ripening and rotting smells of the stacked bulk produce, the swarming echoes of human voices and livestock, and the screeching violet-ink printers stippling her sums across glossy rolls of paper. She had no idea what would drive a person to hate a building so much. A question only one of the unharmed would have to ask. But eventually she came to reason that as the young second wife of a middle-aged butcher, her mother must've carried inside her the easy resentments of a child and was probably envious of the hold that building had on her husband and, eventually, her daughter, though the woman also had a job of her own, took solo trips to visit her sisters in Brussels and Amsterdam, and confessed to Meta that if life had taught her anything it was that love never really runs out, so you could use it on anyone or anything for as long and as much as you liked. But the assessment never sat right with Meta, and after her father's death, she finally had to ask her mother. "What was it all about?" she said. "The animal parts? The blood?" The butcher shop. Her father. Her mother's shame and embarrassment for having married an old man covered in meat.

She was unprepared when, without hesitation, her mother said, "No. It was all the coming and going. The selling and buying. I thought it said something disgusting about people."

Meta had already begun her studies in economics.

She decided to return to the Großmarkthalle that day in 2011 because her father, dead several years, had whispered to her to go. It is a gift certain fathers possess. My own father, while he was still alive, was able to whisper across many nations; six years after his death, his helpful voice continues to keep me up some nights still. In the middle of the tour, to indicate roughly where the ECB planned to insert the first-floor lobby, the guide pointed to where Meta's father had kept his stall.

At a nearby café afterward, Lou reflected on the National Socialists' temporary conversion of the Großmarkthalle into a depot for human cargo and Coy went on about Expressionist architecture. Meta was twenty-eight, finishing graduate school. Both men were handsome and attentive—she'd have given either a few weeks of her life. Her mother had already moved away to Amsterdam and probably wouldn't have joined her for the tour anyway. Having people to share this place of her father's with meant a great deal to Meta.

"I could feel them," Lou said, instigating something Meta didn't understand at first. "The dead."

Then, understanding his intentions entirely, Meta said, "My father had memories of the market from when he was a boy, from before the war. He said it was unsettling even back when it was nothing but fruits and vegetables. He called it the Gemieskersch, the vegetable church."

"How old is your father?" Lou said.

Before she could answer, Coy set down his beer and said, "Expressionist architecture seeks to evoke unease, an uncomfortable level of awareness to shake you from the daydream of complacency."

Meta figured he must've read something to the effect in an exhibition catalog. She thought the men's phony fearlessness and erudition were kind of cute.

FOUR NIGHTS AFTER his arrival, Meta found Lou sitting on the Thai mattress with his back against the wall, staring into a laptop. Coy had turned out the light on his side of the bed and she had her first day of work in the morning, but she couldn't fall asleep.

"Do you mind?" she asked.

"It's your living room," Lou answered.

The digital confetti of an explosion reflected off his glasses, and Meta asked what he was playing.

"*CS:GO*."

"Coy can't stand those games," Meta said.

He snapped a button and tilted the screen down to look at her.

"I didn't serve, so, blowing up terrorists in computer games is the closest—"

"I didn't mean . . ."

He smiled. He had been born with a heart defect.

"I'm joking, Met."

She didn't engage, having developed the ability to recognize his distortion from afar. Sometimes, he meant for it to be playful. It was no matter. She had only to resist the urge to apologize.

"It is kind of sick, I guess," Lou added a moment later. "After seeing a bunch of people all torn up, my own best friend nearly killed—playing a game about war, I can't explain it, but it relaxes me."

"Beer relaxes me," Meta said.

Lou stood from the mattress. He was wearing shiny blue athletic shorts.

"Allow me, then," he said.

As he walked past, Meta couldn't help looking at his legs, covered in hair.

He returned carrying two green bottles of beer.

"Nervous about tomorrow?" he said, handing Meta a beer before sitting back down on the Thai mattress with his own.

"I wanted to hear the girls get in," she said.

On the internet, Meta had seen pictures of Syrian cities like hanging gardens; the same cities like scorched curtains.

"Going to try to have a look at them?" Lou said. He picked at the gold-foil label of his bottle.

"No, I'm just going to listen. The Amblards are stompers," she said. "You're feeling jet-lagged?"

"Nah."

He shook his head.

"Just not tired?"

"I'm tired," he said, a drifting wish in his voice.

"What is it?"

Lou smiled again, two bean-shaped reflections of lamplight sitting in his glasses lenses.

"Bad dreams," he said.

"Since when?" Meta said. She got to her feet.

"Relax."

"About the fall?"

"Yes."

"Since the first night in?"

"Since my first night in."

"Lou."

"Coy and I are going to drive by the hotel tomorrow."

"Coy knows about these dreams?"

"Met."

"This is not a boy's club. This is the same shit you guys would—"

"Met."

"What?" Meta said. Her voice was loud enough and the apartment quiet enough that she was able to catch the word's reflection bouncing off the living room's sterile drywall and humming and buzzing in the glass bowls and cups in the stainless-steel kitchen. The effect startled her and caught Lou off guard. With a look of desperation on his face, he said, "Coy doesn't know. And I don't want him to know. Forget I said anything."

Meta told Lou to keep playing his stupid game. Once he resumed, she sat back on the couch, the beer pitched in her hand, listening to his keyboard commands and staring at a woodblock dove that had once lived on a mantle in her childhood home. It took her a moment to realize she wasn't as angry as she'd sounded. She wasn't very worried either. Rather, she had something urgent of her own to confide, only she couldn't share it with anyone because it wasn't her secret to tell. In January, Coy would be returning to Iraq to serve as an advisor to the Iraqi army. In Texas, Meta had refused to hear anything about it. When the ECB called, Coy wagered a twelve-month contract in Baghdad in exchange for a life in Frankfurt, children, impossible agendas. Lou had no idea, but Meta suspected it was the whole reason Coy had invited him, to tell him in person. She hoped that if Lou asked him not to go he wouldn't.

Meta stared at the dove and the room tilted and fuzzed. An indeterminate amount of time later, she awoke to cold liquid spilling on her right foot and a fizzing cloud of foam climbing the carpet's nap.

"Time for bed?" Lou said, without looking away from the computer screen.

"I suppose so," she said, looking at the spot of beer she'd left.

"I'll let you know what time they made it in," he said.

"Okay."

"And I'll finish that beer."

THE INVESTIGATION HAD been brief. None of the Americans present at the hotel party, all of them military, had very much to say. Lou appeared very drunk. The Germans—cheery, red-faced businessmen brought up from the hotel bar and women who'd followed some officers from the club down the street—made only the slightest mention of an argument between Lou and another man. Though, to their own admission, they couldn't be sure if that wasn't how members of the US military interacted all the time.

And so, once compiled, the report was simple: a cook falling from a seventh-floor balcony, ruining a rosebush near the valet booth. Without cause or context, the incident was a display of physics, deemed an accident.

In their written accounts, the valets, twin brothers, the ones who found him, marveled over the sound.

Like an animal tumbling through the crown.

But how could a man falling all that way have made such a small sound?

Following the rustling behind their booth, the twins discovered Lou with his face tangled in the root system. They thought it was their first dead body. He wasn't dead, obviously. But at the foot of the hotel, the impact had cracked an irrigation line that turned the clay-rich soil to russet-colored mud the twins mistook for an ox's worth of blood.

Watching a team of paramedics load the body into an ambulance, they thought: This is how curses are made. Every night, while cash is exchanged for keys: a military jacket drifting down the hotel's façade, the roses always drowning below.

In his own report, Lou said he awoke to an old doctor bleeding his penis. He had no peripheral vision. The old man mumbled. He wasn't bleeding his penis. A group of doctors, men and women, chatted in German around him. The doctor held up seven fingers. Glancing down at his right leg, Lou saw it had turned into something resembling a burred crustacean, spines and rivets graphing it out. The doctor told him he had shown up looking like a tango dancer, with his spine thrown back at a dangerous angle and a rose in his teeth.

He woke up like this twenty times before he was able to maintain consciousness. The blond valets, he was told, had come around for proof they hadn't seen him fall again the night before. When he was up for good, Coy said, "Look who's going to rehab now," and started to sing.

"LOU, I HAVEN'T met them yet, how would I know what kind of tastes they have?" Coy said.

The three were touring the outdoor market at Römer Square, and before they could leave—the sun was setting—Lou had suggested they buy my sister and me a gift. Bread-colored, medieval-style timber structures loomed over them. The square had been reconstructed in haste after the war, and certain buildings were under restoration again for greater historical accuracy. Meta and Coy had donned heavy coats for the outing.

"What about hijabs?" Lou said. "Nice ones?"

"We don't know if they wear the hijab and maybe it's culturally insensitive even if they do," Coy said.

"They teach you that stuff in Iraq?" Lou said.

Meta suggested it would be like buying an American a cowboy hat.

"If the cowboy hat also had a religious connotation," she said.

"Well, I'd love a cowboy hat," Lou said.

"We're from Texas," Coy said. "And it's nothing like giving an American a cowboy hat."

"What about toys?" Lou said.

"Fatima is a teenager," Meta said.

"What about food? Some chocolates or something?" Lou said.

"They might have food allergies," Meta said.

"Jesus Christ, I thought America was uptight. I'm gonna find these kids something cool and it's gonna be from me, all right? I don't want you two trying to jump in and saying it was a group gift," Lou said.

"Judging by what you've suggested so far, I don't think I'll want to be associated with your gift," Meta said.

"I am a master of gift giving, and you will rue the day you were not supportive of my goodwill," Lou said, and walked off.

Fall had deepened in the week or so Rima and I had been in Frankfurt. The Amblard couple, and their three children, once common fixtures in the indoor pool and game room, had stayed in every day and night since our arrival and took us nowhere. They weren't being cruel or negligent. I believe they were scared. A growing part of the country no longer wanted refugees around, and our increasing numbers made everyone nervous. The Amblard home, what had been meant to serve as a warm, protective nest, hummed with anxious energy. We would've told our hosts we understood their hesitation, that we were witnessing their lives change too drastically, that we forgave them, but they were rarely personal with us and withholding any sort of commentary of our own, even compassion, became a way of reciprocating the courtesy. Their distance was a kind of respect. They were trying their best to be insignificant—to suggest our time in Frankfurt, in Germany, in Europe, was only temporary—and so we remained mutually indifferent about our solitude until our boredom consumed us.

A dinner party wasn't exactly what we had in mind, and we'd hoped for people our own ages, but the Amblards said it would be simpler to do something on their own terms. They confessed that they didn't know anyone else with children. The way they explained it, to be friends with people who had children too would be to miss the point entirely. However, after going over the short list of potential guests, Rima and I thought it was more likely that they didn't have any real friends at all. In the end, the Amblards settled on the couple across the hall and their strange friend who was visiting from America.

The choice was startling. By then, Loïs had led us to believe that Meta was a certain kind of witch. Not in the folkloric sense—stories of witches had been used to warn us away from Alawite households whenever we visited family in Damascus—but Meta, it had been suggested, was a woman who derived her power from the suffering of others—a practice apparently so common amongst the Germans, we were told, they even had a special term for it.

"For instance, Meta would like to know how difficult these first few days have been," Loïs had said early on. And then, "Not to mention all of the hardship you two have been through," amending and repairing her statement.

The truth was, the charming French couple who'd picked us up in their Mercedes-Benz and driven us from Berlin to Frankfurt in the dead of night so that their neighbors would not witness our arrival had transformed into hunched-over figures before our very eyes. Like science-fiction cyborgs, they glowed in front of screens all day. The Egyptian woman who kept their apartment in order was asked to stay away for a time, and dirty clothes and dishes piled up everywhere. How different this was from their usual life, we could only assume, and we assumed the worst.

But Loïs also spoke negatively about Germans in general. For example, she said that ever since taking command of the European economy, Germans resented other EU nations' grievances and missed the days when they did not feel responsible for everyone from the UK to Croatia. The twenty-first-century German, on account of the twentieth-century German, was also cripplingly modest and had low self-esteem, an inheritance that complicated their resentments. And yet all of their anxieties were misplaced, we were told. Long before a reunified Germany became heir to the spoils of the Cold War, long before Adolf Hitler's marauding and beguiled bureaucracy took over most of Europe and committed greater atrocities than Bashar al-Assad and his people could ever dream of, people had disliked Germans for being boring rule-followers with no sense of humor. And, therefore, Loïs said, Meta was "perfectly German" in both the historical and modern sense. Her last name, Loïs explained, was also the state's name.

"We're starting small," Loïs said when she saw the looks on our faces.

It was more than a shock, actually. I thought Rima would cry. That the German witch was going to shake our hands and feed off our suffering was one thing, but that any German citizen would come to know what a burden we'd been to this poor French family was another. For days, we dreaded Meta's visit, and perhaps we'd have run away before the evening arrived had Meta not sent Loïs a text message the morning of the party, which Loïs then shared with us. It read that if there were any reason Germany existed at all, it was for Rima's and my sake. Loïs and Elias never talked about France, and though they'd never call themselves refugees in Germany, they did once describe their emigration as self-exile. Responding to Meta's text, Loïs said the displaced millions could exist no other place but Germany, and concluded her message with an expression of gratitude and belonging, gemütlichkeit, another special German term.

With Lou off buying Rima and me the perfect present, Meta and Coy walked alone holding hands as the outdoor string lights of Römer Square snapped on all at once. The vendors illuminated the internal lamps of their kiosks shortly after, and the market appeared to pull the last of the sun's energy from the sky. Within the closeness of the light, and the little pockets of warmth breathed from roasting nuts, boiling cider, and the small space heaters vendors kept to stay comfortable, Meta sensed the dead, and the lights abounding in the market took on the sudden glow of a conflagration as seen from afar, perhaps the burning of one's own village.

"When are you planning to tell Lou about Baghdad?" Meta said.

"Soon," Coy said. "Soon."

WITH EVIDENT SHAME that put Meta at ease, Loïs and Elias opened the door to their guests, our guests that evening, and said, like true mortals, "Excuse the mess," in both German and English.

The Egyptian woman had not been able to clean the apartment on such short notice, and there was a vegetal smell in the air. The media rack had been pulled from the wall to fiddle behind and not put back in proper order yet. Dishes still crowded the sink. The three Amblard children—less prim, a bit sweaty—carried themselves with the mild despondence of handsome but under-groomed show dogs. Véronique stumbled about aimlessly with a Blu-ray case in her hand, wearing on her face a look of such bewilderment, Meta was convinced her parents must have talked her down with a promise to watch a movie the grown-ups had since forgotten in the chaos.

"The girls," Meta said to Loïs in French, "are they nervous?"

"As soon as you knocked on the door they ran to the bathroom to check themselves one more time," Loïs whispered in German.

We heard them over the bathroom fan. Meta was whispering in English to Coy and Lou when we appeared in the living room. I remember my sister and me wearing alternately colored versions of the same outfit, clothing Loïs had purchased us: long, tapered capris; boxy quarter-length-sleeve silk shirts; and jute-sole canvas flats. We'd pulled our dark curls up and to the side in voluminous but casual bushels. No hijab. We'd said no thank you to makeup. In twisting body and shaken nerve, we were

clearly girls, and yet, I think, to German, French, and American standards, we possessed certain features that only belonged to adults. Our
eyebrows, for example—Western women were always commenting on
them, saying they wanted them. Our matching eyes, which Meta met quietly with her own, which no age could measure.

"Guten tag," we said, starting in German, shaking hands and smiling, petting the little Amblards as the children stumbled forward too, a
little like drunken adults, and then we drifted into French, prompting
Meta to apologize. The men spoke only English and very little German,
but she could translate. We offered the men how-do-you-dos and Coy
and Lou both said "Howdy" with laughter in their mouths. Lou asked
Meta to tell us there were Syrians living in the old Benjamin Franklin
Village these days, where he and Coy had used to live themselves.

When Véronique approached with her movie again, I excused myself
and put the movie on for her. Coy nodded approvingly. It was an *Ice Age*
sequel Meta had never heard of. Elias poured wine and opened beers,
handed my sister and me Italian sodas that stuck to our lips no matter
how carefully we sipped them. Loïs had Jacob, her eldest, bring out
boards of charcuterie and bread and cheese, all halal. In the midst of
eating, children screaming, and four languages, including our own
mumbled questions and giggled comments to each other in Arabic, Lou
stepped back across the hall and returned with a paper bag. He handed it
to us. Inside were cookies, assorted ma'amoul made with dates, pista-
chios, walnuts, every kind the vendor had sold, Lou explained.

To everyone's surprise, Lou's especially, Rima and I were momentarily stunned, and we couldn't help staring into the bag of treats as if it
contained some news from home.

"Thank you," we said in English to Meta, Coy, and Lou, and Meta and
Coy pointed to Lou to indicate that it was all him, that it was his gift.

"Thank you," we said again to Lou. "Thank you."

We ate the cookies as if ravenous.

. . .

AFTER THE CHILDREN were put to bed and we disappeared into the guest room to watch YouTube videos, the adults huddled in the outdoor courtyard to smoke the last of Elias's cigarettes. A bottle of brandy circled and, hiccuping, shivering, and stuttering through English, Elias, with cigarette curling in his eye, explained that there was in fact a third Qabbani sister, our big sister, Anjali, who was still living in Berlin.

"Elias," Loïs begged. "It's been a wonderful night, very successful. These people don't need to hear this."

And maybe they didn't, but Meta had moved close to Elias's shoulder and asked him why the eldest Qabbani hadn't come too.

"The organization in Berlin advised against it. She needs to be under close surveillance. She could hurt herself or others."

"What happened to her?" Meta said, and she felt it, emanating from the Amblards, what someone had done to our big sister.

"Well, in addition to fleeing her war-torn country, she was violated," Elias said, and Loïs made a guttural, animal sound.

"Here? In Germany?" Lou said.

"Yes," Loïs said.

"By who?" Meta asked.

"She won't say. They've tried many times. She won't say. They know it happened is all."

"That's awful," Coy said and put his arm around Meta.

Rima and I let YouTube drive. Syrian comedians doing stand-up in Istanbul. A husky male voice narrating the actions of a woman's hands as she slices cloves of garlic, paper-thin, with an enormous knife. Masked youths doing cartwheels and backflips in the desert to video game music, bombs exploding in the distance.

HER THIRD WEEK at the ECB, Meta took Rima and me to show us her office. Our host parents' home office was one European future; Meta said she wanted us to see something else, something very different to aspire to. A life with others. We'd yet to make any friends at school, even with other refugees, and she suspected we were lonely and quite lost, perhaps already prepared to move on to thinking about adulthood, with all of its autonomy and possibility.

Her office overlooked Frankfurt's skyline, the wistful Main and its bridges. Directly behind us, thirty stories below, was the Großmark-thalle, a concrete lattice from above.

"This building is the center of the European financial market," she said in French. "Germany has maintained a very strong economy, which means it shoulders the brunt of the European financial crisis, which has decimated economies in Greece and Spain. The fate of the EU rests here."

Already the light was looking like winter, sharp and bleaching, and we had to step away from the view and were trying not to look so bored at Meta's desk. Like with the dinner party, a tour of an office building wasn't exactly our idea of a good time. Meta neglected to mention Germany's market was starting to slip as well.

"My boss drives an Audi R8. Do you know what that is?" she said, trying her best.

"Yes," Rima said. "We saw them in Damascus when we visited our cousins. Exotic car collections are popular in Damascus."

"Of course," Meta said.

It is difficult to divide the feelings I experienced back then; in that very moment, especially. I was a teenager. I was a refugee, kilometers and kilometers from home. My parents were dead. Standing in the seat of the European financial market, blinded by the shining reflections of a foreign city, I saw how blurry the lives of others were from up high, and had begun to despise, in a way, anything safe and comfortable and with a future, let alone luxurious and in control of the future. I was realizing that to a person like Meta, I was simply the victim she had nothing to do with but would be apologizing to for the rest of her life. A more thorough explanation is probably warranted, but the simple truth is, listening to Meta talk about money—money that we too could have, she believed—I suddenly wanted to hurt her. Maybe Rima did too. Meta wasn't sharing something with us; she was flaunting it. Every attempt she made to bring us closer inside her world only left me feeling farther outside of it. But I'll leave my motivations there. This is a story about Meta, not me.

"German banks have been very helpful offering groups loans to assist Syrian people," I said, turning to look at the river again, flat, green, and so placid you could confuse it for something solid and unmoving.

"That's true," Meta said of the loans.

She seemed very proud of this, very German, equal parts self-righteous and glib, and mistaken.

"I learned in Berlin," I continued, "the ECB has also made life very difficult in Syria."

"How so?" Meta said.

"Sanctions on the Central Bank of Syria stop all financial transactions. No one is being paid. There is no way to buy anything. Syrian humanitarian workers, without pay, can't continue helping. Other sanctions stop medical supplies, transport vehicles, things that save lives."

"I understand what you're saying, but the bank was frozen to stop Assad and ISIS from gathering funds."

"If our father had access to his savings, he might have gotten himself and our mother out," I finished, feeling better, amused, having inflicted pain.

THE INTERIOR OF the Großmarkthalle, renovated and converted into conference halls, press rooms, restaurants, and an art gallery, obviously no longer meant a thing to Meta. Only the fired bricks of the building's façade held any of her memories.

A crew had been laying an English garden between the headquarters and the Main when fall arrived and stranded the grounds in mud and excavation equipment. Outside, tracing the Großmarkthalle's perimeter, taking in the building's exterior as we walked through the turned earth, Meta was still trying to make amends and complimented me on my incisive perspective. She wanted me to know she was on my side, and confronted with this woman's indiscretion, her shameless expression of guilt, I came to regret how I'd acted in her office. She was a childless analyst married to a man with withered legs, she hadn't killed my family, she just had no idea how to talk to teenagers, refugees or otherwise. But try as I did to assuage her guilt, I must've appeared so tired and sullen, and my French, translated in my head before it was spoken, must've sounded so scripted and unnatural, I eventually found myself listening to a long diatribe on how disgusted she was with the nationalistic rhetoric painting every refugee as a potential threat to Germany, and it did not take her long to reach a point of such ideological despair, she actually said, "You believe me, don't you?" recoiling so quickly afterward that she bit her lower lip, drawing blood.

Polite but incapable of hiding our shock, Rima and I made faces better intended for each other but had neglected to turn our necks, and so Meta saw it, the impatience and exasperation we'd have shared appropriately in private if she weren't standing right in front of us, a full-grown woman begging for our approval.

I said, "Of course, and we appreciate everything. It cannot be easy. We do not expect to be taken care of for the rest of our lives. We want to go home, we want to live in Syria, study in Syrian schools, get jobs, marry, raise children in Syria. We shouldn't be a burden long."

And Rima added, "Germany saved us. But I want to go home."

"Of course," Meta said. "And you're no burden."

She must've known then there was little chance of us ever returning to Syria, and that Germany had no idea how to make our lives successful here. Not yet.

"This building," I said, changing the subject, "you said it was important to you, personally."

"Yes," Meta said, and standing in mud, obviously glad to have something else to talk about, she had to search, nonetheless, for the ability to speak of her father's Großmarkthalle. She moved slowly across the wet earth as she started the story, and asked us to picture a massive vaulting market filled with produce and livestock, iron rail carts carrying tons of food from one end of the building to the other, vendors, stockists, restauranteurs, chefs, the thousands of people gathering each day, speaking in every European language, exchanging the stuff of life under tall windows of light. She explained that the ECB had purchased this space to preserve it, with the hope that this older, more essential market could serve as a constant reminder of what their models, projections, and abstract transactions actually meant in real life. We asked her about her father, and she told us how he was born in 1928 with his umbilical cord tied around his neck, of his many brothers and sisters and how they'd all liked to play tricks on their own father in the Groß-markthalle, who was often here as a grocer. Her father loved pigs, enjoying their intelligence and amicable nature, so much so he raised piglets all throughout his childhood, save for the war years, when the animals were hard to come by. Much to the entertainment of his brothers and sisters, he eventually became a butcher. As often as he tried to explain it, her father could never quite reconcile to the satisfaction of himself or others his love of those animals and his passion to dismember them. A young, childless marriage to an American officer's daughter took him to live in Chicago for a time, and after their divorce he happily returned to Frankfurt, where he continued his work as a butcher and did not marry again until he was much older, which was why, Meta explained, she had a father who knew so many shades of history, having arrived physically by this point in her speech at a concrete footbridge belonging to the Großmarkthalle's Holocaust memorial. The bridge overlooked the former train yard where roughly ten thousand human beings had been transported from their holding place in the Groß-markthalle's cellar to their atrocious destinies, the darkest shade Meta's father had ever known.

"I think you are right," Meta said as we peered onto the track field, a concrete expanse now, but still lined with the polished tracks the Deutsche Reichsbahn had once used. "You must count on having a home to return to in the future, you must count on having a future. And not everything you have ever known is past."

She looked back at the mud field, teeming with dump trucks and bobcats and exposed irrigation line. Germany, not unlike provincial Syria, is in a constant state of repurposing or repair. Meta asked about our father. He was a doctor, we told her. He was kind to us. But his life, like his voice, was a happiness of the past, and ghosts are the nightmares, it just so happens, we aren't ready to wake up from.

IN BERLIN, RIMA, Anjali, and I were the girls who rarely spoke. A young German woman, an employee of the state, our caseworker, asked us to write down the things we were not saying. Handed a sheet of lined paper, I pictured the page already covered in writing, the details of my short life blackening the sheet front and back, spilling over onto the table and the floor, running the lengths of my arms and legs, coloring the woman's white forehead. I thought: If I won't be able to say everything, why say anything at all? I'd heard us on the radio, seen us on the news. We'd been chopped up, our voices smeared in the voices of translators. They had each of us saying the same few things. Then I thought: You're not stupid, you know what this woman, what the country of Germany, really wants to know. Had we been trafficked? Were we brides of ISIS? No, no. They wanted to know if we were fit to stay. Psychologically and ideologically. I told my sisters not to write a word. Staring at the pages we returned, all of them blank, the caseworker asked Rima to draw her memories and lent Anjali a camera, instructing her to take photographs of Berlin. To me, she said, "You, you can write," and handed me more lined pages. I had been the one to fill out all of our forms, from Istanbul to Berlin. Anjali returned one day with photos of the charred remains of a church, which someone or some group of people had burned down before its congregation was able to receive eighty new Syrian guests. Rima submitted drawings of our family, a horizontal band of wobbly cartoons, fires blazing in the backgrounds. Receiving nothing but more blank pages from me, the caseworker suggested I write about someone who'd made a difference in my life. "Unless, of course, you are unable to write, after all," she said, in Arabic. "Unless you have a disability of some sort." I could write about my father, I thought. Or, I could write about Bashar al-Assad, which would be easy, given that I'd already written a lengthy report on him for school before the war started, on his glories and his passion for ophthalmology. I could write about the nameless young man who'd look up at me and smile as he passed under my window back home, even after he'd begun carrying a rifle, taken the oath, quit smoking cigarettes, and ridded himself of every other joy in this world. Back when I could still daydream, I had imagined the young man was my future husband come to visit me. As I contemplated him in Berlin, I decided he had already known he was dead and just wanted someone to remember him. I never wrote a word, and eventually, the German caseworker stopped asking me to.

Months later, a few days after our trip to the ECB headquarters, I came upon Meta and Lou sitting beside one another near the entrance of our apartment complex. It was the one and only time I would ever see the two alone. Lou was playing a song from his phone—a scattered, electronic piece, with little bits of Arabic voiceover, though I could not make out the words. Meta was leaning over to listen better, smoking a cigarette, her hair falling from the side of her head onto the face of the device. I was only a few meters away from them, but they didn't see me at all. Meta, seated on the concrete perimeter of an empty garden box with her legs crossed, flicked her right foot in time with the beat. Lou stared into the crown of her head. When Meta drew her head back, Lou stared into the bone and muscles of her throat, laughing and swallowing as she smoked. He was waiting for something, the phone still glowing in his hand, though it no longer played any music. The music had called birds into a barren tree behind him, the only semi-living thing inside the raised plot, and now the birds started to sing. Lou put his hand on Meta's arm. She shook her head, and he took his hand away.

Back in the Amblards' guest room, I opened an empty notebook, a gift from Meta, and started writing. I wrote what I had just seen. I wrote, *I hate these lives, my old life and the new, the lives of everyone around me.* I didn't know it then, but I'd begun working on this, this thing you are reading, whatever this is, which I finished my first fall semester in Grinnell, Iowa, when I felt nothing but homesickness and guilt, and rewrote in the spring, when, guilty still, I asked myself: What are you homesick for?

META, COY, AND Lou were each seated at their mats, watching the street through the yoga studio's front window, when Loïs Amblard passed holding several bags, followed by Rima and myself. We'd had our chins tucked, and were in a hurry. Two men appeared quickly behind us, pointing and shouting. Lou stood first, and then Meta, who helped Coy to his feet and found him his cane.

On the street, shoeless, the wind quickly freezing her sweat, Meta watched Lou launch ahead, grab the men by their shoulders, and spin them around. They looked oddly like twins, I recall. Heavyset, midforties, taller than Lou. Behind the men, dark, naked trees scribbled the sidewalk as far as the eye could see. The cars all had gray clouds shaking from them. The sky was a single, colorless slab. Loïs, Rima, and I had vanished. One of the men shouted, in German, "They're sending us back to the Dark Ages!"

"What's the problem, guys?" Lou shouted back, in English, pushing the men with his chest.

"Lou, cool it!" Coy shouted from behind Meta.

One of the men shoved Lou back, and after regaining his balance, Lou leapt at him like a monkey, knocking him to the sidewalk, clambering on top of his body and pinning his arms down with his knees.

"Lou!" Meta shouted, and felt Coy rush past her.

The other man was reaching over Lou when Coy caught him with his cane and pulled him into a brick wall. By now a crowd had gathered. From against the wall, the man charged at Coy, shouting wildly, and Coy thrust his cane into the man's gut, sending an explosion of blood up the collar of his jacket, flooding the man's neck and face. Meta and the rest of the crowd screamed as the man tore off his jacket and peeled a large plastic bag from his bloodied shirt.

Lou let go of the man on the floor and jumped to his feet to stand beside Coy. They both said, in unison, "What the fuck, man?"

The German men doubled back. Behind them, two female police officers were approaching. Coy looked to Meta, horrified, shaking. She rushed to him.

"It's pig's blood," she said. "Honey, he's not hurt, it's pig's blood."

AFTER QUESTIONING, AND making it abundantly clear that Coy and Lou could just as easily be stepping into a police car themselves, the officers let the Americans off with a warning to leave these matters to police in the future. Returned to the apartment, the three warmed up and rehashed the fight several times. Lou was still raging, shadowboxing in the living room, referring to the men as Nazi scum.

"Did you feel it?" Lou asked Coy. "Your Marine instincts? If one of them had pulled a gun or a knife . . . I think . . . I think—"

He bolted for the door.

"Rima and Fatima," he said. "We've gotta check on them."

"Lou, let's wait," Coy said. "Let the Amblards reach out. They might be pretty shaken up still."

Lou looked at Coy like he couldn't believe what he was hearing. He turned to Meta.

"And maybe wait until you're a little less excited too. You might end up scaring them," she said.

"We saved them, Coy," Lou said, dismissing Meta and turning again to his friend.

"I know we did," Coy said.

"We didn't do anything wrong," Lou said.

"We didn't. They might be scared is all."

At noon, Coy took Lou to the Galopprennbahn to bet on horses and drink beer. Less than an hour later, I knocked on Meta's door. We were both equally surprised to find one another at the threshold of her apartment.

"Your heroes have left," Meta said, gesturing for me to enter.

"Yes, I heard them leave," I said, and then, "Your husband's cane makes a distinct sound."

I came inside, sat on her couch. I couldn't tell you what color it was, though it's been suggested more than once that I should fabricate details in my writing to fill in the blanks. I'll say it was gray. It probably was. But what I don't remember either and can't seem to make up no matter how hard I try is what had driven me to Meta in that moment. How I knew she was going to be the one who understood. I'd only just started writing about her. But some distances only make voices louder, and perhaps I was hearing more than one—my father's, echoing from the land of the dead, and Meta's, amplified across the distance of the hall.

"Americans are noisy people. How is Rima?" Meta said.

"She's okay. One of the men kept reaching into his jacket. We thought it was a gun."

"It was blood."

"Yes, the police told us. It would have been gross, an insult, but we are not so religious."

"They don't know what a Muslim is. It's a trigger word. It means different. It means enemy. Do you know what I mean?"

"My country is at civil war."

Meta asked if I was hungry, if I wanted tea, but I was content. I wanted to talk. I wanted her company. I felt at ease with her insecurity now, how it was prone to little fevers and spells. It made her honesty more recognizable, a blinking buoy on a dark sea of kindness and humanitarian responsibility. I needed someone who could relate to my guilt. My sister in Berlin; my whole country still dying at home or roaming the streets of Turkey or Europe without hope, or else washing up dead in their life jackets on a warm shore; and me with a sudden growing wish to leave it all behind, my sisters included, to begin a life that was my own—I hated myself. But I knew I wasn't alone. I was convinced that Meta's life was more complicated than the Amblards could ever imagine. Letting her life get so complicated was Meta's greatest regret.

Though I'd had no part in bringing on any of the complications in my own life, I regretted them just the same. But Meta unraveled complex global financial problems at work; resolving her own conflicts at home was only a matter of time. If she stole away from them, onto the other side of the Main, for instance, I hoped I could convince her to take me with. Into the future, into the present.

"When the war started I was interested in economics. I liked math a lot," I said.

"And you were eleven years old?"

"You know that I have another sister."

"Yes, Mr. Amblard told me."

"And you know why she's not with us."

"Yes."

"We were living in the Tempelhof Airfield."

"It is an infamous airport."

"Everyone was scared. No one knew anyone. You don't know who you can trust. You think everyone is together, one, because of what they have been through. You think the people who are feeding you, giving you blankets, will protect you."

"That's not always the case."

"Two men attacked my sister. They pulled her into a closet and left her there and a janitor found her."

"Guards did this to her?"

"No."

Meta leaned forward on the couch to look out the living room window. I wish I could say how big the window was, what there was to see outside of it.

"My sister said nothing. She stopped talking. But a female guard, a German woman who spoke French, came to me and said they knew who'd done it. It was up to me to decide what happened next. The men could be arrested, detained, prosecuted, and returned to Syria, or there was a group of angry men who could take care of the situation."

"It shouldn't have been up to you."

Everything was up to me.

"If the attackers were arrested, there would be a record of the crime. People in the camp already knew what the German public was saying about us. That we were criminals, the men were terrorists and rapists. That we would destroy Germany. The guards could arrange to make it look like an accident. Illness. Anything. It wouldn't matter. Refugees die all the time," I explained.

After a moment, I told Meta that I knew why the airfield was so infamous.

"Hitler said the Tempelhof was going to be the gate to Europe, the way the world entered Germania," I said.

And Meta said, "Someday, if you're comfortable, if you want to, I'd like you to tell me about your sister. About who she is."

THIS WAS THE past I would learn Meta was trying to escape: the investigation into Lou Crimshaw's near-fatal fall from a seventh-story balcony at the Grandhotel Hessischer Hof concluded when Sergeant Coy McCormick-Hernandez came forth and disclosed that he was the man with whom Lou was embroiled in a bitter argument shortly before the incident. In a ten-page testimonial, Sergeant McCormick-Hernandez also disclosed the nature of the argument, regarding a German citizen named Meta Hesse, a woman with whom he and Lou were both in love. Lou and Meta had dated for a time, while she finished a graduate degree in Frankfurt and Lou managed the base kitchen in Mannheim. Meta terminated the relationship after six months, and Lou decided he would return to the United States when his service in Germany came to an end. The base was closing. On the night of the event, after receiving a text message from a mutual friend that reported Sergeant McCormick-Hernandez and Meta Hesse arriving at the hotel party together, Lou Crimshaw drove the forty-five minutes from Mannheim to Frankfurt to confront the two. According to the hotel bartender,

Crimshaw drank several shots of hard alcohol immediately upon arriving and then ordered two cases of beer, to be delivered to the room in which the party was being held. In Sergeant McCormick-Hernandez's testimonial, the altercation that ensued was not long and purely verbal. Lou Crimshaw seemed mostly interested in airing grievances and hearing his old friend apologize. He offered no stipulations on Coy and Meta's relationship. When it was over, the couple departed, but Crimshaw decided to stay and keep drinking. At some point between 2150 and 2200 hours, Lou ventured onto the hotel balcony alone, to smoke a cigarette, and soon after fell. All of this, Lou Crimshaw corroborated as fact.

LOU WOULD LEAVE in two days and Coy had yet to tell him about Baghdad. There was no use leveraging Coy's cowardice against him; not even a divorce would keep him from leaving. He had been part of ruining a country and now it was his duty to build it back up, lest the whole world move across the hall, knock at Meta's door, and ask her to mend its life. She'd been blamed for Lou's injury and that was enough. She'd been blamed for uprooting Coy from his life in Texas, which sent him seeking comfort in Iraq again, even if that wasn't the correct order of events. She'd been blamed for darkening my mood. Meta blamed herself for calling back old horrors to roost, sitting in a glass office perched over the historic trading grounds from which humans were led to slaughter. If Coy died in Iraq, she would never forgive herself.

But Loïs had also texted Meta that morning to suggest, as a send-off for Lou, and to call to an end the fall season, a night out. And Meta, with her million reasons to run and disappear on the other side of the Main, where her childhood home was, which had been quartered into student apartments years ago, couldn't find a single excuse worthy of spoiling everyone's fun. There was music at the museum, and a restaurant to which the Amblards had been dying to take her and Coy and were sure Lou would enjoy as well. He had turned into a magic American for us and the Amblards, with his dented head and scattering talk and moral temper, as he had for Meta years before. Before Meta could write back, in a follow-up, Loïs wrote that if Coy didn't mind walking the museum, they'd book the reservation immediately, and rather than damage her husband's ego, Meta wrote, *Coy will be fine, but what about the kids?* And Loïs wrote back that Rima and I would watch them.

We watched the five set out in a rideshare van at six that evening. The sky had already fallen and gathered into the city lights. Elias spoke with the driver, a large Congolese man who'd recently vacationed in Carcassonne.

"And what brought you here?" Elias said.

"The war," the man said. "It's what brings anyone anywhere."

Meta tapped Coy to tell him what the man had said, but when he asked her what it was she wanted, she said, "Nothing. Never mind."

What followed was a steady survey of German culture—Strauss and Die Brücke and Der Blaue Reiter—followed by Turkish cuisine and too much wine. At one point during dinner Meta said Rima and I would've liked the restaurant, and Loïs, perhaps already quite drunk, started crying.

"I admit it, sometimes I want my old life back," she said, and Elias began to shush her, offer her some of his food.

"Let me say it," she said, and he settled back into his plate. "It's hard enough having three children. I'm not sure why I've taken in two more. Just a break from time to time, it's all I ask. Is it wrong?"

She was speaking and crying in French and Meta did not think to translate for Coy or Lou, who also seemed content with not knowing what the concern was. Loïs sobbed only a little while longer and retreated back into her food, and by dinner's end everyone was smiling again without any further comment.

After the bill, the group huddled in their coats in the restaurant lobby watching a dot on Elias's phone. The dot represented their ride, moving evenly across a glowing map of Frankfurt in their direction. Outside, Elias reached for the passenger door of a black cargo van, then knocked to have the door unlocked. The window slid down and the man inside informed Elias he must be mistaken. Elias begged his pardon and consulted the phone again. Loïs joined him outside.

"It's gone," he said. "But there are more cars in the area."

In less than a minute, he said, another car would arrive, a white SUV, but then its dot disappeared too.

"It must have a bug," he said, and Loïs opened her app as well.

Three failed attempts later, Elias and Loïs returned to the rest of the group inside, where Elias announced to them that while they'd been enjoying wine and dessert, the world had evidently fallen into the Dark Ages, and though it was a crime against convenience, they would simply have to walk to catch a bus if they couldn't hail a regular cab first.

Walking, Elias and Loïs in front, Lou in the middle, and Meta and Coy in the rear, they volleyed conversation into the air. It had been forever since they'd taken public transportation. Frankfurt was beautiful at night. Perhaps it'd be worth tacking a few extras minutes onto the walk to trace the Main. Along the Main, its darkness dappled with the city's reflection, Meta said it was strange how few cabs were out. Coy remarked that he was freezing and Loïs asked after his leg. Elias fell behind trying to get the app to work again. Loïs, also looking at her phone, disclosed that she'd misread the bus route and they'd have to cross the river to get to the bus they wanted after all. The group reconfigured its order, placing Meta and Lou in front, and everyone else fell behind them.

"His right leg seems worse," Lou said.

"It was always worse than the left."

"I told him I thought he should apply at a base here, get back into the swing of things; they could use someone with his experience. Him sitting around, not doing anything, it's driving him nuts, I can tell."

"He's going back to Iraq, Lou," Meta said.

Lou fell silent and looked to the ground.

"He wants to train the Iraqi army to fight ISIS," she said.

"He knows it's not West Point, right?"

"He knows how dangerous it is."

"And that he'll be a target? And that kids are joining the Iraqi army to blow it up from the inside?"

"He knows."

"You can't stop him?"

"I tried. I worked out a deal. I could either leave him and he'd go to Baghdad anyway, or he'd go for twelve months and I'd get my life back. I went with the deal."

She didn't say it, but to keep him alive, she might have to stay married to him forever.

The two looked back at Coy, doubled over in his black leather jacket, his stiff boot-cut jeans swiveling one leg over the other, his glistening cane stabbing the pavement beside him.

"You all right, bud?" Lou called.

"Just bringing up the rear," Coy said.

Then, after a moment, Lou said to Meta, "I jumped off that balcony on purpose, you know that, right?"

"Stop it, Lou."

"And you better believe it had nothing to do with you."

"Lou, we don't—"

"I wanted to serve, do you understand? That's how bad I wanted what he had. To be blown up. That's why I jumped. Because no one was going to blow me up. Now look at us. Our liberated Iraq. Our free world. You guys have Nazis marching in the parks."

"Look at Syria," Meta said. "Look at Syria."

Lou looked at her instead, at a complete loss. These two men had always been at a loss, seeking her perspective or approval. She'd nursed them through their love for her, their jealousy over one another, their injuries and their regrets, and now their guilt. When would it end? With men like these in the world, how would there be anything left for girls like Anjali, Rima, and me? With girls like me and Rima and Anjali in the world, how would there be anything left for a woman like Meta Hesse?

ANJALI QABBANI LOVED and still loves French fashion magazines. Anjali Qabbani loved one dog and two cats, animals the Alawite witch living at the end of our cousin's block in Damascus kept outside in all weather. The witch left her kitchen window open so that the animals could hear the Qudūd Ḥalabīya she played on the radio all day long. On the road to Reyhanlı, in front of a dozen women, Anjali Qabbani, starved for a bath, stripped naked and washed herself under a waterfall. Anjali Qabbani, the daughter of a doctor, a science nerd, delivered two babies on the road to Reyhanlı, welcoming them into the world with a poem by Maqbula al-Shalak and cutting both their umbilical cords with a pair of scissors belonging to the second mother, a hairdresser from Killi. In Berlin, before she stopped talking, Anjali Qabbani told me she heard the voice of our father and I did not tell her that I did too. Anjali Qabbani still loves science; she quietly pores over French and Arabic textbooks all hours of the day. She has taken thousands of photographs of Berlin, not all of them brutal, which she uploads to a cloud for me and Rima to see. After she stopped talking, before we left for Frankfurt, she told me something our father had only told her before we left Hama, something he has never whispered to me. She writes me emails, she talks to me and Rima, she says she will talk to everyone else when she goes to university, that she will talk when she becomes a doctor, that she will talk to her patients, whom she will heal, that she will recite a poem to every newborn baby she delivers.

ELIAS DEMANDED EVERYONE enjoy a nightcap. In the living room Loïs apologized to us for being late. I could tell Meta felt ugly being drunk in front of us. We felt ugly in front of her, in front of everyone. Germany had sung a song together about taking up the broken hearts of the world.

"Did everything go well?" Elias asked. "We hope we didn't scare you."

Keeping her eyes down, Meta heard a whimper in the hall. Véronique, huddled in her Care Bears pajamas.

"Véronique," she said, and lowered to her knees to have a look at the girl.

A shining film of sweat and tears covered Véronique's face and mussed her hair. Her right cheek had a deep redness, like a jewel was lodged in the meat, and her right eye wouldn't stay open.

"I'm sorry," Rima said suddenly, and I almost hit her too.

"For what?" Loïs said, still some kind fogginess in her voice as she stepped past Meta to grab Véronique. "Véronique, what's wrong. What's happened to your face?" she said.

"Did she fall?" Elias said, pouring the brandy.

Véronique shook her head.

"She did fall, we're sorry," I said, lies being only a more measured path to the inevitable, as my father had said when he was alive and whispers to me still.

"She didn't fall," Rima said. "She wouldn't listen. She wouldn't do anything we said. The other two ate their dinner, watched their program, washed their faces, and went to bed, and Véronique did none of it, she just tormented us all night."

It was true.

"What did you do?" Elias said, raising his voice, abandoning the drinks.

"I punished her," I said.

"What did you do?" Elias said again, not repeating himself but demanding details.

"I slapped her and I locked her in the bathroom until she apologized and promised to go to bed."

The way I said it, in matter-of-fact Parisian French, what I'd learned in school, was punishable in itself.

"How could you?" Elias shouted.

"You had no right!" Loïs said, examining Véronique's fingers.

Rima sobbed. "I'm sorry," she said, "I'm sorry," though she hadn't done anything wrong.

"Go, go! I can't even stand to look at either one of you!" Loïs shouted. "We bring you into this house and you act like, like, brutes! Into the guest room. Go! You make me sick! Go!"

"Forgive me," Rima continued to sob, looking so small and meaningless, the face of a crying child abandoned in the street of a war-torn city, her tears parting the plaster blasted across her cheeks. "Please, forgive me," she said again, and it was at this moment, shortly before Elias took us by the arms into the guest room and locked us in, that I searched for Meta again. I realized she had already retreated to watch from the door, and then to listen from the hall, before disappearing into her own apartment, where I know she could still hear Loïs's screams from her own couch. At any moment, Coy or Lou would realize she was gone and reappear across the hall. In a day, one would leave and she would never see him again. In three months, the other would disappear and she would have her own life again for a year, a year to decide what to do, how to be. The year in which I would write her an email from Berlin asking her to adopt me and my sister, a request she would decline, the greatest regret of her life, she claims, though I try to convince her otherwise, reminding her of what Lou had asked of her when they were alone outside the apartment complex, of what the whole world had seemed to be asking of itself then. For now, she had this moment. And in this moment, Meta chose to recall her father at the Großmarkthalle, in the first market days after the war. The meagerness of it all, the wilted fruit and skinny animals; the ghosts, the nothingness, the only thing in full bloom. Portions of the roof are missing. Her father has nothing to sell, few have money to buy, leftover American GIs ambulate with strange smiles and injuries, and her father, my age then, at the whims of history, waits for life to begin again, however it may begin.

YA

PART I: YOUTH

Bush II, the second administration.

BOMBS OVER BAGHDAD . . . again.

THE UNITED STATES is a wasteland of militant gluttony and we've all just been told, "George Bush doesn't care about Black people," though it's something we all know rather intuitively already.

MIKHAIL AND I are sixteen and we are deciding between us the three greatest novels of all time, this being part of our wartime happiness. We wrestle with the topic over lunch, which we take at the center of the periodicals section in Maine Tech's library, at a gray, low-lying table strewn with *New Yorker* copies clipped in clear plastic magazine covers. In 2009, we're foppish little hipster mods draped romantically over the library's fire-retardant furniture. We'd wear argyle even if the school uniform didn't require it. Our hairstyles match the hairstyles of several members of the Strokes. We'd prefer low-top Chuck Taylors over our black dress shoes, but everything else in our lives is perfect (in a wartime sense). Our matching messenger bags clasp around our torsos (identical swimmer's bodies) with straps made out of seatbelt buckles.

Dipping a pale Bosco stick into a cup of marinara sauce, Mikhail makes the case for *Don Quixote*, *Ulysses*, and, maybe, *Infinite Jest*. We've read none of them. But these three have the instincts in them that literary greatness demands.

"The moral omnivore's roving indifference, precocial indecency, and an obsessive caretaker mentality," Mikhail says. Where does he get it? "All of it alive and well in these three books."

All three are also long as hell.

"No Tolstoy?" I ask, swigging from a bottle of Pepsi Blue. "He's pretty encyclopedic."

There are so many new colors in soda products all of sudden. The orange Live Wire, the red Code Red, that purple Pitch Black. We'd read *The Death of Ivan Ilyich* in AP English and been affected by its bourgeois afflictions. Our parents, factory workers, want us to be doctors or, at the very least, pharmacists. I've pictured myself sustaining a minor but mortal injury while choosing from one of our vending machines' endless pop assortments, a nick on my finger, and dying many excruciating and well-documented months later.

"He writes like style hadn't been invented yet," Mikhail says.

"And wasn't he sort of a Jesus freak?" I say.

"Probably."

I want to ask if the lack of style is a translation issue, but there's rarely any contest between Mikhail and me. I am to blame for our infinite peace, which I keep not for fear of upsetting him, or out of outsized respect, but because not even slipping into his shadow would be enough. With Mikhail, I seek a perfect parallelism. We wear each other's clothes, eat each other's food. We are a sustainable commune of two.

Maine Tech is a science magnet on Chicago's West Side. Girls were first introduced in the late seventies. Boys, fearing that the girls would bring down test scores and the school would lose its prestige, protested and occupied the library in which we discuss these male writers. Test scores went up. The humanities weren't emphasized until the late nineties. No one protested. Test scores have been going down ever since.

It means something that one of the books on the list was written in a foreign language and another book was written by a decolonized mind. Mikhail is Bosnian, bused in from Ukrainian Village. I am Mexican-Puerto Rican, bused in from Humboldt Park. Both of us consider ourselves perfect Maine Tech boys. We wear our classmates' clothes as well. But we sense culture leaving the harbor, we feel ourselves assuming future positions aboard.

Doña Alejandra dos Cosimas, master of the house, keeper of the key, the library's Madame, Maine Tech's head librarian, visits us in periodicals to say it's passing period. Roughly thirty, roughly six feet tall, she makes for an imposing school marm, but we are her babies and can do no wrong.

"And I told you, no food in the library," she says, dismayed by the amount of marinara sauce we've managed to spill.

"What are the three greatest novels of all time?" I ask Doña dos Cosimas, not moving.

"*Their Eyes Were Watching God*, *One Hundred Years of Solitude*, and *Speedboat*," she says.

We'd actually read *Their Eyes Were Watching God* in accelerated sophomore English.

"What's your criteria?" Mikhail asks, skeptically.

"Readability, relatability, and accountability," she says, restacking the *New Yorkers*. "And, for goodness' sake, plot."

We aren't sure of this measure.

"Zora Neale Hurston, really? She turns African American Vernacular English into a lyric, sure," Mikhail says.

"And I dig the especially American DIY attitude of its feminist individualism," I add.

Maybe that's *The Color Purple*.

"But isn't it really too soon to determine whether or not it fits into the canon?" Mikhail says.

Doña dos Cosimas looks at us each individually for a moment, as a military doctor might. She shakes a plastic trash can at us to break the spell. As we toss, she asks us what our top three is. Is, not are, because she knows we will share the same.

"You realize *Ulysses* was published only five years prior to *Their Eyes Were Watching God*, and *Infinite Jest* came out in 1996?" she says.

"Zora Neale Hurston is clearly a genius," I say.

"There's no mistaking it," Mikhail says.

"The Ivy League is going to love you boys," Doña dos Cosimas says, feeding the trash can the remainder of our mess. "Now leave. Calculus awaits."

Actually, it's study hall. It's held in the computer lab—the composition computer lab, to be exact; another computer lab exists for programming and CAD, while yet another one is used solely for graphic design. Unsupervised, in the composition computer lab we've noticed girls sometimes spend entire periods staring nervously at empty search bars and scrolling up and down blank Word documents, while boys mostly succumb to a strange Japanese online game, the goal of which is to take a female hentai character on enough successful dates to trigger a pornographic Flash animation. That they can do this publicly without so much as adjusting their dress slacks or breaking off for the men's room confuses the hell out of us. Like, is it just gaming, are they just gaming? After, we have gym. Kayaking in the natatorium, an activity I've been avoiding all week. I shaved my underarms late last week and haven't wanted Mikhail to see. I think enough has grown back that he won't notice. If he does, he doesn't say anything. Instead, he practices rolling his kayak, capsizing and then recovering his craft with his paddle, over and over, until our gym teacher tells him to stop, and his eyes are so messed up from all the chlorine in the pool he looks like he's been crying and throwing up for days.

.   .   .

DOÑA DOS COSIMAS comes to us at our lunch table in periodicals the next day. She is looking for two literary ambassadors to show a visiting writer around campus.

"Who is he?" I ask.

"Who's to say it's a he?" Doña dos Cosimas says.

"Is this person famous?" Mikhail asks. "Have I read them?"

"Not at all. Probably no. He works for a publishing company that specializes in hi-lo literature."

"Hi-lo?" Mikhail says.

"So, he is a he," I say.

"High interest, low reading level," Doña dos Cosimas says. "For struggling and reluctant readers."

I gag, theatrically at first, but then it feels actually reflexive.

"Check yourself," Doña dos Cosimas says.

"Sorry," I say, choking now.

"Drink something," Mikhail says, and I obey, taking a swig of Baja Blast, which looks convincingly like floor cleaner and doesn't not taste like floor cleaner.

"So, are you two interested or not?" Doña dos Cosimas says.

An awful curl of pain peals from my abdominal sphincter, licking the back side of my sternum and cauterizing my throat.

"We are," Mikhail says, looking at me strangely.

MY MOTHER SUGGESTS I start carrying Tums. I'm on Prilosec by the time Herman Lowery, the writer, lands at Midway Airport and begins doing his rounds through Chicagoland.

"It's his diet," my dad says. "He eats like an idiot. I told you that shitty diet would catch up with you."

My dad is a vegan, eats like a bird, and is exercise obsessed. For as long as I can remember, he's always envied my metabolism. Of shitting, the man once said, "I'm tired of it. Every minute I'm sitting on that toilet, I'm being kept out of the game." I can tell he's taking some pleasure in my acid reflux. We're sitting around the dining table in our kitchen. We're not eating, but in such close proximity to my food—my Hot Pockets, my Lunchables hot dogs, my glowing two liters of soda—he can't help himself.

"My diet is fine," I say. "I eat the same as everyone else."

"You never drink water. I don't understand how you're not dead yet," he says, laces up, and goes for a run.

He jogs around Humboldt Park Lagoon, convening with HP's ghosts. He swears he sees my mother's sister's husband standing around every so often, the man a coroner's report swears froze to death in the park three winters ago.

"Why doesn't he ever go home then?" I asked my dad once. He'd supposedly conversed with Elio during a water break.

"Because your aunt's a ballbuster and your cousins are brats," he said.

And then he looked at me with that hungry envy.

"Don't even need to be sensible, just gotta be skinny," he said. "Life's so easy for people who are skinny."

Herman Lowery turns out to be a beauty, a man in a liquid blue suit, tobacco-colored leather suspenders and brogues, a hard white shirt, and an apple-red tie like a political talking head—the kind of men I wait to watch on *Meet the Press*, the kind of men who give me public policy dreams. Without him saying it, I know he lives in an industrial Philadelphia loft with exposed brick older than our country. I know he drinks from spotless, streakless wineglasses, blushes stiff, white dinner napkins with the droplets of merlot the wineglasses leave on his lips, that he welcomes comraderies of men, all orphans, into his home for dinner each Sunday, that he jogs in tube socks, though it's no longer the fashion—my dad jogs in booties—that he still washes with bar soap, though the rest of the world has moved on to gendered body washes with microbeads, that he writes for a living but not a purpose.

Mikhail and I walk him from the bus stop on Western to a coffee bar near campus. We have hall passes for the day. How cool, I think, and then that only two dumb kids from Maine Tech would think they need hall passes to roam freely the streets of the world.

"You guys are with the newspaper?" Herman Lowery asks.

"No," I say. "We're friends with the librarian."

"Oh."

Mikhail and I order dirty chai lattes and Herman Lowery orders an americano.

"You want to study literature, writing, in college?" he asks.

"Political science, I think," I say.

"Psychology," Mikhail says.

"Cool cool. Considering any HBCUs?" he asks, looking at me.

"Like, bank loans?" I say, and all the cardamom, cinnamon, ginger, black pepper, and clove in the world comes riding up so fast, my knees buckle.

Our campus sits alongside a forested park. We take Herman Lowery up and down its walking paths, point out different places various classmates have been discovered passed out drunk in the past. He understands we are not a party school. We are a school of high-functioning neurotics. We fear failure. We understand we will have to engineer and nurture a more healthy planet. Eventually, we too will be complicit in a foreign invasion. A man in a trench coat carrying a briefcase blows past and Herman Lowery raises his eyebrows.

"Poet laureate, or something?"

"Nah, just some neighborhood guy. We call him No Time for Birds," Mikhail says.

Herman Lowery's eyes follow the man as he disappears into the woods.

"Yeah, we like to pretend that he thinks he's on his way between meetings and that he pulls a pistol from his briefcase every time he sees a bird and shoots it because, well, *There's no time for birds*," I say.

"Where *are* all the birds?" Herman Lowery says, realizing now that the woods, save for sounds of nearby traffic, are silent.

"I don't think our theory is half-bad," Mikhail says.

Herman Lowery's writing process is strange. He calls himself a content creator for young Black and brown men's souls. Each novel he creates triangulates a new set of specific data points—vocabulary and reading levels, timely issues, demographic trends within specific demographics, and additional information culled from surveys, student essays, and parent and teacher feedback. Characters and plots are workshopped in focus groups before the first draft is even written. Subsequent drafts are filtered through schools and rated by how many complete reads they earn. Revision and editing are conducted by committee. And the whole process is completed within twelve months before it is repeated, again and again. The finished titles get zero publicity and no reviews but are meted out through contracts with public school districts all over the country. It's all very cutting edge. He is salaried, works nine-to-five five days a week, and gets five weeks of vacation a year.

"It's a good gig, and, on the whole, the books are well received. People love them. And we have so many series now. We write books for every age group, from grade school to senior citizens," he says, proudly.

We try our best to look unimpressed.

"Do you know what it's like to read something above your comprehension level? A high school senior with the reading skills of a seventh grader reads at the national average of American adults, which is about fifty-eight percent below their grade level. Check this out, this is what it looks like to read at about thirty percent below grade level—that's a C average, according to American grading standards."

Herman Lowery extracts a page from his briefcase for us to read.

    ■ *came out* ■ *today very* ■ *to meet the* ■ *student whose* ■ *told a* ■ *of mine* ■ *his son's* ■ *had been* ■ *real value. It* ■ *his mother* ■ *bragging about* ■.

    I have come ■ *from the* ■ *of your* ■ *to the tranquility* ■ *your campus* ■ *speak about* ■ *future of your* ■.

    The purpose ■ *protecting the* ■ *of our nation* ■ *preserving the* ■ *of our* ■ *is to pursue* ■ *happiness of* ■ *people. Our* ■ *in that pursuit* ■ *the test* ■ *our success* ■ *a nation.*

    For a . . .

"Can you tell me what I'm looking at?" Herman Lowery says, the paper shaking in his hand.

I want to say he's looking at something beautiful, an erasure poem, but I say nothing, neither does Mikhail, and Herman Lowery tells us that it's his job to fill in the gaps.

"Would you call what you create literature, though?" I say, still dismayed by his description of his writing process. "It's content, sure, but isn't it kind of like painting by numbers?"

Herman Lowery laughs and puts the paper away.

"Hey, Charles Dickens was paid by the word. And haven't you always gotten the impression that *literature* is gatekeeper terminology? Another thing to keep us out? And the highbrow/lowbrow distinction is so passé, it won't be long before a comic book wins a Pulitzer," he says. "Besides, ever heard of an MFA program?"

Mikhail, who hasn't said very much at all, asks why Herman Lowery has decided to come to a school like Maine Tech.

"We don't exactly have low reading scores," he says, and Herman Lowery looks at his feet.

"Well, that's the rub, boys," he says. "Because Ms. dos Cosimas didn't invite me to Maine Tech, and neither did the English department. Your Computer Science chair did. And that's because my firm has started experimenting with a new artificial intelligence tool to compose novels at a faster rate. AI can just as easily analyze the data that focus groups and writers and editors can. Algorithms can affect voice and writing style. We're currently training a computer to write a sequel to one of my most successful books. I'm not here to give a reading or promote our titles or the importance of books, but to pitch a future career path to kids interested in computer programming and artificial intelligence."

"But you're not a programmer," I say.

"No, and I assume neither are either of you, but they sent me for the same reason they asked a couple of book nerds to greet me, and that is our ability to communicate ideas. They're already downsizing our writing team. I figure I might as well pivot and get into marketing. The future of our kind of storytelling is in sales, my friends. The machines are going to dream up the next big idea, a war or a new kind of car, but they'll still need real live people to sell it, and nothing sells better than a good story."

TRAINING AN AI to write low-cost books for mostly low-interest audiences is not nearly as exciting as training an AI to hunt down cancer or terrorists, but Herman Lowery's presentation to the CS department works like gangbusters. Applying for their spots in the publisher's pilot program, asked why they are interested in the opportunity to train an AI to write books, the applicants say things like, "I like to read. Tolkien is my favorite." "It sounds fun." "It sounds easy." "It could be my way of giving back."

Mikhail and I shudder at the thought that these are the people who are going to be the engineers of the engineer of the human soul. Maybe because he feels the same, Herman Lowery, before he leaves, pairs us each with a three-person team of programmers to help see it through. It becomes our responsibility to teach the programmers what makes a good story, to provide them book lists to feed the AI, and to help edit and revise the AI's stylistic approach. We never interface directly with the program, we have no idea what it looks like or how it works—we don't want to. The programmers' first task is to have it write a five-page short story in the naturalistic style at a seventh-grade reading level.

On my team are Reece, a sophomore from Bridgeport; Carlos, a junior, like me and Mikhail, from Pilsen; and Liliane, a senior from West Loop. At first, I consider giving them stories from *Dubliners*, which I have read, but figure those stories go above reading level. I search "great short stories for middle school" on the internet and most of the results refer to O. Henry. However, I refrain from submitting O. Henry stories because of their ironic twists, not believing that a machine can handle irony. Like the subtlety in the Joyce stories, O. Henry's twists, however tight and mathematical, require familiarity with life. I finally settle on Hemingway, the first forty-nine, some of which are very beautiful and very good and possessive of a brutally invisible resonance, such as "A Clean, Well-Lighted Place," and all of which perform evenly and clean from start to finish regardless of what you think they might mean and are quite fine. I am ashamed when Reece comes to a meeting one day having read "The Killers" the night prior and shares his feeling that we shouldn't be training the engine (everyone has a different name for it) on racist language.

"The N-word appears twenty-four times in the story—practically as many times as the word 'the,'" Reece says, a little angry and visibly hurt.

Carlos says, "Yeah, that's not good for the machine. It's probably not good for you either, Felipe."

I had forgotten somehow, or, somehow, I had never noticed.

"I'm sorry," I say.

"The engine is very sensitive, very impressionable," Reece adds. "Frequency of use demonstrates priority. You feed it enough words like that, it'll be a part of its function."

"Yes," I say, "in the future, we'll make checking for this kind of stuff part of our, um . . ."

"Protocol," Liliane suggests.

"That's great," I say.

"We can call it fitness of language," Carlos says.

"Perfect," Reece says, no longer looking so upset, and then, "And we can keep the story, Felipe. It's an interesting piece. We just need to clean up the language. And not for *me*, but the engine."

"Of course," I say.

"Do you think you could go over the text tonight, Felipe?" Carlos asks. "It's not just that story and it's not just that word."

"Sure," I say. "Sure thing."

After the meeting, on my way to meet Mikhail in the library, Liliane comes up from behind me and asks if I've ever read Borges's "The Wait."

"Have you ever read 'The Garden of Forking Paths'?" I say.

"Sure," she says. "But have you read 'The Wait'?"

"A long time ago, and I don't think I finished it," I lie.

"You should reread it. And finish it this time."

"CERVANTES JOYCE WALLACE Rivera," I say.

"Or Wallace Joyce Cervantes Abadžić?" Mikhail says.

We're trying to decide on what our future child's name is going to be.

"So, you two are *dating* now?" Doña dos Cosimas says.

"Dating sounds so juvenile," Mikhail says.

"Engaged?" dos Cosimas says.

"Kind of military-ish," I say.

"You're soul mates?"

"Without souls," I say. "We don't believe in the soul."

"I kind of believe in the soul," Mikhail says.

"Okay, so you're Australian," dos Cosimas says, and heads back to her desk.

I read Borges's "The Waiting" aloud to Mikhail—not sure why Liliane called it "The Wait."

Four pages later, when the story is over, I say, "David Foster Wallace called it 'marvelous' in the *Times*."

"The Waiting," it turns outs, is a remake of Hemingway's "The Killers," like a really good piece of fanfiction.

Mikhail stays silent for a time, a pant leg riding up to reveal he is not wearing any socks.

"You should wear socks," I say.

"It is marvelous," Mikhail finally says. "Because Borges only really focuses on the transcendent moment in the Hemingway story. The whole drama of Hemingway's first act—Nick Adams getting tied up by mobsters in the diner's kitchen with the cook while the mobsters await the arrival of the Swedish boxer so that they can kill him—doesn't exist at all in the Borges version. The tension of the first act dissipates in the

Hemingway story, but only once Nick is let free and discovers that the boxer is simply lying in bed at home awaiting his fate, but that's the dénouement, not the plot."

"Yes. The genius of the Hemingway story is his unraveling of the hero's purpose. His original hero. But that's only possible because we spend so much time with the hero hoping that he'll be able to escape and save the boxer's life."

"As soon as he steps into the Swede's room, it's like stepping into Elysium."

"Do you think Nick Adams is dead in the rest of the stories?"

"He seems pretty dead in 'Big Two-Hearted River.'"

"But that's because of World War I."

"Joyce liked 'The Killers.'"

"Weird," I say.

"Borges really does focus *entirely* on the transcendent mystery at the end of the original," Mikhail says. "It's fascinating."

"And he goes full-on Borges by being anti-Borges in this story."

"Yes, he swims in the lacuna, he fills it. By replacing the Swedish boxer with another mobster outrunning mobsters, there's a moral fairness to his impending demise. We sit with him within the condition of destiny. It solves the mystery of the boxer's inaction in Hemingway's original."

"How can somebody live in opposition to the inevitable?"

"Borges's mobster is consumed by the inevitable, too—he dreams of his own murder almost every night, the killers suddenly arriving and killing him. It's as if he's just as afraid of losing power as he is of death."

"But he's never actually without agency."

"No, but he tries to be."

"Yes, when the killer finally does come for him, he asks that he can turn away before he shoots him so that he can return to the blindsided state of his nightmares."

"But because his nightmares are of his own making, he isn't blind-sided, he's making this moment happen."

"And because the killer is after him for something that he's done, his death is literally of his own making."

"Which is why, when he arrives at his final hideout, he assumes the identity of the man who is after him."

"Because he is his own killer."

"Just like the Swedish boxer."

I realize my mouth is dry from reading and all of the talking. I open a bottle of Live Wire and, for a moment, before the pepsin pumps awaken and begin hosing down my innards with acid, I feel cool inside.

"Twenty-four is a lot of times to use that word, though," Mikhail says.

"Yes," I say, feeling the pepsin rush. "I wonder how Borges felt about it."

PART II: ADULTHOOD

Biden, the early administration.

. . . Bombs over Iraq, again.

> "To have compassion for those who suffer is a human
> quality which everyone should possess, especially
> those who have required comfort themselves in the
> past and have managed to find it in others."
> —Giovanni Boccaccio, *The Decameron*

Welcome, one and all, to another episode of The Book Murderer *Podcast. I'm your host, Mikhail, aka Micky, and this hour, or this hour and fifteen minutes, or these forty-seven minutes and twenty-two and a half seconds—not sure how long it's going to take—I will be taking to task yet another book that is rotting the minds of America's youth—as well as the minds of quite a few adults—in part six of our series:* Why YA? Why God, Why-A?? *Today, we are going to be toppling a very*

*popular book, a very popular book that I think all of you may already
know, called . . .*

THE PODCAST IS, I'm not afraid to admit, my real life, and the rest is something else entirely. I stumbled upon my real life some years ago. I was broke and dispossessed of any interest in the waking, walking parts, so I started to read again, after a long break, and soon after found myself stepping into a Best Buy for a desktop microphone and a wind sock. Recording my thoughts on the withering state of contemporary literature—and not just YA, but the whole enterprise—became a way of diluting the pepsin in my gut, getting the real blood pumping again. Whenever I find myself growing despondent—I can't normally tell myself, I usually rely on the looks my wife and son and supervisor at work start to give me—I fire up Audacity, a free and easy to use digital audio workstation that I cannot recommend highly enough, and . . . *pontificate.*

There is a way of knowing who is listening, but I choose not to look. It's none of my business. YA is none of my business, either, I admit, but with my son bringing home so many titles from the library, I have not been able to keep myself from taking a peek and gasping. I'm no *Catcher in the Rye* kind of guy, but I do recall, on occasion, being made out to be so much, whenever I've snuck a real novel into his reading stack. "Let the boy read what he wants to read," the wife tells me. Yes, let *the world* read what it wants to read, let the world *vote* for whom they want to vote, let the world rot and await the day a band of scrappy survivalists shows up on your doorstep, holds your family hostage, and raids your pantry, and don't you once consider offering anyone an ounce of criticism, not an iota, even if it might help those willing to listen to lead richer, fuller, *longer* lives. Just don't. Just let. *Just podcast*, I say.

I'm podcasting down in the basement when I am awakened to the humbling presence of my own body. Aboveground, I discover that I am alone. The empty fridge and the pantry's unstocked shelves persecute me. I consider ordering in before deciding I am going out.

I live in one of America's most walkable medium-sized cities. The restaurants and shops are open again. And there's a decent club at the diner around the corner. I'm seated, I'm situated, I'm settled within seconds. Eschewing the menu living inside a QR code, I tell the server—who had been my host, will bus the scraps I leave behind—about the club, water will be fine, and they take my order to the kitchen. Through the window, I see a man walking in a certain light of day and think, I *have* to be happier than you. I have to be happier than *you*.

My water comes. It's been years since soda. In the booth behind me, I hear two adolescents conversing, one sounding male, the other female—I didn't catch a look at them on my way in. Drinking my water, I think I'll put the podcast to rest. There's mold in the basement. The family could drive out west. Out west, with the family, I could seek some clarity. It's not going to turn out well if I keep making space for disappointment and anger. I want to love a book, the way I have loved books, I want to see the world through the boy's eyes. I want the boy to look into his own eyes and see his father's eyes and not see anger and disappointment. When my meal comes, the server says, "Careful, toothpicks in da club," and does a dance move and smiles.

If I were the regular in a short story by Raymond Carver about a regular in this diner, this kind server would be my salvation. We'd smoke and talk for hours in the story. I'd offer them a nip from my flask, which in real life I do not have, and they'd shudder as they swallowed and say, "Motherfuck." Neither of us would be generous with our words but we'd both be very sincere. They'd be much older, a lifer, and a woman. They'd show me a picture of the surly cook when he was young and he'd remind me of someone I used to know. Oh, yes, myself. "He's not so bad," she'd say. Her nail polish would be the same shade of powder pink as her uniform. Despite the twenty-four-hour sign out front, around 1:00 A.M. the cook would come out and announce that it was quitting time. He'd hook his thumbs toward his smock, which would read KISS THE COOK, and the waitress would kiss him on his hard, clean-shaven chef jaw. Then he'd hook his arm round her rump and heave a good chunk of butt, in a Popeye the Sailor Man kind of way but consensually. In the parking lot, after our goodbyes, I'd hear him ask, "Where to, baby?" and she'd reply, "I'm in the mood for diner pancakes," and he'd say, "You've got it." Semi-drunk, seated in the darkness of my car, I'd hear the engine roll over three times before waking up. In the final scene, the story would jump to my wife waking up and rolling over to look at me in bed and me saying, in the dark, "I want to talk. I'm ready to talk."

The one who sounds male says, "I don't blame Felipe for what happens to Mikhail."

The one who sounds female says, "No, not at all. He doesn't know who he is, he's scared, he doesn't really know what Mikhail has been going through because Mikhail doesn't tell him. Oh, it's such a beautiful book."

Da club is still intact. I turn around like a character in a Carver story—a quiet man with his heart on his sleeve like mustard on his shirt, a drunk man with his furniture on his front lawn—and ask the two what they are reading. They flash a yellow paperback with the title *No Time for Birds* slashed across its face.

"What's it about?" I say.

"You really want to know?" the femme says.

"Sure," I say.

They tell me it's about two high school book nerds attending a private school in Chicago during the early stages of the Iraq War. They are trying to decide what the greatest book of all time is when their librarian asks them to aid a pilot program teaching artificial intelligence how to write novels. They are each assigned a group of computer science students to assist with the design and composition. The two, Felipe and Mikhail, might be in love, but they don't know for sure, it doesn't go into a lot of detail, it's more inferred. A lot of the book is just them talking about books. Despite the fact that they are both the sons of working-class immigrants and probably gay, their literary tastes are very conservative, very old dead white guy. They despise YA literature, which the AIs they are helping to train are designed to write. Together, they devise a plan to sabotage the pilot program by feeding their AIs books that are too subtle, too ironic, too amoral for an algorithm to interpret. However, when Felipe starts to fall for Liliane, a girl in his group, he changes his mind. Liliane is studying computer science but loves literature too. She introduces Felipe to a new way of looking at stories. "They can enlighten you in positive ways," she says, and cites some stuff Nabokov said. Felipe decides then to feed his AI simple, morally legible stories, but he doesn't tell Mikhail, afraid that Mikhail will think he is a coward. Meanwhile, Mikhail is struggling at home. His parents are going through a divorce, his mom has lost her job, and he overhears the two arguing one night about how best to address his sexuality. In an act of defiance, and self-liberation, he pins a pride flag to the lapel of his school blazer. It's not against school policy, but his classmates start bullying him, which reaches its apex when a kid pushes him in front of a city bus after school. Distraught, he turns to Felipe for support, but Felipe argues that it's too dangerous to be out in this kind of environment. Their librarian comes to Mikhail's defense instead and ends up getting into a physical altercation with the lead bully and is fired. At the end of the year, each AI training group is asked to share their AI's short story with the student body. Felipe's tells the simple story of a father-and-son fishing trip. Mikhail's ends up being a vitriolic, racist, misogynist, homophobic screed featuring a walk-on by George W. Bush. Mikhail feels betrayed by what Felipe has done and swears he'll never forgive him but winds up asking him to junior prom, a proposal Felipe promptly rejects. Instead, Felipe goes to senior prom with Liliane. Over the summer, Mikhail kills himself, and Felipe struggles with his guilt. Liliane goes to college in Michigan. Felipe visits her one weekend and the two take a canoeing trip with her friends near where Ernest Hemingway set some of his early stories. Felipe flirts with one of her openly gay male friends, but when he gets drunk one night, he tells a homophobic joke that rightly upsets the whole group. In the morning, Liliane tells Felipe that he has a lot of growing up to do and they shouldn't see each other anymore. His senior year, he writes a poem about Mikhail that earns him a college scholarship.

"And you like this book?" I ask.

"It's my favorite," the masc says.

THE FAMILY HEADS east for a trip. Out east, one can achieve clarity as easily as out west. The boy wants to see NYC. I leave them in Dumbo, rent a car, and drive into New Jersey for a day. New Jersey is where I've tracked down Herman Lowery, his name having appeared slashed across the cover of the beloved yellow book too.

The internet tells me *No Time for Birds* was published in 2012 and nobody noticed. Shortly after, its publishing company filed for bankruptcy and *NTFB* fell out of print. Over the years, however, the publisher has developed a bit of a cult following amongst high school teenagers, and *NTFB* first editions (never released in hardback) sell for upward of $150 on eBay. It was Herman Lowery's last book.

A jovial fifty-something-year-old man answers the door of Herman Lowery's apartment in New Jersey.

"An old coworker, wow, I thought you guys were ghosts," the man says. "He's in the living room."

When I find him, Herman Lowery is lying on his couch thumbing his phone. He doesn't get up.

"Who are you?" he asks, turning his head toward me on the armrest.

"Mikhail," I say.

"No, Mikhail was the white one," Herman Lowery says. "Mikhail died."

He spins his body to face the couch. His shoulders, draped in a blue dress shirt, rise and fall as he says, "I've been waiting for you, Felipe. I've been dreaming of this moment for years. Please don't hurt Blake."

"Why would I hurt Blake?" I say.

Herman Lowery turns around and sits up on the couch.

"I didn't write it," he says. "They just put my name on it. I tried to delete it and they put my name on the cover."

"Who wrote it?" I say.

"The machine, the engine. I told them to get rid of it. I told them your friend, a young boy, had killed himself, that it was a horrible, dishonorable thing to publish. They wouldn't listen. And now kids are eating it up. Mikhail. They're eating him up."

"Mikhail didn't die. *Our* Mikhail didn't die," I say.

"What are you saying? You're lying. I followed it in the news, a boy from Maine Tech named Mikhail killed himself. I saw his picture."

"It was another Mikhail—there were two Mikhails at Maine Tech at the time. Our Mikhail *tried* to kill himself but his mother saved him. Fall of our senior year, the other Mikhail, a junior, killed himself. I know the picture you're referring to. The paper mixed up the two. Mikhail tried to have it changed but the paper never answered his emails. The AI made a mistake. But the AI, it worked?"

Herman Lowery looks at his hands.

"Did you and Mikhail ever talk again?" he asks.

"Only once. He asked me if I thought it was his fault that Mikhail had killed himself. We'd heard so much about copycat suicides. I told him he had nothing to feel guilty about."

"Did he believe you?" Herman Lowery asks.

"I don't think so."

Our Mikhail, of course, did kill himself. I just can't bring myself to let Herman Lowery think himself a monster. I know the condition all too well, having written the phrase *I am a murderer* many times on strips of paper, strips of paper I have burned, buried, tossed into various bodies of water, swallowed whole. I pray that Herman Lowery will not go digging, will not call Maine Tech to confirm he'd been lied to. I hope he knows the scent of compassion, whiffed it on the still air of his home, and allows himself the human right to breathe it and hold it in.

"That excerpt you showed us," I say, "I knew what it was, even with a third of the words missing."

"It was a dream," Herman Lowery says.

"It was part of LBJ's 'Great Society' speech."

"A dream," Herman Lowery says.

I stay for a drink Blake prepares in the kitchen. Their home is small and artless. The drink loosens me up. It gives me heartburn. Blake is an interesting man and a terrific conversationalist. I have awakened couch man, and Blake is grateful. He cuts cloth at Jo-Ann Fabrics. His outfit, a billowy shirt and short ensemble, is all Jo-Ann, a solid swatch of planets and moons.

Before I leave, he asks me, "I hope you don't mind me asking, but were you and Mikhail in love? The book is very ambiguous. Herman says it was a content filter's fault. That the publisher didn't want to publish explicitly gay love stories. Not like YA books today. I've always wondered, though. You wrote that poem about him in the end, but it's also sort of vague. It's more of a eulogy than a love poem. It could be expressing platonic love."

I say, "I don't think we had the confidence to know anything then. We were children. We loved books we hadn't read. We wore other people's clothes. We never touched. We never kissed. How would we have known?"

Blake's drink looks like a watered-down brass pipe in his hand. He says, "Oh, honey. You can love a book you've never read. If a robot can write a story about being human . . ."

III.

ILLNESS

CONCERNING THOSE WHO HAVE FALLEN ASLEEP

ON THE EVE OF THE parade, Hanna Schröder was asked to have the Allerton sisters ready for the party in under an hour. It would be difficult, given the girls' general recalcitrance and specific disregard for the help, especially those with whom they lacked any consequential rapport. When Hanna appeared in their bedroom and asked that they please wash and clothe themselves, the children called her a stranger and told her to go away.

"I may be unfamiliar, but I'm no stranger," Hanna said, stepping toward the girls. "I do your laundry every day. We've spoken before. You're Alice, and you're Rose."

"I've honestly never seen you in my life," the older one, Alice, said, and Hanna did not advance any further into the room, dark like the father's library and silky and moody like the mother's boudoir.

Hanna was nineteen; Alice and Rose nine and seven—but she was disturbed by their coldness just the same. She'd been warned that the girls could be peculiar and cruel but was not prepared to be pronounced invisible. It was a childish notion, Hanna admitted, but the way Alice had delivered her statement—sharp and mannered—carried with it no silliness at all, and this stung. However, unbeknownst to Hanna, Alice wasn't being silly or cruel—not intentionally, at least. The child wasn't lying. She was barely exaggerating. The truth was, like the nocturnal creatures that wreaked havoc on their mother's garden at night, even on the clearest day, the sisters could register only the silhouettes of most people. The woman they sometimes found crying under the wrought-iron trellis of the rose arbor during her breaks was nothing but a pair of trembling shoulders, nameless and faceless and somewhat comical in her composed despair, her only companion a dusky water spigot cast in the shape of a squirrel. Even a helpful voice warning them away from a braid of poison oak or a nest of yellowjackets, when the sisters turned to find its source, would somehow originate from a scratchy mirage, a ghost but not a ghost. But unlike their rodent counterparts, God-given myopia and sensitivity to sunlight could not be blamed for the girls' poor eyesight.

When the two discovered the old chauffeur laid on his belly in a copse of trees a year ago, they knew the man was in trouble, quite possibly even dead, and yet they simply turned away from him and did not utter a word to anyone about what they'd seen until the chauffeur's nephew, a boy no older than twelve who worked in the Allertons' stables, interrupted their breakfast with screams that he'd found his uncle dead in the woods. Worst yet, the nephew thought his uncle quite bloated and a little mean in appearance. Alice, who'd barely looked up from her plate of toast when the boy burst in, calmly replied that she didn't think so at all, finally breaking the sisters' silence on the matter.

"I thought he looked rather small and very shocked, like a child," she said.

Before the nephew or any of the other employees standing around at the time could think of what to say, the cook ushered the boy away and a pair of footmen departed for the woods. The story circulated through the household, and eventually, it became widely agreed amongst the staff that the girls must have something wrong with them, though whether they were evil or deranged remained the question.

Hanna was not present for the event, but she'd heard about it and been advised never to find herself in trouble while the two were around. Watching them carry on with their dolls, she couldn't help feeling a little like the chauffeur herself, not quite dead but dismissed, which somehow meant something worse. She could not be made to quit so easily, however. Standing her ground in the darkened, silken room, she reminded them of their parents' party and the import of the following day's festivities, and they suddenly turned their eyes toward her.

"And I know that you girls have been warned what would happen to you if tonight turns out to be anything short of a complete success," Hanna said, and without further protest, the girls put down their toys and marched to their bathroom.

The evening's event, as had been suggested in the invitation, would feature a six-course meal, champagne, dancing, and an opportunity to show one's own winning, patriotic resolve in tasteful and familiar opulence. Typical of any Allerton affair, there was no reason to believe it would not be well attended. Little had changed over the years amongst this crowd, save for the hats. Joining a world already at war was simply another cause for celebration, and investment.

Until that hurried hour, Hanna, a washer girl, had spent little time inside the main house, but the au pair, Astrid, a robust Swede with degrees in botany and literature, had recently fallen ill, and at risk of contagion was asked to stay away and needed replacing. No one on staff knew for sure where Astrid was being kept. She was missing from her apartment; no doctor had been seen coming or going in the past few days. Like a turnip selected from the market, Hanna was told she would do and had been whisked inside.

James, the girls' ten-year-old brother and Hanna's third charge for the evening, though reliably more amenable than his sisters, was quite their equal when it came to dressing up for guests. He hated formal garments' yet more restrictive qualities. Most days he spent out of doors, regardless of the weather, aping the part of the l'enfant roi and terrorizing the gardener, but James fell in love with Hanna upon discovering her in his bedroom and proceeded to lose every ounce of wildness. To him, her mouth resembled that of an enraptured female saint featured on a funeral card he kept hidden between the pages of a Jules Verne novel beside his bed, and so he allowed himself to be directed without protest as the woman hand selected his attire and did his best to be mannishly self-sufficient when she departed to tend to his little sisters again. Once fully clothed, however, he stomped into his sisters' dressing room distraught and with shoes untied. The first guests were just arriving. His shirt was misbuttoned, and his bowtie was horribly knotted, but he didn't look ridiculous at all, Hanna assured him. Attractively helpless, she claimed, like a brooding little artist who simply had more important things to attend to. Her smile revived him, but only momentarily. When she told him she may need a pair of scissors to release him from his bowtie, the boy stiffened. Her nails were soft as shrimp tails after all the boiling water and bluing.

Hanna wore a bland perfume excited by her sweat. It swelled with the smudgy oil odor of her hairline. Wet boughs and greasy baseboards. This too revived James. He looked for his sisters' mirror to find himself and wavered in his reflection. He had a malformed hand—some impatience in the womb, his mother had been told—and for this he was impatient to grow up, wear leather gloves, and mostly be left alone. Hanna watched him hide his hand in his pocket, concealing it from his reflection.

"You can tell people it happened in the war," she whispered, and James nearly hugged her.

"You see, our family came over on a great big flower," Rose explained as she paced and watched the woman re-dress her brother. In their matching emerald dresses, amongst their chalky dolls, taupe quilts, and wilted undergarments strewn about the room, both she and her sister glowed like manure flies.

"Daddy says we created society, the greatest society in the world. Which is why we're rich and you're poor," the girl kept on.

Choking, James tore away from Hanna's beautiful hands and said, "We came over on a ship called the *Mayflower*, you dunce," and, with his good hand, swatted at her for saying such a thing and at Alice for giggling.

Hanna pulled him back and, on one knee, shook her face in his. Releasing him from his bow tie finally, Hanna said, "We all come from boats," and went after the rest of his shirt buttons.

The Allertons were a Philadelphia steel family. At that very moment, dignitaries from New York, Boston, and London were being dropped in front of their palatial Fairmount Park home from chauffeured cars. The family had tried to stay noncommittal to the war in Europe, even citing a cousin's standing in a local Quaker house to defend their steel-for-all stance, but the *Lusitania* had changed just about everything, and by 1918 the United States was engaged in full-fledged military conflict with the Kaiser and Congress was charging treason.

"Let's see you," Hanna said, and James, with his shirt corrected, admired his own reflection. He let his bad hand hang at his side this time.

"Now, go make a mess," she said, and the young man disappeared.

She hissed at the sisters and they, too, departed.

Downstairs, the guests accepted refreshments and showed each other their teeth. Hilda, the woman with whom Hanna had interviewed and who had shown Hanna the ins and outs of the Allerton home, an esoteric mansion with hidden rooms and places to spy from within the walls, gathered coats at the door, nodding politely with an American flag pinned to her gray smock. Hanna adjusted her own as she passed her in the foyer. Nearly every woman who worked for the Allerton household was German; earlier that day, Marin, a cook, in a respite between meals and the evening's preparations, had nervously painted them each a felt flag to wear on their breast. She had told Hanna Mrs. Allerton had thought she'd done well, even if the stars and stripes were blurry and ill counted. Accepting her pin, Hanna had thanked Marin for her efforts and told her her pins were very handsome. Marin hoped Mrs. Allerton might bring attention to the pins during the event. It was an important expression of solidarity, after all, Marin had said. Hanna had said nothing more. The night prior, depositing a stack of napkins in the kitchen, she had overheard Mr. Allerton tell his wife that it might behoove them to hire Negroes for the event, for appearances' sake. But Mrs. Allerton had responded with a scandalous story a member of her bridge club had told about fifty dollars in missing linens. This, and only this, had swayed Mr. Allerton's opinion, and without these suspicions, Hanna knew, she and the rest of the Germans would have been asked to spend the night at home, pins or no pins.

From the foyer, Hanna disappeared through a servant's door and squeezed herself past a menagerie of vested male servers waiting with hors d'ouevres in the darkened wing. A wall of exposed wire and plumbing scratched at her arms as she hurried along. Summoning bells whirred and tined. In the darkness between and beyond the walls' mechanics, Hanna detected something or a family of things breathing, a fur-covered lung lifting and falling. She had five minutes and she'd give them to the new washer girl, who, too, had been discharged from her usual duties, to fold the napkins Hanna had washed the day prior. Fifteen or so, a few years younger than herself, Hanna could not recall the girl's name. Irish, though. After, Hanna would reemerge on the ground floor and tend to the young descendants once again. Being deep inside the house, she'd tried explaining to her father, wasn't like being inside the hull of a ship, where the ceiling bows with every step overhead and drops its salt. Inside was deeper, farther below, the bottom of the sea. Inside were secret nibbling fish. The place she'd always been from. In the dark, she felt for her pin, adjusted it once more.

SHORTLY AFTER THE last guest left, Mr. Allerton approached Hanna in the drawing room to ask if she knew where the children were. Though she'd have worried if he were drunk, Mr. Allerton did not imbibe. Still, his composure and officiousness, so late in the night, startled Hanna just the same. She had put all three children to bed hours ago and did not know what to make of his question.

"Be that as it may, Ms. Schröder, Mrs. Allerton just went up to check on them and said that none of the children are in their beds," Mr. Allerton said. "She cannot seem to find them anywhere."

"I'll find them immediately, Mr. Allerton," she said, and headed outside.

The children had given her none of the grief the others had promised. They had eaten, the littlest one had danced, and the night had concluded without any commotion or complication. But when Hanna put James to bed, he had asked after Astrid, clearly worried, and Hanna suspected that he may have gone in search of the au pair.

Moving through the night, starless and without a moon, was like traversing a sea. The darkness a hard body to push against. The rise and fall of the Allerton grounds, the dips and swells of cresting waves. Hanna stumbled more than once as the lights of the household shrank behind her. Not a night bird spoke. Passing the garden, she caught no thieves. Like the world, thick with essential elements everywhere, was still unfinished in certain places, and she had come across one such area. Then, nearing Astrid's apartment, a tiny, stone bungalow with a view of the Allertons' swimming and skating pond, she spied a human figure peering into the bungalow's front window, marking an end to her strange and unaccompanied journey. It turned, spotting her as she approached.

"Ms. Schröder," it called out in a whisper, and she knew by the measured timidity of its voice that it was James.

"Ms. Schröder, I swear it wasn't my idea," James said when she reached him.

"James, what are you doing out here?" Hanna said. "You should be in bed, fast asleep like I left you."

"I woke up. The party was so loud. I'd had a dream about Astrid. But it wasn't my idea to come, I swear. I went to see if Alice and Rose were still awake, to ask them if they knew anything about where Astrid had gone, but they weren't in their beds, so I went out looking for them. I'm telling the truth, please believe me."

She couldn't see the look of exasperation on James's face but she could hear it in his voice. He was so little in the light, even smaller in the dark. His hand was back in his pocket.

"Did you find them?" she asked.

"I did, but they ran off."

"Where?"

"The pond. I told them not to."

Hanna looked back toward the main house. It was too far to ask the boy to head there alone. His parents would not like to greet him without her by his side.

"Show me," Hanna said.

She took a step in the direction of the pond, but James did not move.

"They said they saw Astrid," he said.

"Astrid is here?"

She tried to get a look inside the bungalow herself.

"They said she was leaving."

"Leaving? Leaving where to?"

"She was packing her suitcases, they said. They saw her through the window."

"She's gone, then?"

"They knocked on the door to ask her where she was going. She answered the door and . . ."

The boy turned his shadowed face away from her.

"And what?"

"They said she told them that she was dead. They said she said she'd died and she was going away."

She heard the child begin to cry.

"If she was dead—" Hanna started.

"Astrid was my friend," James said, choking as he had in his bow tie. "Astrid was kind to me."

Hanna heard the cloudy sound of laughter on the water.

"Your sisters," she said.

She heard the echo of a rock skipping across the water's face.

"Oh, your sisters are such devils," she said.

"Is she dead?" James asked, sober suddenly, like his father. "Is Astrid dead?"

"She most certainly is not," Hanna said, though she had no idea. "Now, let's get your sisters."

By the time they reached the pond, the girls had quit skipping rocks and laughing. A cool wind flew across the water, invigorating Hanna's lungs. She was about to call to them, calmly but sternly and without shouting, when James screamed, "Hurry! Hurry!" Hanna jumped and the girls came rushing.

"James," Hanna said, "What is the—" but the boy put his partial hand in hers and she fell silent. In the dark, in her mind, she tried to picture what she was holding, the form of another thing. Was it not unlike a bird? More like a mouse?

"Mother fell," James said, crying again.

"Mother fell?" Rose repeated.

"She's dead," James said, and bawled.

"Mother is dead!" Rose wailed.

"Mother is dead?" Alice asked Hanna.

The early parts of James's fingers gripped at Hanna's hand.

"I don't know what any of this could mean," Hanna said.

"Mother is dead!" Rose screamed again.

"Mother is dead!" James cried.

James tore toward the house, his sisters in tow, Hanna trying to keep pace behind them. The landscape rolled like a wave, but the darkness lessened in the strengthening light of the home. Birds called at them this time. Dogs barked. In the garden, the thieves scurried. Mounting the paving stones of the patio, Hanna could imagine the bones of the girls' toes dragging the meat of their bare feet, the pads scraping and tearing and bleeding.

Inside, their mother was still in her evening gown. The color of champagne. The cut in the silhouette of a champagne flute. The girls flew to her. Hanna thought they'd tear her to pieces.

"I simply had no idea what any of them were saying," Hanna said eventually.

"Yes," Mr. Allerton said. "Perhaps it was a bad dream."

HAD ANYONE BOTHERED to ask Abel Schröder his feelings about the war before last April, he would have said what was happening in Europe was someone else's issue entirely. Wishy-washy Wilson, for that matter, was someone else's president, too, someone who could actually vote, however mindlessly. And yet there Abel Schröder was the morning of September 28, having arrived early, freshly shaved, and with Wilson's long, Scots-Irish head floating on the charcoal weave of his twill vest, at the parade grounds to ribbon lampposts with his daughter, Hanna. Half the German raw-hands of Southwark were there, having made a show to their employers of asking the day to take part in the loan parade. There were German men hanging from trees in the North.

With their leftover ribbon, Abel instructed Hanna to give herself a smart little loop and pin it to the breast of her smock. She'd lost her flag from the previous night. The smock was stiff and cut darkly into her white neck. He had not seen much of her since she'd been hired at the Allerton home a year ago. When he dreamed of Hanna, she was a child in ripped stockings. She'd be a woman in servant's clothes for the rest of her life.

"You should have worn a dress," Abel told his daughter.

She glowed against her ribbon.

"Your mother and I met at a parade."

She looked at the ribbon, what it was doing in the early fall air. It was the most he'd ever told her about his courtship with her mother.

Three of them now, Abel, his wife, and Hanna. The boy having withered out of uniform in a bed in the French countryside before returning in full military dress to be interred in St. Peter's Cemetery three months ago, dead from illness. Igor, swimming in the folds of his costume, was the reason no one bothered to ask Abel why he'd come this morning, why he called himself a Republican, though he couldn't vote, why he'd told Hanna if she couldn't take the day off as well he'd beat her into an infirmary. Igor had brought himself to an American death. It was America's war now; it was Igor's parade.

In Germany, Abel had been a master tailor. In America, he made alterations in a shop owned by a man named Yeats. For almost a year now, not a week had passed when a young discharge would not appear in Yeats's shop and ask each of his suits be altered to accommodate a wooden appendage or conceal a shrunken or missing limb. Abel would line a sleeve or leg with stiff cloth, lending body and fullness to the emptiness there, and the boys would appear almost whole again as they stepped into their altered suits in front of his mirror. Abel said to them, "As you will appear in the Kingdom of God. At your peak strength and beauty," these luckier versions of the ghost still haunting him.

Had Hanna been beaten into an infirmary, she'd have discovered more than three dozen infantrymen shuddering in cotton beds right there in Philadelphia, each praying dignity and courage be restored to him, too, in the Kingdom of God.

The world, as it is concluded in the Bible, Abel knew, would be consumed in several ceremonies.

"I'll be checking in with Mrs. Allerton this evening," Hanna said. "To make a good showing, I plan to hurry in and do the evening load. And I'll see if the party still needs cleaning up after."

He wanted her home but never stood in her way to persist in this world. If it turned out she were one of the countless seeds the neighborhood had warned against, a generation of youths with so few ties to their origin they might as well have traversed the Atlantic by wind or wing, so be it. He wouldn't have beaten her into an infirmary. He'd never once laid hands on her. He'd played a small but meaningful part in giving her life. He'd never considered being part of her destruction. All over Philadelphia microbes were tying their shoes and combing their hair in front of mirrors, assuring that he would be.

"Your mother misses you dearly" was all he said.

The girl's mother had been captured—like a bird, docile, almost ornamental with indifference—by grief. She had helped Abel with his work. The men worrying her stitches in their repaired pockets and women for whom she'd let out gowns wearing her double seams down their engorged backs had no idea the trouble she was in. They never would. They'd simply say Yeats's work was never quite the same after America joined the war.

"I'll make you dinner next week. Marin will have some neckbones for me," Hanna said.

Abel said nothing.

The city filed in, two hundred thousand American souls. Buoyant heavenly bodies with German, Dutch, Irish, and Italian tethers, but red, white, and blue leads dashing in the air overhead. Floats carrying biplanes and cannons to "Stars and Stripes Forever." Faces sneezing and kissing. Pacts were being made with freedom: if you sealed your earnings with freedom's fate and freedom reigned, both would be everlasting. Heaven on Earth. Hanna had had her mind on a pair of boots. Abel had wanted to buy Hanna more time, a few free nights a month to have a man over for dinner, a different kind of future. But the boys overseas needed boots, the boys overseas needed dinner. The war bonds would bind Hanna to a lonely but perhaps sturdier fate, Abel thought, and he signed off as much as he could without his wife noticing. In her rare moments of lucidity, his wife had sworn off all countries. The whole world owed her her son.

When the parade was over, at the end of the line, Abel would remember seeing horses standing like vagrants outside fruitless orchards, looking for work. A woman pinching a white rag to her face and yanking away a boy who'd been standing beside him, watching the horses, too. The boy keeping stride with his mother as she beat him. The boy not crying out once, his mother wailing all the way home.

In two months, when people wrestled Abel, weeping in the wet street himself, they'd yell, "You didn't know. None of us knew. They said, 'Go out to the parade.'" And he'd quietly fold his hands because this was what memory was determined to do, and who was he to stand in its way? He'd only say there were idle horses waiting at the end of the line, primed for riders never to return. Though at least three newspapers had warned readers to avoid crowds, stay indoors, and prepare for quarantine. Why had he insisted his daughter accompany him? For the moment, however, watching the city celebrate its unity, Wilson's promise to make the world safe for democracy, holding his daughter's tiny blued hand, Abel simply enjoyed himself, the colored paper and screams coating the air.

TWO WEEKS LATER, in place of the horses and human feet, happy screams and colored paper, the streets filled with Red Cross trucks. The world brimmed with fumes and engine sounds, like the twentieth century had arrived at last in all its shining vulgarity. Despite the trucks, piles of dead were beginning. The war had reached the American shore, battles were being waged in sick beds, ammunition in everyone's saliva. The dead, before they died, wheezed and vomited a bloody lather. Hanna came over and made dinner, more bone broth. After, she gave her mother a hot bath. At midnight, with the women asleep, Abel stepped out onto the front porch to find every head of household doing the same. All along the street, the long boxcar corridor of porches contained one man apiece, each man illuminating his mustaches and spectacles with the fairy sprite of a wooden pipe or lobbing cigar, the little smoking flames acting as censers, forbidding the contagion entry into their homes. Abel was tossing a spent match into the darkness when Hanna appeared at his side.

"The Irish girl is sick. The children are sick. Now mother is sick," she said. "The Allertons managed to have a doctor pay them a visit. He says we are its harbingers. We've done this. It's a plague brought unto us by God for our sins."

Her words wrapped around a nameless globe in his head, a rust smoke spewing from a crater in Europe. All evening, she'd withheld her alarm. He knew his daughter was without sin. His wife, the Allerton children, too. He had sinned. Pride. If God had really smote those prideful tower builders by slicing their tongues into the tribes of the world, America was nothing but modern man's attempt to undo His ancient vengeful scattering. Better to live as an enemy to his newfound countrymen than to die at peace with everyone but God.

"The children can't breathe. The doctor says little can be done."

And for what reason had he taken Hanna to the parade? To offer Igor dignity in death? Shouldn't a man's name be dignity enough? Because Igor Schröder, son of Abel Schröder, meant nothing in life, he had to die for a country he hardly knew.

"You'll stay home. That house is cursed," he said.

"Mother."

"We must protect ourselves."

"The Irish girl, she's only a lamb. She'll make her whole family sick."

"I'm going to protect you," Abel said.

God had already assigned him his tribe, and his tribe was dwindling. The rest of the city could go on dying without them.

IN THE MORNING, there was hardly a scene at all. Abel's wife was brought down the porch steps and placed inside a wagon. There were some medical students left in Philadelphia, doctors and nurses in training, and churches had been converted into hospitals. The driver told Abel they'd have to make a few stops; hopefully, there would be an open bed somewhere. Hanna tried to follow behind, but could not manage. The neighbors did not look from their windows or from the sidewalks, it being the belief of some that one could contract the illness just by looking at it. There was a revitalization of privacy and dignity in even the city's most cramped quarters since the nude bodies had appeared, belly-up and swelling in the street, as a queer family of right whales had on the shores of New Jersey a few years prior.

SIX DAYS HANNA suffered her father's reign, who, like Prince Prospero, sealed them off from contamination behind the brick and wood of their home. They ate meal after meal. With her idle, repairing hands, Hanna stripped and re-dressed the beds several times a day. If someone knocked on the door, Abel begged Hanna to hide. Poor souls coming in search of suits old Abel had been commissioned to alter prior to the outbreak of influenza. Garments that hung completed in the drawing room but Abel refused to return until one of the mounted dailies on the porch declared the rapture finally over.

Hanna, in her hours between redress and unwanted meals, located an old book in her father's library. *The Secret Garden*. She recalled her father having purchased the book to help her and Igor with their English when they were young. Four times, Igor had tried to read the novel to her before giving up. She'd plucked it from the shelf believing it contained nothing but magic and wonder.

Had she been able to remember anything from Igor's attempts, she'd never have reopened it. But there it was all along, her own life and everyone else's, inside the pages of a book, for children, no less, and contained within its opening chapter. In the contemptible Mary Lennox, she discovered the Allerton children. In the Ayah, herself, Astrid, and the Irish girl. She marveled at what simple work the author made of Mary's condition. Though it had never been any mystery to Hanna where the tempers and dreams of a child derived from—her own she knew were born out of her father's heroic work ethic—reading the fact of a person's whole makeup, stated so plainly and with such authority, Hanna failed to breathe for several sentences at a time, as if the novel were a spyhole into the Allertons' deepest inner conditions and she was on the other end, standing, watching, and needing to hold her breath so as not to be discovered.

When Mary began to transform, her heart thawing with the kindness and misfortunes of those around her—those working for and living in the shadow of her hunchbacked uncle—Hanna almost couldn't bear it. She remembered what she'd allowed James to do to his sisters at the pond, their helpless climb across the wide estate, the regret and confusion James would feel if his mother or father or both suddenly did die, as so many were. She imagined the children succumbing to the illness themselves, not a single adult around to care for them, to see to their last rights, to bury them at the family plot.

Where had their secret garden been hiding? In Astrid's apartment? At the bottom of the pond?

The death of those children was not a regret she could accept idly. She stood from her reading chair and found her father replicated at every exit, wearing the same mustache and solemn expression but a different suit. Herringbone, tweed, double-breasted pinstripe.

Back in the library, *The Secret Garden* open again in her lap, Hanna's mind moved to the Irish washer girl. They could have been friends, Hanna thought. They could have been each other. They were probably lonely in the same way, the way so many serious young women from boats are. Frightened and untouched. But maybe the Irish girl was different, maybe she'd had a man. Perhaps she'd have even told Hanna about him. The facts of his touch.

Hanna couldn't finish the book. She tried to finish the world from the confines of her father's home instead.

Had the Irish girl the chance to kiss her man once more before departing? Hanna wondered. To gather a bit of warmth to carry on her journey to the other side? Hanna had carried a corduroy rabbit with great big amethyst eyes on the ship from Juist to New York all those years ago, the ceiling bowing and dropping its salt. If the girl did, and she'd killed him with her lips, as Hanna was compelled to believe the Irish girl had, abandoning the book and rushing to her room for the rabbit, how then should the poor man be restored in death, as all good men were in the passages concerning those who have fallen asleep? Was he to be returned to the Irish girl as someone she had lost, or his self, and if he were returned to his self would he not be chagrined to give his former darling the time of everlasting day when she eventually appeared to him in heaven, her having severed his bountiful American life so early for a simple Irish kiss? In a book for the bereaved, Hanna had read that arms, legs, memories, wives, and favorite birds were returned to their rightful owners at day's end. But surely, in the whole history of death and dismemberment, there were some who were better off alone in the afterlife. In such cases what justice was God offering in promising a reunion? And if all were designed to be forgotten, and each is forgiven their role in life, such that the cause of death, the print of the kiss, a lie told beside a pond at night were erased for harmony's sake, what silly bitterness was living, Hanna thought, combing her rabbit's corduroy ribs, remembering an umber mange of sand sedge bending seaward along a northern Juistan shore. After the several days' journey from the country's interior, she'd thought their arrival on the island, by way of ferry, was the end of it. It was already a different world, but it would have somehow made less sense to stop early than to keep going forever.

THE YOUNG MAN, when he entered, said he didn't see anybody. He'd been coming by for the past three days, knocking, waiting, walking away. He didn't look like anyone who might have business on this side of town, and even with everybody indoors dying, he said he felt eyes on his back. But he was due in DC to do some speaking—what a Negro GI could manage after losing an arm—and this Abel fellow was supposed to be fast, which was the only reason he hadn't gone to a tailor in his mother's neighborhood. And he only broke into the old tailor's home because he thought the man was dead. He didn't see anybody at first. The house was dark. But then he saw someone in another room, standing there, not moving. He crept toward the drawing room and swore it was a gathering of spirits, shapely but empty military uniforms floating in a circle, discussing something serious the way they were all dressed up and stiff like that. It might've been a coronation, a welcoming of a new spirit into the fold, his own soul, perhaps. He gathered air to scream but sneezed instead. Wiping his nose, he saw the wooden hangers, the clothesline, the ticks of tailor's chalk. He found his uniform, pulled it from the wire, and made to get out of there. All he'd needed was to have the shoulder brought in. Abel, the old sonofabitch, when he turned around, was in the living room waiting for him. He said, "She just left us this morning. She's upstairs, if you care to see her."

"What was that ribbon tied to her dress for?" Bingham Tomlin asked police, who'd arrived after a neighbor reported a break-in and discovered the two men hovering over the young woman's body in a cramped bedroom upstairs, a one-armed Negro holding a military uniform and an old German tailor wiping his face with a corduroy rabbit. They didn't know.

WATCHING BINGHAM TOMLIN roll a cigarette is a sight to see. People watch him roll the cigarette, pop it in his mouth, light it, smoke it, and say, "I like the way you do that. You do that real good." He learned to manufacture a smoke one-handed on the edge of the Argonne Forest at the age of eighteen, right hand on the rifle trigger, eyeball suctioned to the scope, left hand pinching and massaging the cigarette from canoe to chrysalis. Stateside, one-armed, he bought Lucky Strikes and learned other party tricks, like fastening a bowtie with one hand. W. E. B. Du Bois had asked him to do a tour of the nation's Negro colleges telling his story. He'd stood up there in the first year after the war with a black rose blooming from his freshly shaved throat and told young Black intellectuals what it was like being a colored man in the US military, a colored soldier hero. Scary, sad, difficult, but it was meant to inspire the audience. Their race needed decorated heroes, Du Bois had said, but the veneration of one Black man did not mean the fight was over—returning soldiers needed to continue the battle at home, in this shameful land called America, against lynching, disfranchisement, caste, and brutality. It was a part of the war best fought in a tailored suit. Speaking engagements, newspaper interviews, and half a page in a forthcoming book on Negro American GIs helped his mother with the bills for a while, but Bingham Tomlin quit the circuit before that book even came out. White men had started waiting for him outside of venues at night. As punctual and present and constant as the Bible's most loyal wives. They watched him like he couldn't see them, like they were family and had swam naked together as boys. And he realized that flying across the ocean to kill perfect strangers before they killed him had not made him any less susceptible to being killed back home. Had he come from a military family, someone might've told him a man was supposed to join seeking a selfish need and return in search of a selfless desire, not the other way around. He moved back to Harlem, where he'd worked as a bellhop before the war, bringing his mother with him this time, and started donning a bow tie for the express purpose of presenting individuals with trays of food and sparkling drinks—a job with a long history of one-armed performances, waiting tables arose as the perfect vocational transition. Every few months he'd ask himself what his story was supposed to mean to those eggheads. Hadn't even needed to get his uniform altered.

When trouble in Europe started up again, and he was called upon to stand in front of Black audiences once again, this time by the US military and to sell his young brothers on the falsehood that war really was the great equalizer, Bingham Tomlin recalled the posters he'd seen in occupied France made special for African American soldiers. They'd said, in so many words: Germany's never done anything to you, your real enemy is White America, what are you doing over here fighting a white man's war? Funny that the Germans, for all their race arrogance, and Du Bois would end up saying the same thing for a time. *No, thank you*, Bingham Tomlin wrote back. *Bingham Tomlin is done doing other people's work, done using their words, white or Black*. He thought maybe the Kaiser had been trying to say *Let me have this one and save yourself the trouble of the next guy*. He figured the world was just old and trying to die anyway, we were just too stubborn to let it go with any dignity.

Bingham Tomlin was fastidious with his attire and checked himself in a mirror only to admire his reflection as he smoked. July 1941, twenty-three years since he broke into that old German tailor's home in Philadelphia to retrieve his military uniform, Bingham Tomlin was forty-one years old in the basement of a brick-and-steel behemoth teetering on an island, smoking in front of a mirror and readying himself to weave toast points and baubles of caviar and flutes of champagne through a frenzied crowd of philanthropists and war profiteers while Franklin Delano Roosevelt and Dwight Eisenhower tapped glassware from the stage, a party trick that raised millions of dollars for the war effort. Every few years, the effort had to be made. Bingham Tomlin recognized this, finished his smoke, and passed a corridor of steamy condensation for the stairs, seeking the kitchen, the port of entry into the swarm. He never made it. On his way, on a landing between basement floors, he collided with an old man rushing yellow tailor's tape down the steps. Pin cushions, sleeves, chalk, and scissors came flying out of the man. He grunted in the European tradition, a grunt Bingham Tomlin had heard the enemies mutter while they heaved French and American bodies into a pile overseas.

"So, this is where we wind up?" he asked the tailor.

"Come again?" the tailor heaved, collecting his appendages.

"Here?"

IT CAN BE difficult to picture Manhattan, in the same century as Philadelphia's horse-drawn Liberty Loans Parade, overrun with blue and black and yellow automobiles, but it was as Bingham Tomlin and Abel Schröder left the lobby of the Waldorf-Astoria, abandoning their work to hail a taxi for Long Island, where Abel said they could have a quiet place to sit down and talk.

"Your jacket," Abel said in the taxi. "Whoever did it did a very fine job. Usually, you see the sleeve and it's just folded over, like a brown paper bag, a sack lunch. Yours is done with some credit to what was once there, this is important."

Bingham looked at the vacated sleeve of his coat, which had been stitched to his side to prevent getting caught in revolving doors.

"Your uniform, does it still fit nicely?" Abel asked.

"No, but I went and got fat, you see."

"I do see," Abel said, disappointed.

The taxi delivered them to a dingy clapboard.

"This your house?" Bingham Tomlin said.

"My sister-in-law's," he said. "But I've lived here since leaving Philadelphia."

Inside, the men were greeted by a heavyset woman who spoke no English. She treated Abel with motherly suspicion and glared at Bingham.

"This way," Abel said, and ushered them through a small kitchen, onto a screened-in porch.

Green, ornamentally reflective, plastic carpeting covered the floor of the back porch, and through the lazing gauze of the gray screen, which sucked and sailed in the breeze, Bingham eyed the sliding hunchback of the sea.

"Who do you work for? I've never seen you at the hotel before," Bingham said.

"A man wanting to look his best before paying to join a war," Abel said.

"What'd you wanna talk about?"

"Mr. Tomlin, forgive me, but perhaps I must ask you something strange."

"Perhaps you do."

Abel appeared pained, as if he anticipated something awful was about to happen to him, but said nothing.

"Do I owe you something?" Bingham said, growing impatient, and checked his surroundings for any sign that he might be the one in danger. "You asked me here, old man, now out with it," he said, recalling the loyal men who'd trailed him when he was young, who could have done anything to him.

The look on Abel's face eased into a smile and he sat back in his metal chair with relief.

"Then you've forgotten," he said.

Bingham had not. The uniform. The mirror in Abel's house. If that's what this was all about. But what else could have brought them together again?

"No such luck," Bingham said.

"Then you still don't understand," Abel said.

"Never tried to."

"We return to them," Abel said. "Their souls ask for us to rejoin with them and we do. It took me many years to understand. My wife, when she reappeared at my side, I thought she'd returned to haunt me, when in truth it is I who has come to her, a promise from God."

"So, that nice woman in the kitchen?"

"My betrothed."

"And you thought I was?"

"Not that I would have been unhappy to see you. But I'd hope you'd wish for someone more important than your tailor."

Bingham remembered returning to his mother's house in Society Hill that night, unknotting the boxing gloves he'd made of the uniform Abel had altered and laying the wrinkled, tailored mess on his bed. His mother, up, listening to the radio, had given him hell for being late when he'd first walked in. From his bedroom, he strained to hear some news about a parade but heard nothing but "Krauts did this, Krauts did that." Spanish flu. His mother didn't like to see him in uniform, so he stayed in his room to try it on by himself to see if it did it again, if it'd repeat the trick he'd seen in Abel's mirror. Du Bois's letter lay on the desk, reading: *The Lord has maimed you so that our race may rise.*

Before that, he'd walked his mother's old neighborhood. The prim lots were quaint and reminded him of a miniature train village in a storefront window after hours. People were dying quietly again. Where ambulances and makeshift hospitals made a fuss elsewhere in the city, Society Hill had never gotten a thing. You need not worry, it just gets you.

On his way north from Southwark earlier, things couldn't have been more different. Midway through his journey, he'd discovered the whole city out and about again with wagons and horses and ribbons and wreaths, marching in a nocturnal parade. Strange, it being dark and their bodies and faces making no adjustments to the absence of light, as accustomed as cats. Beautiful girls cartwheeled and screamed, and men with mustaches gave out fliers and accepted plain cash donations. They were eating and drinking and screaming under the streetlamps. It was Philadelphia, the whole lot of them. Paper waste stuck to his dewy boots. He'd bent down to pick a scrap from his toe but couldn't read the print, the words kept shooing to the margins. John Philip Sousa led a march to his "Stars and Stripes Forever." Bingham started to run to escape the mad contagion of the crowd, their kissing, sneezing faces.

Before the crowd, back in Southwark, empty save for him, the policemen long since gone, as he'd left the steps of the Schröder house a free man, his aloneness was first interrupted by orange ladybugs—not ladybugs, but mimics who'd run out of paint. Two, at first, something to notice, there not just being one, and then dozens and dozens, feasting their cellophane wings on the air. He'd remembered his mother telling him they bit and felt them in formations cupping the back of his neck. If enough of them hit heads, they made noises. He parted sepia curtain after sepia curtain of them, like he was lost in a jazz club downtown, drunk and out of money.

But then he recalled it having been dark yet and so still when he first came off Abel's porch. No bugs to speak of. He was free to go, free to do as he pleased, it having pleased him to be alone in the night air, to be young and alive—to be young and armless was nothing in comparison to being young and dead, he'd just been reminded of this. His first steps on the street in front of the Schröder house had felt like those first steps on France. It was the same scorched Earth, the same endlessness of anything and death. 1918.

He felt the cup of the scope's eye cap on his face again. His vision darkened to a theater, the single illuminated screen. This isn't the one where he loses his arm. The sky is open around him in that memory. In this one, he is laying in mud watching an American soldier dig a grave five hundred yards away. A single German soldier stands guard over the American. Bingham knows who the grave is for. He keeps the German's head in the center of the refractor scope. He can shoot the German, saving the American and giving away his position. He can shoot and retreat and hope for the best. But he doesn't. Instead, watching the men conduct their horrific ritual, he wonders what compelled him to take up his rifle and stare into what had appeared to be an empty field in the first place. In that other reality, he'd have been caught off guard by the sound of a single pistol shot in the distance. In this reality, he sees the American finish the grave, rest his shovel on the earth, kneel to face the gnarled hole, and tumble forward into its open mouth before the sound of the German pistol registers in anyone's ears.

Bingham went back inside the German tailor's Long Island house in search of the dead girl but discovered only Abel's hulking wife sweating over an out-of-season neckbone broth, cursing him under her breath. He smelled ramshackle contagion on the air and ran through the front door in search of 1941.

"So, this is where we all wind up?" he asked Abel again, kicking rocks over in the front yard. He'd gotten over the shock. He wasn't dead; other people were. He'd assured himself escape would be easy. This was where all the cabbies lived; he'd just need to start knocking on doors.

"Everything is returned to those worthy of the Kingdom of Heaven, even us possessions who are still living," Abel said.

"Long Island is heaven?"

"For some."

"Not your children?"

Abel sighed.

"Their souls cried out for other people in other places, evidently," he said.

HANNA ROSE FROM the basement to find the Swede and the Irish washer girl reprimanding the Allerton children in the foyer. The children were covered in earth and leaves and looked like little mud sculptures of themselves. They were paying the two women no mind at all.

"We've been looking for these three for over an hour," Astrid explained, breathless, like she had been running.

"They were hiding in the garden," Augusta added.

Hanna looked upon her wards.

"We weren't hiding from them," James explained. "We were hiding from a man, honest."

"With a dark complexion," Rose whispered.

"You three need a bath and to stop telling lies," Hanna said. "Should your parents find you this way and hear you going on—"

"Our parents will never find us," Alice said.

"They're lost, like you said," Rose added. "They can't find their ways back."

Their brother let out a cry and tore toward the staircase before anyone saw that the front door had opened, revealing a man Hanna had never seen in her life standing in the open night air.

"He's found us!" James screamed, cowering on the stairs, covering his face with two perfect hands.

Hanna felt at her back the secret nibbling fish of the basement, all of the Earth's earlier inhabitants. She stepped forward to place herself between the man and the women and the children.

"This is a private residence. You are trespassing, and I will—"

"Go home," the man said.

She saw now that he was missing an arm.

"What did you say?"

"Your father misses you. Go home," the man said.

Hanna looked to Astrid and then to Augusta. Water lilies of blood floated to the surface of Augusta's cheeks.

She had seen her father a week ago, at the parade. No, he had come over carrying her corduroy rabbit again. There was work to be done, she'd explained. There was always work to be done.

"I can't," she told the man. "Guests will be arriving soon."

The guests were in a perpetual state of arrival. They would surprise her with their sudden presence again any minute now. This man knew nothing of searching for secret gardens, the work she and Astrid and Augusta did restoring these people to wholeness, what it was to fulfill the promise of heaven.

"You asked God for guests?" the man said.

"I asked God for forgiveness," Hanna said.

She told Astrid to draw the children a bath and Augusta to clean up the mess they'd tracked in. Alone with the man, she felt strange, never having been alone with a man. She walked with him to the pond. There was a moon this night. There were stars.

He asked, "Is that true, what you said about their parents?"

"Their father sneaks in for clean shirts once a week. He asked for his office," she said.

"Their mother?"

"She's alive. She lives in California."

"But I thought . . ."

"It's a choice whether or not you do as the ghosts ask."

She could tell the man was hurting. It no longer had anything to do with his missing arm. Augusta's lad had worn the same face when he appeared at the Allertons' front door stinking of leather and tan.

"It's not so guilty-making forever," she said. "Most nights I come here and the pond is only a pond. It's lovely in the rain. Look now how it's caught the moon."

He looked.

"Most days, the laundry is only the laundry. I watch the children swim in the summer, skate in the winter. And like tonight, the new owners, they're never home."

BACK IN HARLEM, Bingham Tomlin struggled, one-armed, to enter his old military uniform again. Buttonholes pinching, pockets bunching, he had to remove all undergarments and try again from the nude. The shoes still fit. A soldier appeared in the mirror.

Bingham Tomlin still lived with his mother, had never married, carried people's food around with the last arm he had left, but he'd been an American soldier, he'd seen Paris. He was that man again.

The Great War had returned to claim its many still living possessions. Calling all belligerents, calling all belligerents. What he saw in his mirror was the same image he'd seen in Hanna's mirror twenty-three years ago. His arm, returned. But now he knew the truth. His arm had not climbed out of a mass grave in France and inch-wormed and freestyled across the land and the sea to join him. Rather, his body, which had only been a remainder all these years, a fraction of what it had once been, had been compelled to reconvene with the missing arm, the left arm that had awaited him. From beyond the great divide, Bingham Tomlin's eighteen-year-old arm had wrenched its body back and sewn it, with a German tailor's precision, in place. It had nothing to do with the uniform. It had everything to do with his arm, the dead, their wishes. The inside of his uniform, like the inside of the Allerton's house, was only a safe place to ask.

Bingham Tomlin left his room for the living room, to touch his mother with both hands. She screamed at the sight of his uniform, who knows about the hand? Holding her close with both arms, he told her he had to go back. He was going back. A forty-one-year-old fool, his mother called him, letting himself feel sorry and dreamy again.

"Igor and the other boys are asking us back, don't you see?" Bingham Tomlin told his mother, filling with pride. "That's why he doesn't live on Long Island. I can't leave my arm over there all alone. I can't leave my brothers all alone. Igor needs me. They all need me."

THE BOX

I.

A box is crafted with no consideration to its contents. Negotiated dimensions, red cedar, and the shadows they catch together on the workshop floor in Sierra Leone. When the box crosses the border into Nzérékoré, however, it comes carrying nine bottles of palm wine packed tightly in straw. The Guinean who ordered the wine has agreed to pick the shipment up from the bus station. The man is a musician, and the wine is for a concert he's playing that night. A young lorry driver slides the box of palm wine beside the electric organ in the back of his van. The musician gives the lorry driver a free ticket to the concert as a tip; the lorry driver tears it up as soon as he drives away. All night long the man plays music under a row of floodlights like a firing squad. Two meters away from him, an invisible crowd dances. Heat and drunk breath rise from the dancers. Then, between songs, when everyone is still, a cool night air washes over the audience and onto the stage. After the show, the musician asks for a friend's keys to use her car lighter to light a cigarette but walks into the forest instead, stranding her. He is a bellicose man, and when he returns, two hours later with a story about smoking with a gang of guerrilla soldiers he met in the middle of the woods, it is easier for his band to say they believe him. "They were only boys when their commanding officer abandoned them without a compass," he says. When they finished the joint, the men evidently led him to where they'd buried their enemies by memory. "Where are my keys?" his friend asks. "They were only boys," he says, and, moved by his own lies, cries himself to sleep. In the morning he turns the wine bottles over to a liquor store. The band is going on tour. He looks at the box and leaves it to the café owner across the street from his home. For a while the box sits on the broken sidewalk like a beggar. The city gets rain and from the box a great hatch of mosquitoes rises like smoke. It subsists as a door wedge. The owner elects the box to carry drinks to a large table of doctors sitting in the big yellow rays of the sun. The doctors are overheated and distressed. The owner remembers the okoubaka patrons ate under before the neighborhood voted to cut it down and grow purple horsewhips instead. But the tree's poison had stayed in the soil, and every flower planted since has died in its first season, the horsewhips included. She looks at the barren ground where the flowers die and thinks: What a waste.

II.

The box becomes a half-Liberian, half-Belgian doctor's laundry basket. It sits beneath her desk all winter. At night she turns on a soft paper lamp to write observation notes and letters. At some point she writes: *I am sorry I came this time. I will be back before the spring. The work has always been challenging and meaningful.* But now it is also selfish, she has realized. *The hiccups*, she writes, *they will haunt me forever.* In early March, she leaves. She returns to Brussels, where her husband and son are. It was not like before, she explains to a colleague over coffee, when it was only her, the work, and the long solitude of memory. "Of course not," he agrees, tearing open a packet of sugar, staring at the plinths of rain outside the restaurant window. "The oath to your son should be greater than the one to your patients." She feels put off by this comment. On the train back to her apartment, an anxious and angry young Belgian grips his bicycle handles and mutters at her in French. The halls to her apartment building are covered in makeshift electrical wiring. They are like infected stitches and they remind her of the continent. The other continent. In the living room her son kisses her all over. Her husband puts on Charles Bradley, which means he will be starting dinner soon. It was about time she hung up the hazmat suit, she admits. The rain falls at an unchanging angle. In bed she tells her husband she is coming to terms with things. "I didn't want to be alone anymore—I understand these are the consequences of no longer being alone." "We have our whole future ahead of us," he says. She thinks of that future: How will I make it mean anything now? she wonders. All that time. When I have seen so many fight to make just a few weeks, days, hours mean anything. How can there be so much time?

Before she left she treated a man for MRSA. He took an interest in her because she was part Gbandi, like his girlfriend back in Liberia. He was only doing seasonal work in Nzérékoré when he got sick, and while she met with him he asked her to speak to him in Gbandi. "A ridiculous language," he said, and closed his eyes to listen. "Do you understand any of it?" she asked that first time. "Not a word." She had a hard time taking the language seriously herself. Her mother had insisted she learn it after the woman returned from a church retreat, and she always thought it sounded a little hysterical coming out of people's mouths. In Gbandi, over the course of three visits, she would talk to this patient about things around the room—irrelevant things, things he didn't need to understand. *Thermometer. Syringe. Floor. Ceiling. Blood.* Until the Gbandi words began to take on the incantation of alarm.

The man's name was Jonathan Durham, and she implored him to leave once he was cleared of infection. He refused to leave before repaying his debt. He took a job washing linens. When she departed, she left him with the box. In Brussels, where she has never spoken Gbandi, she thinks of him sometimes.

III.

Jonathan's father calls upon his eldest son to return home in late March. Business at the garage has picked up and he needs all the help he can get. The box travels with Jonathan on the bent roof of a lorry to Lofa. His first night home, he sands the box and then lacquers it to the color of grapefruit. He will give it to his girlfriend as a gift. His girlfriend cleans houses with her aunt and little niece. She is so meticulous; no one can make a house clean like she can. He goes to her late that night, shows her the box before he even walks through the door. The full moon snoops over his shoulder. His girlfriend is surprised and confused by this gift. Most men bring their girlfriends dresses or perfumes, mobile phones or dance tickets. She knows her friends would laugh if they knew this was the gift he brought her after all these months. They will see kind Jonathan Durham coming to call on her and say, "There goes Jonathan Durham, the man with the box." She looks at this man blocking the moon in her doorway, reeking of grease. "Jonathan Durham, the man who is always away and too sickly to bring his woman any joy." He has no idea the kinds of things her girlfriends tell her when he is gone. How before bed they tell her he is kissing his Fula girlfriend goodnight. How when she told them she was no longer a virgin they warned her about his plan: to go on dating her and the Fula girl until one of them gets pregnant, then cross the border in whichever direction is away from responsibility, and keep that mistress for as long as she is without child before heading to Nigeria, telling every woman he meets he loves her along the way. "Then you will shrivel up with jealousy and regret for having picked an Igbo man for a boyfriend." He has no way of knowing it, but, like his absence, this ridiculous box, his lovely, smiling face, are injuries. They laughed at her when she said love is as porous as the borders, that we are all immigrants in each other's hearts. They called her a fool. And she's about to send him away, back to Guinea with his stupid box, when he puts the smooth wooden shape in her hands. It weighs so little it is like passing a kiss. It is rather beautifully crafted. "This is where we'll put our hearts when they are too heavy with love," he says. "We'll put it on a shelf in our house." She takes the box inside and positions it on a bench where it can collect the moonlight like water. She runs her hands over his arms.

IV.

Mr. Durham dies from throwing up too much blood. Teenesee does as instructed and buys twenty minutes at an internet cafe to transcribe a handwritten note he'd prepared for the half-Liberian, half-Belgian doctor. She logs into her email, composes the note, and hits send with less than two minutes left on the computer's timer. Panting, she stares at the list of emails advertising generic medicine.

Hidden somewhere in the spam is a message from Mr. Durham. The computer resets before she can find it, and she wonders about the urgency surrounding death now. Just six months ago death was still a lazy walk in sandals, a stroll onto the other side, taken so slow by some, their ghosts sometimes lingered a week or two to finish a hot bottle of Coca-Cola or to laugh at jokes as old as time. Two days later Teenesee returns to the internet cafe. The doctor has replied in Gbandi. Teenesee is devastated. The doctor will not come. She has a son in Brussels.

Wealthy women begin to clean their own homes. Soldiers stop harassing civilians for money. A man throws a party no one attends but plays his music loud enough to keep everyone up until morning. Teenesee's little niece bumps elbows with a little boy to say hello one afternoon, and Teenesee recalls how amputees shook hands after the war. There is a rumor that no one has been kissed in twenty-two days, nine hours, and fifty-seven minutes.

V.

Teenesee, your name is not Gbandi, the doctor writes.

It's Kru, Teenesee replies.

To protect you.

It means time does not pass.

Jon said you were so beautiful you could stop time.

I wish time would run itself into the sea.

Every day I wish I could be there.

This morning, when the doctors came for the sick, family members threw rocks.

VI.

Teenesee meets with six fat nuns. A tent city, a necropolis of tents, has popped up on the edge of an orange road. The nuns tell Teenesee that her patience and attention to detail will serve as the wells from which her bravery is drawn. She dawns a white frock she ties to her contours with a rope. They give her light blue rubber gloves and a face shield. Her first day at the camp she learns she will never know the pleasure Mr. Durham knew, the beauty of washing one hundred linens in a big pot over a wood fire, like boiling a soup of clouds. "Not until the new shipment of disinfectant arrives," a woman tells her. For now, everything is burned. The blankets and the bodies.

On the outskirts of the village of tents is the water pump. It burps and mumbles to itself like a mocking drunk. Teenesee cannot use it. She ventures to the wells of perfect penmanship, bare corners, and taut bedspreads every day instead. She walks where the other girls dash. And every walk, no matter the direction, always ends slowly with the fire.

Eventually, her frock loosens to a sexless robe. She blooms into a great traveling tent revival. Inside, she fills with the crackle and feedback of an old PA system, the band's untightened drums and mistuned guitars. By day's end her heart is too full to hold and she places it in the box beside Mr. Durham's: all swollen and bursting with blood.

VII.

A knot of toads keep Teenesee up one night. She thinks of her girlfriends mocking her with kissing noises. "Oh, Fula girl! Oh, Fula girl!" they sang. None of her girlfriends speak to her anymore. There are no jokes. There is the chorus of silence, the hiccups and the toads, now.

VIII.

Her detachment is a form of grace. The devastated, moonlighting as nurses, take turns with a disinfected DVD. It's a World Health Organization production and the cast is made up mostly of Nigerian doctors living in Europe. On the tiny, scratchy screen, the doctors stand in lab coats, explaining how many will not make it. One doctor says, "You are treating then their whole life, suddenly ending in a strange tent." And Teenesee thinks, Yes, I am the woman who appears when grown men cry out for their mothers. I am the ferryman who rows them to the other side. And because the disease is in them and stays in them long after their hearts and brains and souls depart, the disease is also in my care.

By now Mr. Durham has dissolved into the cloudy broth of so many memories formed all at once. A boy or a woman is admitted and Teenesee tells another attendant, "I meet them for the first time and I instantly feel I am already remembering them."

One pop-up ward reminds Teenesee of a house she used to clean. The house was rented to a diplomat, and in the seven months she lived there the woman had a gravel driveway laid and a greenhouse put in beside the kitchen. After they finished working, Teenesee, her aunt, and her little niece would sit in the greenhouse, sunbathing like birds. There was a plant inside that lived off nothing but detritus and light in the air. It's the way light reflects in the pop-up ward that reminds Teenesee of the greenhouse. The thin geometric panels. She looks through a clear wattle of IV drips and sees Jonathan in a nearby copse of trees, running for his life in a pair of black Nikes.

IX.

Tell me what they are not telling me, the doctor writes.

The disinfectant hasn't come.

And?

It is like they are just waiting for us to burn ourselves out.

And?

The painkillers have run out.

I should have said things of meaning to him, the doctor writes.

X.

The orange road brings a mother and her infant child. The child is torn from the woman's weeping breasts. The woman is quarantined. The constant ceremony of fire casts a shadow play against her tent at night. Up all night, she watches the story of a body. Not as good as the original; however, it is the necessary sequel to life, she thinks. The fire is so eternal, while they wait for more trees to be cut, the attendants begin burning useless supplies, furniture, and heartfelt things.

The child is quarantined. It is so new it requires a vessel to keep it in place, from collapsing and killing itself. Teenesee finds a vase, a plastic bag. Then she runs home, grabs the box, and lines it with blankets. The child is placed in the box. The box is placed on a counter. A sign, written on medical tape, is applied to the box. *Quarantined Do Not Touch.*

One day she can go airing its cries from her tenting frock, simmering across the dust, telling the others to feed and wash the thing. Sleeping for one minute in the sun, she dreams of the box floating at sea, the baby inside the box, drowning in a pool of its own bloody feces. She finds a rag, drenches it in pump water, and runs it over to the child. She cleans the child as Mr. Durham had lacquered the box, to a shining perfection as deep and uniform as midday shadow. The child can stop crying for as long as it takes to catch its breath. Hand and baby go soft. The crying stops.

And still she keeps returning to the pump over and over, and each time the plumbing seems to whisper: Washing, washing, washing. Teenesee, dear Teenesee: we shan't ever sicken, we shan't ever die, should we never stop washing. Teenesee, sweet angel of hygiene: keep washing, washing, washing! Lest we burn all that which is living for carrying all that dead inside.

IV.

FIRES

SLEEPY THINGS

JOSEFÍN HAD BEEN IN HER coma for less than a week when she started popping up in Magdalena's dreams. Josefín was Magdalena's son's girlfriend. Like the coma, the two's relationship had been sudden. Tony had only gone on three dates with Josefín, and the jodona was already lounging on Magdalena's couch watching her cable in Tony's old track-and-field gear every night of the week. Magdalena was preparing her son an ultimatum—*If you want a lazy live-in girlfriend, fine, but you need to get your ass a job and a place of your own to keep her*—when Josefín got sick. She would have taken pity then, except whatever-it-was put Josefín to sleep with a smile on her face, no less. Maybe it was nerve damage, but posed all saintlike in her hospital bed, adorned with space-age tubes and instruments, flanked by her loving, devastated, forty-eight-year-old parents, Josefín looked so damn peaceful, Magdalena had to resist the actual urge to reach over and pull the child's hair. Illness or not, la mala had basically up and abandoned her son, leaving him in ruins, like it was nothing. She knew it from the first hospital visit—Tony crying these racking sobs while Josefín just chilled there, her doctors and nurses hugging metal clipboards and tablets to their bellies. Her son's own life was slipping under, too.

Magdalena used to tell people she had Tony back when she was stupid. She was sixteen, was what it was, and the condom broke, and she ended up being more Catholic than she'd previously thought. Actually, she was a nearly straight-A student. While the other teen moms were all crying over losing the best years of their lives, Magdalena worried what her son had to lose. A boy needed a mother's expert hand to guide him; holding baby Tony, her own felt shaky and constricted, like playing a piano recital in the snow. When his dad stopped coming around, she pictured Tony flying, up high above, blind in the clouds, with no ground control. Tony was twenty-two now, an impossible age, but he needed his mother's guidance all the same, and Magdalena still didn't feel old enough to help him. Josefín's parents, older, wiser, only smiled at him politely.

"Mijo, mijo," Magdalena had said to him on their way back from the hospital that first time. Tony had insisted on driving home but was throwing his body all over the steering wheel, like a dolphin at SeaWorld doing tricks at the edge of the pool. He was crying so crazy, Magdalena worried they'd crash. "Mijo, you can't get too mixed up, you two barely knew each other."

Struggling to catch his breath, his voice shuddering, Tony said, "I told her I loved her and she told me she loved me."

And all Magdalena could think to say was, "That's good. It's brave to talk about your feelings like that."

"She makes me feel important. And special."

On their second visit, Tony cut Josefín's fingernails, brushed her hair. It bothered Magdalena that the girl kept growing while her son was stuck waiting. She didn't go back a third time.

"HOSPITALS ARE FOR sick people. Eventually, even healthy people get sick when they spend too much time in hospitals," Magdalena told Tony.

He'd packed a night bag, a lumbar pillow, and a wireless speaker for his phone. Unfortunately, the girl's parents had found it in their hearts to get him an overnight pass.

"They're breeding grounds for superbugs," she said. "Look, watch this video, it explains everything."

She had her phone in her hand. Her whole life she'd had something in her hand. A doll, a CD player, a compact, a little boy's hand. Now this.

"Ma," Tony said, turning away from Magdalena's beaming palm.

She lowered the device.

"What?"

"I'm going."

"But why?"

"The doctor says the music helps her."

"Then let the nurses play it."

"The music is helping me, too."

"Chacho, we have a stereo."

"I'll see you when you get home from work tomorrow."

"You'll be here?"

She'd wanted him out of the house, and now that he was at the hospital all day and night she wanted him back, slow breathing in his boyhood bed, demanding breakfast in the morning, bumming around while she was at work, making a mess of things.

It was summer. A fire was spreading south of the airport, this time started by a Boy Scout leader. The boys had watched as one of their dads flicked a cigarette out the window on the drive home from a campsite and now they were all famous. There were warnings that Flagstaff might have to evacuate. The boys, on the *Today Show*, made the flicking motion with their hands. It looked like a strange salute. Alone, Magdalena stood in the backyard of her rental, kicking over rocks. The wind, when it blew, felt like a straw broom against her face. For a second, she thought she heard booming thunderheads, godsends, but it was only her neighbor's car's subwoofers flexing their bowels in the street. Smelling of seven or nine types of smoke—one for each genus on fire—the air made Magdalena's eyes itch, her nostrils burn. Pretty soon, they said, you wouldn't even need to flick a cigarette out a car window for the fires to start, they'd begin out of nowhere. Down in the valley, even when there weren't fires, in all directions, butter-colored smog crowned the horizons, hiding the mountains from view. The desert, impossibly hot, was getting hotter. If it didn't burn down first, Flagstaff would eventually need air conditioners, and how did people keep their eyes open with those machines constantly blowing in their faces?

Back inside, with a plastic cup of tap water, Magdalena lay in bed listening to the distress of her neighbor's car. In the dark, she texted Tony:

<WHAT R U 2 LISTENING 2 2NITE>.

Seconds later, her phone made a water droplet sound and lit up the whole room with its dry ice light.

<SHOSTAKOVICH QUARTETS. DON'T TEXT IT INTERRUPTS THE MUSIC.>

After, in quick succession, he sent:

<GOOD NIGHT>
<LOVE YOU>
<YOU DON'T HAVE TO WRITE BACK. I KNOW YOU LOVE ME.>

She tried listening to an overture on her phone, but it was a little too dramatic, and she turned on her white-noise machine and a small fan instead. She felt afraid as she fell asleep. A talon at her chest, a squirrel at the foot of her bed.

"MIRA, JODONA, GET up," Magdalena said to the girl on her couch.

The girl stretched like a cat: shaking, assuredly in love with itself. The light had a medical zeal to it. Her spine realigned, the girl turned on the TV.

"Where's Tony?" Magdalena said.

"He had to go to work," Josefín said, sitting up, the light keeping her hidden sutures clean.

"I wish," Magdalena said.

Tony's blue sweats were like Aladdin pants on her. Letting her feet down off the couch, the pant legs rolled up and revealed her pale ankles, shin stubble cuffing a straight tree line above the bones. There was dark jam under her toenails. Ui, no, Magdalena thought. At least she could try to be presentable. Tony wasn't wealthy, too smart, or even funny, but he was handsome. Didn't girls go crazy over good-looking guys anymore? Couldn't he have landed a pretty, lazy girl instead?

"It's better if he's not here anyway," Josefín said, changing the channel.

Jerry Springer popped on. A 9/11 widow was confronting a United Airlines stewardess before a live studio audience. Across the bottom of the screen were the words: *In-flight floozy messing with your man?!* Magdalena reached for the remote.

"Enough with this trash," she said.

The TV powered down like a state-of-the-art computer. Magdalena remembered when the picture used to suck down into another dimension, the little beeping sounds at the start of the VHS tape.

"Always have to cut out the juicy parts."

"Those people died, that's not even funny. Jerry should be ashamed of himself."

Josefín started laughing.

"Quit that."

"You talk like Jerry's a real person. He's just a character. That's like getting mad at the Joker or something for being the bad guy."

"Jerry's real. He was a lawyer and a mayor and he ends each episode with a special message that some people really listen to. He needs to watch what he says."

"Sounds like you're a real expert on trash TV," Josefín said, and began walking around the kitchen.

"Let me guess, now you want something to eat?" Magdalena said, feeling trapped but less lonely. She peered into her bedroom. The house was like a dog after its own tail: living room, kitchen, a hall with doors to two bedrooms and a shared bath, repeat, round and round. Her bed looked smaller and taller than she remembered it. Once, she'd gotten up to crap and heard Tony and Josefín messing around. To save the universe the embarrassment, she didn't flush, and Tony gave her a piece of his mind the next day because Josefín had been the first one up that morning and jumped out of her skin at the sight of what'd been left behind.

"Who eats at a time like this?" Josefín said.

"At a time like breakfast time?" Magdalena said.

Magdalena tried filling herself a plastic cup of water from the sink, but the water kept disappearing.

"Dummy, they're evacuating everything south of I-40," Josefín explained.

Magdalena gave up on the cup.

"What should I do?" she asked.

"I'll tell you what I'd do," Josefín said.

"What would you do?"

"I'd pull out some cash and take a little trip."

"Yeah?"

"Yeah, I'd get out of here."

"Like you'd ever have any money."

MAGDALENA HAD WOKEN up with a sore throat. Tashana, her coworker in the Safeway's Starbucks kiosk, shot some mocha concentrate onto a banana for breakfast and told her it was probably the particulates in the air.

"I thought I got sick from sleeping with the fan on," Magdalena said.

"Ain't sick. It's the fires. I've had to cut back on the cigarettes. It's just too damn smoky."

"Should quit altogether."

The Starbucks kiosk was shoved in one corner near the store's south entrance, the Wells Fargo in another, and between them, across from produce, they shared a beautiful LCD screen that was always playing CNN. Their own little Flagstaff, Arizona, had center stage, on account of the fires.

"Do you think?" Magdalena said.

"Not in a million years. And you know what? I wouldn't budge anyway."

"That's crazy."

"And you would?"

"I don't know."

"Think of what you're saying. That's your home."

"So, you wouldn't leave if the whole town was up in flames?"

"Listen, my own husband used to beat me in my house, my son ruined his life in my house, if none of that kept me from leaving, even for a stroll to air my own goddamn head, you know damn well some forest fire ain't going to either. Besides, this is just the beginning. Global warming, bitch, get used to it."

Tammy Pham, senior teller at the Safeway's Wells Fargo branch, walked up to the kiosk lint-rolling her pencil skirt. Magdalena started on her tall soy latte. Tammy Pham told fantastical stories about Manila nightlife and still carried toilet paper in her purse wherever she went because you never know. She'd recently married a doctor with a kid in college she'd never met and a boathouse on Lake Pleasant she'd never seen.

"So slow today," she said. "Nobody's shopping."

"Fine by me," Tashana said.

"Not me, I work for the thrill of it," Tammy Pham said, taking her latte. She turned to the TV, the bending flames.

"Now *that's* thrilling," she said, sipped, and left her maroon lipstick on the sculpted white lid.

Over Tammy Pham's shoulder, Magdalena saw a man in a rubber Hillary Clinton mask step up to the Wells Fargo kiosk and pull out a black pistol. Enrique, the junior teller, made no sudden movements.

"Oh shit, Tammy Pham," Tashana said.

Tammy Pham turned, latte in hand, to catch the robbery in progress.

"Hey, get out of here, asshole!" she shouted.

"Shut up, bitch!" the man yelled, and turned his gun toward the Starbucks kiosk.

Magdalena and Tashana crouched under the bar. Hiding behind the milk fridge, Magdalena heard Tammy Pham warn Enrique not to give the man any money.

"He's a fucker! Fuck him!" she shouted.

"Man, bitch, I'm gonna shoot you if you don't shut up!"

Two shots rang out. Gripping Tashana's mocha-syrup-sticky hand, Magdalena whimpered, "Tammy Pham."

A cackle rose from the other side of the bar.

Now vertical, Magdalena saw Tammy Pham standing where she'd abandoned her, lint roller in one hand, soy latte in the other, laughing. Glen, the sixty-year-old security guard, was hunched over and shaking, his sidearm dangling from his right hand. At his feet was the crumpled body of the Hillary Clinton–masked man.

"Oh shit," Glen was muttering. "Oh shit. Oh shit."

"WHAT'S WITH THE monkey suit?" Magdalena said.

Tony was wearing black Dickies, a black polo, and a black cap.

"Got a job, Ma," he said proudly, and opened a Tupperware of sliced honeydew.

"Yeah?"

"RadioShack, sales technician. Mobile specialist in training."

His thumbs hooked chest-ward.

"They hired you on the spot?"

"I've had a few interviews."

"And you weren't going to say anything?"

"Wanted to surprise you."

"You sly dog. About time."

"Yeah."

"Mobile specialist, that sounds complicated."

He popped a pale green melon sickle in his mouth.

"It is. And mobile technology is only getting more and more complicated."

Clear juice candied the wet banks of his lips, his stubbly chin. His whole life, his salivary glands had asked too much of him.

"It's good to have the chance to learn things at work," Magdalena said, fighting the urge to wipe his face.

"Yeah, there's all these different tutorials I'll be able to take."

"That's what I like about Starbucks, they're always coming up with new drink recipes you have to learn."

"Exactly."

"We need to celebrate," Magdalena said. She'd refrained from texting or calling him all day, worried she'd interrupt the one bit of Mozart that'd get Josefín to wake up. She wanted the girl out of her dreams. She wanted Tony to be happy. Now, looking at her son in his RadioShack getup, she decided it would be best to forgo discussing the day's trauma altogether. Keep the boy's spirits high. Don't frighten him away from the world he's finally embarking upon. She knew he never bothered with the news.

"I don't know," he said.

"Fratelli's delivers."

She called in an order for a deep-dish spinach pie, dressed two bottles of Dos Equis, and handed one to Tony in the backyard.

"Could you push the lime down? My thumb always gets stuck," he said.

"Big baby," she said, and the citrus lit up an invisible cut on her finger.

"How long they say it's gonna take?" Tony said, moving rocks with his feet.

"Forty minutes to an hour."

"I might have to take mine to go."

"Tony."

He gazed at the smoke in the distance.

"I wonder if the fires have something to do with Josefín getting sick," he said.

"She got sick before the fires."

"Maybe they're keeping her sick."

"Then maybe you should go put them out. Come on, Tony, stay home tonight."

"Ma, what do you think this job's about? Hospital bills are expensive. I gotta help out."

"Her parents and their insurance are paying for those."

"It's important to be able to provide for the person you love. It's part of being a man."

Magdalena sighed, licked salt from her lips.

"I wasn't going to tell you this, but there was an attempted robbery today at the grocery store. The man had a gun. I thought I was going to die. Glen nearly killed the guy."

Tony stared into the gauzy clouds of smoke again.

"I guess we don't know how blessed we are until bam, you know?" he said.

"What?"

"Until you're dead or asleep," he said.

She stared at him, baffled.

"I'm not being philosophical. I really could've died. Have a heart."

"Jeez, okay, sorry," he said, putting his hands up in indignation. "You obviously weren't bothered by it enough to mention it until now. I was just following your lead."

WHEN TONY WAS six, his teacher, the teacher's aide, actually, called a conference to discuss the academic challenges he was facing in the classroom. It was one of the rare occasions in which his dad was also in attendance. Sitting in tiny plastic chairs around a kidney-shaped table covered in finger paintings and loping curves that would one day yield written language, the teacher and the aide talked about processing disorders, how sound and speech worked, how for one reason or another everything was getting jammed up in the Grand Central Station of Tony's brain.

"So, what, he's, like, slow or something?" his dad said.

"Slow," Magdalena said. "Nobody says slow anymore, José."

"I didn't say the other word," José said, crossing his arms and turning away from all three women.

"You didn't have to," Magdalena said. Then, to the teacher, she asked, "Is he ever going to be . . . normal? Is it a phase or is it forever?"

The teacher only shrugged, but the aide, a student-teacher originally from Phoenix—who, Tony said, was very nice, always tying his shoes and putting the straw in his juice box—leaned over the table, touched Magdalena's hands, and said, "Whether it turns out that Tony has a learning disability or a processing disorder, his brain will continue to mature with his age, and one day he will be a full-grown man capable of enjoying all the same pleasures and responsibilities as anyone his own age. But he will need a lot of extra help along the way. He's being asked to learn in a way that is not, well, native to him. But when we figure out what works, how he learns best, he will be able to catch up. Knowing what's right for him and fighting for what's right for him will ensure his success."

The aide, maybe twenty-five, was already older than Magdalena. Years later, Magdalena would sometimes click around Facebook and LinkedIn in search of her. She couldn't remember her name, and so she'd Google teacher awards, scan the faces of the recipients for that wonderful Black girl. She wanted to know if the woman would think Tony was enjoying the pleasures and responsibilities of a full-grown man these days.

But if she ever did find her, Magdalena would like to tell her about Tony's track and field years first, how between the ages of thirteen and sixteen Tony had displayed the attributes of a world-class athlete. How beautiful years she felt the world had something to offer her son. She remembered the training and conditioning being pure madness. All evening long, Tony would sprint and jump and toss, and at first Magdalena worried—was he hurting himself? Was he in danger? But then her worry turned into wonder. Tony was like a crazy antelope on the field. Magdalena had never seen anyone run so fast. Thanks in large part to Tony, their champion pole vaulter, the team won competitions all over the state. José would show up to the meets and sit next to Magdalena and act civil under the bone-colored stadium lights, the green on the field glowing like the grass does in dreams or in scenes in movies or TV shows depicting dreams. She'd look at Tony's shadow leaning against the pitch beside him whenever he was stationary and watch him leave it behind when he vaulted himself into the night sky. Recruitment, scholarships, college, felt not only possible but inevitable. She researched different types of intelligence and discovered her son possessed superb physical intellect. Athletically, he was a genius.

But then Magdalena would have to inform the former aide of how it all ended. At sixteen, Tony peaked. His teammates got faster, jumped higher; Tony stayed the same. She wouldn't be able to explain it any other way. The coaches said it didn't have anything to do with his work ethic or training. But by the time scouts started to appear in the stands there wasn't much left to see in Tony's performance. His dad stopped showing up to meets, and Tony stopped going out with the other guys after competitions. He got varsity letters but no college offers.

Tony had left Magdalena alone again. Honestly, Fratelli's pizza sauce gave her the runs, and so she only nibbled on the crust for a few bites before she wrapped up the pie, put it in the fridge, and dumped the rest of her warm beer in the sink. She Googled nice teachers in Flagstaff. Job postings came up.

"HONEY, YOU GOTTA do something about that bikini line," Magdalena told Josefín. They were on a beach in Magdalena's native Puerto Rico.

"You're so superficial," Josefín said, looking right at her. "You're so vain, I bet you won't even get your hair wet."

"I don't feel like swimming. Has nothing to do with my hair. What you need to worry about is *that* hair."

The sea was swirling like in a lousy painting of a swirling sea.

"And if the whole island was on fire? Would you feel like swimming then?" Josefín said, staring out at the lousy sea.

"Probably not," Magdalena said.

Josefín turned to face Magdalena again, her face looking rather somber suddenly.

"Listen, what if I said I had something serious to tell you?" she said.

"I'd probably be more willing to get my hair wet," Magdalena answered.

"For serious."

"You're always telling me something. Your ass is asleep in a coma and you're still telling me things."

"Listen to me."

"What do you think I'm doing?"

"I need you to tell Tony something for me."

"What?"

"He's gotta move on."

"Damn right, he does."

"It's not working out, you know?"

"Hell no, it's not working out."

"I don't want him watching me sleep anymore."

"Hold on, you make it sound creepy. That boy loves you, you know?" Magdalena said and sat up in her red plastic recliner.

"I know."

"You'll never meet a more honest, devoted man."

"Magdalena, he's gotta move on."

"Are you going to die?"

"I don't know."

"You don't wake up, then?"

"It's not up to me."

"Then what is it?"

"I don't love him. I don't even like him that much."

Magdalena spat, pet the hard plate of a horseshoe crab dozing beside her chair. They weren't so bad if you didn't look at their undersides. They had blue blood that was valued at fifteen thousand dollars a liter.

"We're not right for each other," Josefín said.

"You got another man on the side?" Magdalena said.

"I'm in a fucking coma."

"Mira, jodona."

"Mag, tell him."

DAYS AND DREAMS passed. Tammy Pham was fired for breaking Wells Fargo protocol and putting her coworkers at risk of bodily harm or death. She took out the nearest Safeway aisle, bread, as she left. The kid filling in for Glen while Glen underwent psychiatric evaluation didn't quite know what to do with her, so he just followed her around, picking up loaves, apologizing to frightened customers. It cracked Tashana up and broke Magdalena's heart. Tammy Pham was an excellent, passionate bank teller. She brought these awesome egg rolls in for the Starbucks crew every so often. She didn't love her husband. Her kids, from her previous marriage, never called.

Each night, no matter how hard Magdalena tried to get him to stay, Tony left for the hospital. The salted necks of unfinished bottles of beer filled the kitchen sink; with their lime tongues pointed up, they looked convincingly like tropical baby birds. In the backyard, Magdalena went in search of horrific things. A scorpion the color of earwax, a webless spider, a buried shoe. Josefín grew so nagging, Magdalena started staying away from sleep, downing caffeine pills with cups of coffee—it was like *A Nightmare on Elm Street*. On walks at night the only humans she encountered were people with dogs and drug dealers. She discovered that nothing lived so well and darkly as the coyotes who evidently frolicked in your yard while you slept. The smoke in the air made her cough and cough. The coughs left her like assurances, stranding her, breathless with doubt.

For a while, Magdalena had thought it was possible that having Tony and keeping him to herself had been a mistake. Her big sister had offered to pay for everything herself; instead, in her blown-out Soffe shorts and ballooning camisole, Magdalena had marched all over their mother's carpet like she knew exactly what she was doing. She was a nearly straight-A student, for God's sake, she told herself and anyone who would listen. She was ready to love something forever. When her water broke over that carpet, her sister said, "You're in for it now." Expecting wasn't the same as being a mom, she discovered; equating the two had been her mistake. Motherhood wasn't about what you expect, it was about what you had.

Her worry, like her love, had known no bounds over the years, but it'd been a long time since she'd felt so clearly mistaken. Tony going crazy over his Sleeping Beauty made her wonder if she'd failed to give him something essential. Dignity. Self-respect. A father. Jesus, she thought, how could so much be wrapped up in one fucking thing?

At work, Tashana told Magdalena that she was worried about her. Knowing nothing about the dreams, she said, "You gotta sleep, girl. You gotta sleep," her voice like a lullaby. Magdalena's knees buckled right there in the Safeway.

"And no more coffee," Tashana said, taking away Magdalena's latte before she spilled it.

Leaning over the water fountain between the bathrooms, letting the hard arc of icy water roll over her lips, Magdalena thought perhaps she was being unfair to herself, that she'd taken the most ungenerous appraisal of her life and run with it. Maybe she was being equally unfair toward Tony. This could just be the beginning of empty nest syndrome, she reasoned. Thirty-eight was not too young to feel totally forgotten. But the dreams, what were the dreams? She was bathing her whole face in the water fountain now. Could Josefín be her imaginary friend, come to fill the void Tony was leaving? Magdalena had never had an imaginary friend before but hearing others talk about theirs, they often made them sound involuntary, phenomena almost schizophrenic in nature. Or maybe she was being visited by Josefín's spirit, a sort of pre-ghost. In this case, these types of visitations might've been something the ancients had understood perfectly well and that humans had grown frightened of only recently, sometime around the invention of indoor plumbing. She tried to remember the real. How many nights had Tony spent away? How long were the fires? Tammy Pham had said you could watch them dance a conga line at night from Fremont Peak. *He's gotta move on*, was what she remembered.

"When's the last time you saw any of your friends?" she asked Tony, as he gathered his things that evening. "And how come you don't talk about work anymore? Where's that hat they gave you? Shouldn't I wash your uniform?"

"I can wash it myself."

"When?"

"Tomorrow."

"You'll be home for two minutes tomorrow, just like tonight, just like last night. At least let me have it. I can press if for you and everything. You've got to look nice."

She reached for him but he tore away from her.

"They don't care about my fucking uniform, Ma. They don't care if I'm late or early or on time, they don't care how long a break I take. The managers are always goofing around, smoking weed, nobody ever buys anything but batteries. I've been there three weeks, three weeks, Ma, and I haven't sold a single phone. The job's a joke."

"Honey."

"I'm like that guy you used to bag groceries with. Let's face it, my job exists for two types of people: losers and disabled people. And I know you always told me to never think I was dumb or stupid or anything, but sometimes it's easier to think that I am. That way, at least it isn't my fault I've never accomplished anything."

Magdalena grabbed him like he'd broken something or was bleeding.

"Disabled people aren't stupid," she said.

"Then what's wrong with me?" Tony cried.

"I FEEL LIGHTER," Josefín said, "sleeping alone. It's nice. But now he's in your bed."

She sprayed lemon on her popcorn shrimp and settled the rind on her plate. They were seated in a booth at a Red Lobster. Pink cotton candy clouds floated outside the window. The parking lot was an endless black-top desert.

"It used to be our favorite thing, lying in bed together, watching TV. Comforting one another was like a pastime. It feels good to do it again," Magdalena said, and shooed a live lobster at her feet.

"Grown-ass man in his mother's bed."

"Nothing wrong with it."

"Trust me, I'm not complaining."

Magdalena took Josefín's crushed lemon wedge and dropped it in her iced tea.

"He was just doing what he thought was right," Magdalena said. "He doesn't want to be like his dad."

"I know."

"Wasn't enough, though," Magdalena said.

There'd been a note of regret in Josefín's voice and Magdalena didn't like it. Josefín wasn't allowed to make it about her and her own complicated feelings. She wasn't allowed to change her mind either. Waiting for Josefín's response, Magdalena took a sip of her tea. It tasted oceanic.

"It wasn't," Josefín said, finally, placing empty shrimp tails over her fingertips. "But I really want to wake up, and that's evidently not enough either."

"We only have power in our dreams," Magdalena said.

And though nothing in dreams ever feels dispensable, Magdalena thought her words sounded hollow. She reached for a lobster and when she turned it over there was nothing inside.

MAGDALENA WAS AWOKEN by her phone. Not the watery sound of her text message notification but the alarm of an emergency alert. Flagstaff was evacuating. She stirred Tony awake. It was early morning.

"What should we do?" she said.

He sat on the edge of the bed, rubbing his face. He turned on the TV. It was all right there, all of it on fire.

"I have to go the hospital," he said.

"Tony, what we do, we do together," Magdalena said. "If you want to go to the hospital, I'm going with you. But it says we have to move now."

The map of Flagstaff on TV was waving with animated flames, the hospital in the red evacuation area.

"Tony, they usually have plans for these types of things."

"What if something happens to her?"

"Tony, I have to tell you something," Magdalena said.

Everything was so bright and fresh, like citrus, this early in the day.

"What?"

"It's something I should've already told you."

"What?"

"I love you very, very much. And I've always been proud of you. You've always made me so proud."

He smiled tearfully, having heard it all a thousand times before and having heard this time as well.

THEIR NEIGHBORHOOD WAS being sent to Flagstaff High School, where the Red Cross and some other groups were setting up cots and two kitchens in the gymnasium. Evacuees were given an hour and a half to gather insurance papers and get to the school. Tony drove them past the hospital on the way there. Shuttles were idling at every entrance, and school buses and even one gray prison bus were parked on the lawns. Hospital staff were running in all directions, pushing gurneys, holding up glowing IV bags in the first of the day's sun, which was setting early behind the crumbled black clouds arriving from the south. It could've been rain, if it wasn't so much fire. Police directed Tony and Magdalena away.

Media vans were all over the high school by the time they arrived. All of Magdalena's favorites were out there in their suits and blouses staring into cameras. Dumbass Dale, Fake Tits Magee. A crossing guard she recognized from Tony's school days guided them into the lot, to a parking spot between two minivans. Kids were everywhere, running around and laughing. Family dogs relieved themselves all over everybody's cars. Military and police and fire copters beat the sky, whisking the black clouds, uttering megaphoned allowances under their buffeted breath.

The hanging lattice of big metal lamps was only just waking up when Magdalena and Tony walked into the gym. Magdalena imagined this was what it must be like to come to in an operating room. Beards of smoke clumped in the windows. The sound of people talking wove a heavy atmosphere of noise cut only by the chirping of people's sneakers. Row after row of cots disappeared into the far corners of the gym. People were all over, flowing out of the changing rooms, standing around the trainers' offices, lining the trophy hall; there were even people looking down from the retracted stands. Up there, they looked like nervous gargoyles.

Tammy Pham was seated on a cot across from Tashana. Both women were looking at their feet, doing ankle stretches or something when Magdalena found them. Tammy Pham looked up and told Magdalena to use the cots behind her.

"You guys okay?" Magdalena said. "Where's Sasha?"

Both women nodded to suggest they were fine. Tammy Pham said her husband was at a conference.

"Or something like that," she said. "He wanted me to go, but I'd rather stay here and burn alive."

"Tammy Pham, Tashana, this is my son, Tony," Magdalena said.

The women looked at him and smiled.

"We've heard so much about you," Tashana said. "Good to finally meet you. But what strange circumstances."

He said hello. Nothing registered on his face. Josefín was hooked up to all sorts of devices in the hospital, machines plugged into the wall. How easy would it be to move her? Josefín had asked to be left alone, but she'd asked inside *my* dream, Magdalena thought. For the first time, it struck her that people often used the words "hope" and "dream" interchangeably. What if the girl burned up in her sleep? Was that what she'd wanted for her?

"I'm going to walk around," Tony said.

"I can set you up next to me?" Magdalena asked.

"Sure," he said and walked away.

"He okay?" Tammy Pham asked.

"I don't know," Magdalena said, settling his work clothes at the foot of his cot.

How did it feel to be back in the last place he'd felt like someone, surrounded by green eagles—the mascot—in the old gym where he used to stretch and sweat and dream?

"Are you okay?" Tashana asked.

"I don't know."

She'd returned to her alma mater too, the last place where the unknown felt like trying a door. If something was meant to be known, the door opened; if not, it was usually locked. Since Tony, the unknown had been like holding hands in a labyrinth, a feeling like being lost but not alone. That she could lose Tony in the labyrinth, that she was supposed to, that they were meant to be alone from each other, seemed the most unreasonable thing in the world.

Through the gymnasium windows, she could see the last of the morning darkening to a convincing dusk. The smoke had changed. She could detect plastic, paint, and fibers in the burning. The bloodcurdling smells of someone's house. The McMansions in the forest would go first, breaking down into nothing but cinder and soot bearding a heated in-ground pool. The flames would climb down and take her place next. She looked around to try and see where Tony had gone, but he wasn't anywhere, or he was, just buried by the hundreds or thousands of other evacuees looking for each other in the teeming gym. Some dads pulled out tumbling mats and kids took turns slamming their bodies into the foam. She'd reserved hopes for others her whole life. Here were those people.

"Did Glen come back?" Tammy Pham asked.

"He decided to retire," Tashana said.

"Hm. Some hero," Tammy Pham said.

"Ladies and gentlemen, if I could have your attention, please, I'm Fire Chief Arturo Gomez with House Eleven. The western kitchen will begin serving breakfast to rows A through J, that's A through J . . . "

"Where's it say what row we are?" Magdalena said.

"I dunno," Tashana said. "They're just giving out chips and water anyways. I ain't eating that shit."

Magdalena traced her aisle in search of her letter. Twelve cots up, she nearly bumped into Tony's dad, but she stopped short. He was too busy wiping a baby's mouth, a little girl with dark hair, to notice her standing beside him. Magdalena had wanted something for him, too. She stumbled out of the gym and into the natatorium. The icy glass shell was easy on her eyes and the chlorine washed the smoke from her nose. It gave her a headache, but the chemical also made her feel like she could finally breathe again. Tony didn't pick up his phone. The quaking shadow of a helicopter looked like a shark swimming over the natatorium glass. Tony didn't text back. A gym-teacher-looking guy stood at the other end of the pool and told Magdalena she couldn't be in here.

She pushed against a door and was outside. On the horizon, between the treetops and low black clouds was a bright red crack of flame. On the internet, she'd read an article by a scientist who said the fires weren't global warming's fault. Trees naturally caught fire. She liked what he was saying even if she knew she wasn't supposed to. It felt good to think some things in this world weren't her fault. Ash crests crumbled underfoot, inside the gray were spiny blades of grass, soil, and seeds. Sleeping things, bound to wake up when this was over. Better they stay asleep, Magdalena thought. Her eyes adjusted. Below the woods was the track. A single figure was running a desperate circuit, sprinting, clearing hurdles, in plainclothes. It could've been on fire itself. It was a man. He tore off the track into the field, scrambling around the turf in search of something. From afar, the object he picked up was impossibly large, like the wing of an airplane, only skinnier. He ran with it, and it wobbled like a pool noodle. He pinned the pole down into the earth and climbed into the air holding on to its other end. At nearly ninety degrees with the planet, he let go and flew, eclipsing the red band of wildfire with his body before arcing down onto a mat. She ran to him.

"Ma, did you see that?" he shouted.

"I did! I did!"

"I didn't know I could still do that."

"You were flying. I saw you. You really flew."

They wheezed and coughed.

THAT NIGHT, IT took even longer for the gym lights to quit glowing than it had for them to turn on, and when Magdalena closed her eyes they were will still with her, their color memories, bruises shaped like strange countries. She'd never seen Tammy Pham or Tashana in pajamas before; they both wore slippers. She remembered seeing her girlfriends for the first time in their underwear or swimsuits, when she slept over or when they went to the pool, the shock of their bodies. The overhead lamps finally darkened entirely. She sat up a bit and saw the bobbing lights of a hundred phones, tablets, and laptop computers hovering inches from the watchful faces of people lying in their cots. The fire chief, before turning out the lights, had kindly told everyone good night. Farther off, in the gymnasium windows, was the pulse of the fire. Magdalena turned to Tony. She could not see him, but she heard his sleeping breath.

She closed her eyes. The sovereign bruises had lifted. It was nothing but dark. She did not dream of Josefín. She did not dream at all.

ANIMAL FIRES

HE REMEMBERED HER GOING OFF to live on an island in the Gulf to study marine biology. That's where the university was. He and his wife were from the Texas hill country—college island sounded like a gag, but their daughter had always cared very deeply about fish. She came back in the summer and said she hadn't expected it to be such a party. People would have to get over the fact that they were surrounded by water eventually. "Baby, you just make it to class and you'll be fine," he told her. In the spring of her junior year a professor took her and twelve other students to Belize, where she drank from sliced coconuts on the beach and accidentally discovered a species of salamander only the locals had a name for. He was a tiny fellow and didn't fare well in the lab. When she returned, her father noticed an ear-shaped coral pattern tattooed to her left ankle. It wasn't done well and reminded him a bit of the darkened blood vessels he saw on the surfaces of his own ankles. But she had done it alone and he was proud of her for seeing it through. He found irony or some special providence in her waiting tables at a seafood restaurant these days. Sadness, too. Mainly sadness, in fact.

Something had happened in some transition he could not completely remember.

She came home one evening more upset than usual. He looked for an opportunity to make things better. He was usually allotted one, but he had to be quick about it, or else that was it and he'd have to sign off for the day. He saw his chance and bent down to pull a battered shrimp from the cuff of her stovepipe pants. "Finally caught one!" he announced and wagged the flaking thing by its crispy tail. She lost it. Some things are just too much and she broke out laughing. She was also kind of crying. He hugged her, let go, and prepared the wash. She was twenty-five. When she handed it to him, he discovered a pool of tartar sauce in the front pocket of her server smock as well.

"How's my old friend, Orie the Orangutan?" he asked.

"Still miserable," she sniffed, now changed into a pair of gym shorts and a T-shirt.

They were standing on the back porch, where the washing machine was. *En plein air.*

"Something happen at work?"

"Yeah, I showed up."

He tossed in some of his own work clothes to top off the load.

"There should be worker's comp for that," he said.

She'd moved back home three months ago. He and his wife had been down in Bayside for a few years, having grown fond of the Gulf after visiting their daughter so many times at school. One of her first nights back, watching the dog watch the koi color the metal washtub lily pond on the back porch, his wife told her about an encounter she'd had at the post office. The girl holding her packages was new and said she had some juicy gossip about the farmhouse they were renting if that was her address written on the package.

"Y'all live on a street now, why don't the packages come to the house?" his daughter said.

"That's not how it works," his wife said. "Anyways."

The post office girl had an uncle who'd lived in their house when he was a boy. The whole Gulf had come under a lightning storm one summer and a bolt entered the home, through the metal roof. Her uncle's father was holding to a pipe, and from the father's body the electricity leapt through a portal in her uncle's boyhood heart. With a searing hole in his chest about the size of a quarter pounder, she said, her uncle, who was already lying in a bed, minding his own business when it happened, opened his eyes from the afterlife and saw all the walls alight with a starry firmament of orange glowing nails. Amidst the burning polka dots he said he saw people he'd never seen before. Tree-like men and women stalking about, a family of them. The boy only put it together years later that they were ghosts.

"That boy made it, but his daddy died," his wife said. "Not before they shared that lightning, though."

"That's a messed-up story, Mom," his daughter said.

"I just thought it was funny that she called it juicy gossip."

The koi drew a Japanese watercolor. Braque, the dog, enjoyed it immensely.

"Which room was the starry firmament room?" his daughter asked.

"Yours," his wife told her, and then, "Oh." She put her hand near her mouth. She had a willowy, mischievous look about her. His daughter took after him, more blatant. There was nowhere on their faces where thoughts could hide.

He said, "Why are you going scaring her about things?"

"Not meant to be scary," his wife said. "Supposed to be poetical."

"Quoth the raven," he said.

The starry firmament room used to be his, while his wife slept in the back room with the covered parakeets. He'd moved into the hot water closet to give his daughter a respectable bedroom. The closet was space enough for a twin and his body's overhang and a pile of science fiction paperbacks and the water heater. "Like my days in the army," he said, though he'd never been in the army but was a pacifist who was not afraid to get into fist fights about U.S. military aggression. The room was so humid all his books quickly wilted, but he liked the space, and the parakeets, he was convinced, were all his ex-wives and girlfriends come back to deprive him of sleep. In the starry firmament room that night, his daughter fell sound asleep on the downy bed, in this world, but was soon thereafter awoken by a gentle nestling in the palm of her right hand.

"Braque," he heard her calling, "leave me alone." And then again and again, "Quit it, Braque."

He was still up reading and looked down from his paperback at Braque.

"He's in here!" he shouted.

His daughter appeared in the dewy threshold, and sure enough, there was the dog, drowsy, licking moisture off the cement floor.

"It felt like a head resting on my palm," she said as he tucked her into his twin in the hot water closet. "It's probably that man who was struck by lightning."

"Think it's Chepo," he said.

"Who the hell is Chepo?" his wife asked.

He'd faulted his wife for giving their daughter the creeps and here he went. But too late now and it was an interesting story. Might as well air all your ghosts at once.

"Dennis, next door, said the Guzmans have been living there since before they were Guzmans, back when they had some Karankawa name. Chepo was the only one who didn't die at home. Died here, next door. Properties used be a lot bigger, but our side yard was the dividing line. He's just looking for a little tenderness, baby."

"Now who's scaring her?" his wife said.

"Christ," his daughter muttered.

"Chepo," he said, pointedly.

The washing machine's drum slung as much water from their clothes as it could and then he put the clothes out to dry in the last of the sun. This was now, later. For a while there she'd had a dryer, fabric softener.

Putting on clean pants wasn't like stepping into the brambles in your undies, she said. He wouldn't know. His whole life had been the brambles. But something had happened. If he asked she couldn't explain it. One minute she was continuing her studies on jellyfish in Florida in soft clean pants and the next she was back in the brambles, sleeping next to a water heater that hissed at her like a snake and working as many shifts as she could at a seafood restaurant surrounded by caged exotic animals in Port Aransas. Was it even legal? The animals? He had found it best not to speculate. She speculated. The restaurant was famous for the animals, had bypassed morality by way of sheer spectacle and tradition, the way certain entities in Texas do.

"I wonder if anyone's ever had their death expunged here," she'd said once.

"Whole world's a wilderness," he said, "why shouldn't your home state be one too?"

"Just wish they'd let those animals go."

"Me too, but some things are too sweet to let go."

He pruned his fingernails. Now, later, by the clothesline. He was already saying something.

"Anyways, tomorrow they're going to pump my bladder with the TB. Say I'll have to hold my piss like a racehorse in a horse race and afterward I'll feel sick as a dog," he said.

He was sick. Tomorrow was the day he was supposed to begin getting better, maybe. From time to time, he would forget he was dying, or dying with such precision and ambition. It was hard to think of himself dying when he saw his daughter living in this way, tartar sauce in her pockets, without a lover or a life of her own. Tomorrow he was supposed to start dying in reasonable increments again; it would be better for everyone.

"I'm pretty sure racehorses just pee while they're running," she said.

"Not if they want to win," he said.

The treatment was experimental. Bladder cancer. It had snuck up on him like a cat in the dark. The tuberculosis strand was supposed to jump-start the immune system to burn off the lining of the bladder sack or something, thus eradicating the cancerous growth. If the cancer ever came back it'd feel like TB again, coming at him like a dog in the daytime.

They watched America's Game. She bought so many vowels. Neither of them could guess a single phrase; the hints and letters seemed to suggest things so outlandish and esoteric, they saw only signs pointing to the extraterrestrial. When Vanna revealed the phrases he and his daughter were astounded by how pedestrian they were. *Hoof in mouth. Beggars can't be choosers. A bird in the hand is worth two in the bush.* His wife came home and they set the table. There was fibrous stuff from the garden and they dipped it into two types of homemade hummus. A little yellow flower floated above one bowl of hummus for beauty and aroma. There were mushrooms dotting the other for flavor and sustenance. The mushrooms looked like coral or decayed incisors. He felt their fungal presence in his bladder.

"June will be over in the morning to watch Braque," his wife said.

"Mom, since when are you guys eating mushrooms?" his daughter asked, watching the mushrooms the way he was.

"It was about time," his wife said.

When the girl was eight she'd eaten a poisonous mushroom and died. It was an act of questionable judgment. The doctors brought her back with charcoal, and he and his wife refused to allow fungus any further entry into their home. On her own, outside of the house, his daughter had eaten nontoxic mushrooms freely, discriminately, for years. She ate one now.

"These are good," his daughter said, popping another one into her mouth.

He winced.

Before bed he walked by the hot water closet and heard his daughter say the same prayer she said every night: Dear Lord, please see to it that this Reagan-era water heater doesn't explode in the middle of the night, sending scalding water all over my dead, shrapnel-pocked body.

.   .   .

SHE SLEPT AND dreamed of nothing. She waited in the car fifteen minutes for her father to pick the right shirt for the morning and watched two unfamiliar dogs stalk the yard and dozens of anonymous blackbirds make deft landing on a madrone. It felt like being in a deer stand. Studying the flaying tree, she realized someone was watching her. Dennis, on his tall cement stoop, with a broad plate in his hands. He ate like he was drinking it. He was wearing his usual biker uniform. Wranglers, white T-shirt, and a black leather vest. She thought he looked like a big Edward James Olmos if Edward James Olmos wasn't big—she didn't know. Tree-like. She thought he was looking at her like he'd known her for a long time, like she was all of sudden grown-up. She'd hardly ever spoken to the guy. Growing up, she'd never had a neighbor. In Pipe Creek her parents had property enough to contain not one but two magical lands: a creek with rock walls that spat ice-cold spring water where she swam as a child, and an ashen patch of burned-down old growth where she'd sought escape as a teen. It was so big and wild someone could get lost on the property if they weren't careful. How they'd managed to lose that world, she couldn't recall.

Her father came into the car wearing a guava-colored shirt that pinched his armpits. She knew the shirt. This exact shirt.

"Bury me at Make-Out Creek in my wedding shirt," he sang, like it was a song.

Her mother had a matching one in canary yellow. They'd gone to the courthouse and afterward bought a couple of Squirts from a vending machine wearing these shirts.

"People thought we were a band," her mother had said.

"Scared?" she asked her father, fifteen soundless miles later.

"Yes," he said.

WHEN THEY ASKED him to get up and move around, to swill the liquid in there, he did the Cabbage Patch. He had the nurse laughing; she said it was like watching *Soul Train*. But the TB-like symptoms that came with being injected with TB started immediately and he lost his power soon after. On the car ride home he'd turned river clay-yellow. He was fortunate his shirt still sang. She sat at her father's bedside in the starry firmament room. Her mother wasn't home yet. He nibbled on a mitt of naan. The fever was higher than the doctors had warned and she cracked open the painted window.

"I thought Dennis was looking at me strange this morning," she said. The air from the open window threw her hair on her face. For a second she lost sight of her dad.

"How so, honey?"

"I don't know, just strange."

"Hm. Known him forever, never known him to be strange around you. Maybe it's just that you've grown so much since you last seen each other. You are a striking woman now."

She looked at her delirious father.

"Dad, Dennis and I do not know each other. We've barely been introduced. Maybe he thinks he knows me, with you going over there, drinking and running your mouth."

"My own daughter."

"Hm."

"He let me ride his motorcycle the other day."

"Wonderful."

"Honey girl, Dennis was the one who found you when you ate that poison mushroom. He ran your body back to the house. You don't remember that? That was the worst day of my life. These are things you must remember."

Had he the strength he'd have sat up. He tried.

"I thought the worst day of your life was when Reagan got reelected."

"Nope, the poison mushroom day."

"Fine," she said, and wept.

"Baby, don't cry. I'm okay. High time we share some lightning."

She left him asleep and walked the four blocks to the beach. She could've walked it with her eyes closed, in the pitch black or at the end of the world just by following the sand's nipping at her naked ankles. Like little cat teeth or iguana tails. She was there on the water thirty minutes before sunset. Great, she thought, so he'll live to lose his mind. And her mom, eating mushrooms? Life really had gone on since she'd gone away. She needed to plot a way out, a way back, but the brambles were so thick.

An old hippie couple was out on the bluing sand next to their pickup. From the bed of the pickup they dragged a small gray shed and dropped it onto the beach. The woman tossed necklaces of gasoline over the structure and then the man lit it with a match and the whole thing went up in flames. Around about sunset it began to buckle into big black vinyl boils. The hippies were gone and a poison gas cloud hovered over her head.

Where did I go? she wondered. Where have I gone? How long has it been?

HE HAD PEOPLE down in Corpus and they were the ones who pointed him in the direction of Port A for someplace fun to take the girl for lunch. "It's totally disgusting," his sister said. "The whole place is covered in red shag carpeting soaked with beer and fish juice but the owner's got a zoo attached to it!"

"A zoo?" his daughter shouted. She was seven. This was so many years ago.

"Yeah! With a tiger and a puma and turtles for petting!" his sister told her.

And they were in the Bronco on the way west to Port Aransas for a place called the Big Fisherman on a father-daughter date. Leatherine palms drooped all over the parking lot, a little battered by Andrew or Allen or whatever storm had come through last. From the car his girl could already see them, the heat-exhausted animals of the African plain and South American jungles. A sagely orangutan in a pee-stained kiss-the-chef smock stalked neurotically in a fenced-in grass section beside the path leading to the front entrance. The ape might've opened the door for them if allowed to. Inside, the girl's ecstasy continued. Parakeets dotted the ticket counter, and who cared about their feces when they shouted spraying colors across the ceiling all meal long? She loved her battered shrimp. She said the tartar sauce made her tongue prickle to a peach pit. It was such delirious joy he lost track of his beers and repeated to her the romantically unromantic story of how he'd married her mother. When the story was over, he pointed his greasy thumbs at his shirt, all covered in beer drops and little green and yellow parakeet feathers, and said, "And it all happened in this shirt. All this life, still happening in this shirt."

"That's a beautiful shirt, Daddy," she said, offering him her wealth, her surplus of sincerity. Every moment of life could repeat a hundred times and she'd have love for each and every one of its imitations.

The waitress, who looked a little like one of his ex-wives, was sweet with her and answered her questions. It *was* fun working here. The animals were all *very* happy. Sometimes the monkeys ate fried shrimp *too*. When she left the check, his little girl leaned over the table and said, "I wouldn't mind working someplace like this. Maybe I could go to college down here, work here at night."

"There's a college out here on Oso Bay," he said, and left a poem on a napkin because of the beer and how moving the whole experience had been.

He took his little girl by the hand and led her around the property to pause at each sorrowful beast. The beautiful, tapestried neck of the giraffe. The druggy eyes of the puma. A pale flamingo. A tiger who was no longer frightening.

"What the . . . ?" his daughter said, but was still joyous.

When he found himself on the Gulf again, more than a decade and a half later, this time to live there, he drove out to the Fisherman to see if all those creatures were still around. He had a pair of pliers in his trunk and fantasized freeing them. When he arrived, the palms were a few rags and the whole place had burned down, nothing was left but the stone foundation and the empty metal cages. He went across the street to a place selling double-wides to get to the bottom of things. A gentleman in Bermuda shorts and a clean white polo told him it was arson and insurance fraud.

"What happened to the animals?"

"Charred in their cages."

"Bastard could've let them out before he started the fire."

"He really could've, couldn't he have."

Weeping out on the water, he thought of all those poor animal souls crying out in the dead of night, unable to flee from their unnatural habitats. Some intrinsic memory of running from fires pushed them to the fences, their meat and fur through the small square holes but no more and no further. Their moms and dads had run past flames in the jungle and savannah. Why should it have been so easy for them? A memory barked at him from farther down the beach.

V.

HEROES

IMMANUEL

THE HOUSE HAD AN ODD set of footprints in the dining porch that no one could recall setting down and that could never be swept away. They disappeared from time to time, in certain light, but would reappear just as soon as a cloud shifted or a candle was lit. An infant's left foot and a grown man's right, dark like sweat stains on the cement floor. The white family liked the way the feet moved across the dusty, quartz-speckled grade and padded straight into the wall of jasmine they had running along the porch's southern edge, the cup of a man's heel shining beneath the climbing plant's flowered hem. The jasmine was for keeping the sun out in the summertime, when the white family threw their parties, and sometimes the Caskills told guests that whoever left the prints must've walked right on through the wrought-iron trellis that enclosed the porch; sometimes they said the feet had been there since before the foundation.

In this house of strange footprints, a boy named Immanuel was held captive. Immanuel was a child of nine, tall for his age, and kind with animals. Along with eleven others, he was a slave. Unlike his fellow captives, however, he had yet to be assigned any role or responsibility in the Caskill household, and many regarded him in the same way they did the footprints, as a strange, nearly spectral presence that never went away. Half marked for freedom and half for untold horrors. Either way, he seemed caught in a purgatorial state, which some feared they could be drawn into by simply talking with the child.

The condition was all owing to the peculiar case the Caskills made to their human property. God, having created both masters and slaves, wanted something for each of them, Mr. Caskill claimed, and little good could come from interfering in God's plans. The Caskill home was not a plantation, so God, he said, finding no cause for serious industry, simply asked the dozen Black men, women, and children to be obedient and helpful in certain tasks. This was His hope and His vision, Mr. Caskill assured everyone. A utopia of necessary basic labors Mr. Caskill would take upon himself to describe, as it was often the case a slave would miss God's instructions. To Immanuel, God had yet to say a word, Mr. Caskill stated, though no one could ever recall hearing any of the things Mr. Caskill heard God say. But just as the sun did not rise until God had spoken, so it was that Immanuel was not given a single duty or task for the first nine years of his life.

Immanuel's mother, Pearl, another of the Caskills' captives, personally found it difficult to believe that God had constructed any man for anything less than the whole of life. She knew for a fact that God had told Josiah the stable hand to escape to freedom, and although the Caskills did not intervene when Josiah ran away they paid the bounty to those who did, two men who'd beaten Josiah beyond recognition and returned him to them naked in a small cage. No god could instruct her or any other woman to bear a child so that it might be sold to a white person requiring its labor, but the Caskills had dictated that theirs had asked this of her on three separate occasions. Suspecting that this was the true purpose of Immanuel's idle existence, Pearl dreaded the day the Caskills' god would speak to her Immanuel in a voice only Mr. Caskill could hear and send her son away from her forever. It was the fear that stalked her every waking and sleeping second until the summer afternoon their youngest captor, six-year-old Benjamin, pointed to the ghostly footprints and said to Immanuel, "That is us."

The jasmine, which would come to be known as Confederate jasmine many years after the fall of the as-of-yet formed nation, reeked in the summer heat. No one had ever dreamed of stating the obvious, that the footprints had probably been someone's idea of a joke when the cement was still soft, afraid it would offend the Caskills.

Immanuel, who'd been standing idly by and wondering for what reason, said, "Okay then," it being his nature to be agreeable despite his mother's insistence that he keep a bit of his own mind for himself.

Whatever Benjamin meant exactly by this declaration, little foot, big foot, Immanuel and Benjamin marched from that day forth, through the copse of turkey oak running the eastern length of the property, out of which the boys crafted a fairy kingdom, and around the malarial pond, into which poor souls from the neighboring plantation would sometimes slip and drown in the night. Other excursions took the two through Mr. Caskill's mostly fallow fields. Mr. Caskill, who made his money as a merchant, had yet to partition the fields off to neighbors. On occasion, one of the fresh young Scots he met in town would want to try his hand at an agricultural operation for a season, and Mr. Caskill considered it his Christian duty to help guide newcomers to prosperity, even if their interests and skills resided in areas in which he had little experience or curiosity himself.

On one such adventure, Benjamin, who was normally quite sure of himself, suddenly looked panicked.

"The entrance to the magic cave, it's not here!" he said. "What should we do, Immanuel? We're trapped!"

Immanuel at first did not know what to say. Benjamin's storytelling and directions had never faltered in the past, and Immanuel had never once been called upon to steer their play. The very idea of it disturbed

Immanuel, but before he could protest, Josiah appeared along the field's northern edge and he felt his own panic for escape.

"We need a bulb from your mama's garden to open the cave!" Immanuel shouted.

Benjamin's eyes widened. The boy Immanuel had once heard Mrs. Caskill describe as a gentle child possessing of a lonely imagination.

Breaking character for only a moment, Benjamin said, "That's good. That's quite good," and their game proceeded.

In his talking dreams, Benjamin became bosun to Immanuel's captain, Merlin to his Arthur. Magic abounded; evil, everywhere, needed vanquishing. Life was painful; this game was not. Benjamin was mature and thoughtful for his age, and he never asked of Immanuel anything dangerous or particularly humiliating. But the game was strange, and Immanuel would feel Josiah's and the others' eyes upon him, hot with scrutiny or worry, which had been the real cause of their first bulb hunt in Mrs. Caskill's garden. When Pearl was eventually sold to the neighbor—she was unable to bear any more children for simple labor or sale—these men and women held their promise to keep watch over her son, and no doubt these men and women only worried and scrutinized in ways she'd instructed them to. Each time Immanuel disappeared into the white child's lonely imagination, he experienced the burning shame of an ill-behaved dog and practically had to be coaxed from out of the turkey oaks at mealtime or nightfall, not for want of more playtime but because those men and women, and even some of their boys and girls, would sometimes look upon him when he reappeared as if they'd heard him giggling with the devil himself. Immanuel would know his mother's scorn. And who was he to say he wasn't fraternizing with the devil? A great deal of adventures concluded with Immanuel killing the devil with an invisible sword.

After their separation, Pearl was permitted to visit Immanuel on holidays, and only in her presence would he feel himself untethering from Benjamin. Benjamin called what they shared a twinship. Its properties were something Immanuel found both obvious and elusive—impossible, real, and imagined. There were their spectral footprints, of course, big and little and more pronounced as Immanuel waded into the edges of his manhood. But night after night, in the pitch darkness, listening to the work-earned sleep of the dozen men, women, and children who'd spent their days currying horses, pumping water, tending the little fields, and running the interiors of Mrs. Caskill's great home, Immanuel would replay the time Benjamin had pressed his hand against his and declared that they were the same. His mother had taken the opportunity to clarify that it hadn't been some high-minded proclamation but rather a simple reminder that he, like every other dark-skinned being he'd ever seen, was some white person's property, in both body and soul, and that Benjamin was only trying to own him more deeply by consuming him, as the earth did the fallen chaff, as Immanuel himself did every time he nibbled at his own scabs. But dreams and spirits and hopes and regrets alike walked the Earth on two legs at night. Straining to hear the sounds of his neighbors slipping into the waters outside the sleeping quarters, Immanuel could never be so sure of this assessment, for surely his mother, wise but all alone now in this life, had never known the companionship he knew with Benjamin. Fallen asleep in meadows together, with their hands in each other's hair, they'd awoken tugging for each other, having escaped from the same dream, wherein a great deluge had tried but failed to cast them apart. Benjamin spoke of a future filled with duties—military academy, treacherous and far-ranging travels in Indian Country, a dismal afterlife with a wife and children—and in each vision visited upon him he said he could see Immanuel standing beside him. Relinquished or removed from Benjamin, Immanuel would spend a day or two alone with his mother. She'd curse the malarial waters and hold him in her arms and pick the pieces of his twin from his skin and hair. *Lord, take the boy out of this boy's mind.* But it was more complicated, in a way, to be a son to a woman he saw twice a year, than a twin to a little master he saw every day. Eventually his mother stopped holding him and eventually she stopped visiting and eventually even her surrogate eyes quit worrying and scrutinizing and Benjamin became the only family Immanuel had left in this world.

And so it was for years.

Then, one Christmas, the Caskill family visited a cousin's plantation. Mr. Caskill's cousin Mr. Clarence had a queer interest in the lives of his captives and particularly enjoyed their celebratory customs. So, on Christmas Eve, Mr. Clarence took Benjamin and his mother and father and brothers and sisters and Immanuel to witness a musical performance in their camp.

A group of men and women with musical instruments sang and danced. A group even larger than the players formed a circle and danced and sang along. Immanuel had never seen so many of his own kind congregated together, save for at auction downtown, but those men, women, and children never appeared as joyous and free as the people on Mr. Clarence's plantation on Christmas Eve. A frost, from high up in the air, swept across the dormant fields, and Immanuel searched the crowd for his mother but found no such woman.

A great big woman led the group on an instrument she played from the crook of her neck.

"A fiddle! A fiddle!" Benjamin screamed when she dug at its body.

Benjamin was eleven now.

The fiddle, or so Benjamin called it, produced a fibrous moan, like an animal long of throat, starting and stopping and starting again with dried squawks, pleasant as the sweat dripping from the player's rounded elbows, as the hairs on her chin, as the birthing noises she made with her gut and chest and breath. Ugly, noisome. Mr. Clarence poured the players drinks himself.

"Why, this isn't Twelfth Night!" Mr. Caskill called to his cousin.

"It's twelfth from somewhere," Mr. Clarence shouted.

"Twelfth of something," Mrs. Caskill said. She was clapping.

It brayed, Immanuel decided. The fiddle brayed each time the woman opened it up, and the ass became a bird, but only a fool wouldn't hear it for what it truly was: an ass, a braying ass. He wanted to stop the stomping, the drinking, the screaming. A man drew his clean fingernails through an invisible weave floating atop a tortoise shell slung across his belly. Immanuel felt those notes like jute between his teeth, pressuring an ache in the gums, expressing the dark blood, the jute you used to proof the man teeth beneath. But all at once, with the music in his teeth, Immanuel felt his twin tugging him toward the circle of dancers, he felt Benjamin's joy, he felt the braying ass sprout wings and kiss God. He looked for his mother, a woman who might play his mother in a dismal, dreary pretend of life but found no such woman.

After the holiday, Mr. Caskill prepared for a purchasing trip to the coast and asked his children if they wanted anything for themselves.

"A fiddle," Benjamin said.

Mr. Caskill didn't think much of this request at first, but preparing for his return trip home a week later and checking his stock, he realized he had managed to acquire every other item his children had asked for and felt guilty. It was a Sunday and every business was closed. He appealed to the hotel proprietor for help.

The proprietor said, "There's a Spaniard who runs a shop out of his boat. He's denounced God, I believe, and does business even on Sundays. He may be your only hope."

Mr. Caskill found in the Spaniard shop a beautiful violin. The shopkeeper informed Mr. Caskill that he had acquired it in Italy.

"One troy ounce in gold," the shopkeeper said. "It was made by one of Stradivari's most skilled apprentices."

Returned home, Mr. Caskill bestowed the violin on Benjamin, with surprise but little fanfare.

Benjamin took to the instrument quite seriously, and in the early days of Benjamin's musical apprenticeship, relinquished or repudiated in the presence of this violin, Immanuel tried to make use of himself elsewhere, fashioning his actions after the other able-bodied boys, rotating from the outbuildings and the fields and visiting with Josiah to curry the horses. Then one morning, standing in the stables with Josiah, asking that he show him how to shoe a horse, Josiah became angry with him, tossing his tools about and frightening the animals. When Immanuel asked Josiah why he'd become cross with him, Josiah turned to Randolph, a Shire, and began stroking his long Roman head.

"They won't let my son in here. Don't you think I'd care to spend my days teaching my boy my trade?" Josiah said. "You, they let wander in and out of any old place your feet take you."

Immanuel looked at the day through the stable doors, a bright but shadow-cast object, like a painting in a dark frame.

"I don't know what I'm meant for," he said.

Josiah shook his head and Randolph, a giant, mimicked him.

"Do you know what a lady-in-waiting is?" Josiah asked.

Immanuel said he did not.

"Fancy white ladies circle theirselves with other fancy white ladies so when she got a story to tell or a song to sing, she got an audience. She sit down and eat with Jesus or take a hurtful shit, don't matter, she wants someone to tell it to, and ladies-in-waiting wait til she ready to tell it, and then they wait and listen til she done telling it. Benjamin ain't no fancy lady, but he sure is a fancy boy and he gonna be a fancy man, just like his daddy, and just like his daddy, he will need, for the rest of his life, a boy, who, just like a lady-in-waiting, waits. You Benjamin's boy. You meant to wait. So, go wait someplace else," Josiah said.

Getting up in ages, the boys' adventures had already begun to wain by the time the violin had arrived, and so determined was Benjamin to make quick mastery of the instrument, one might've suspected he'd forgotten his old twin entirely when Immanuel appeared again to wait on him as Josiah had instructed. When Benjamin wasn't taking school lessons with the governess, or violin lessons with Mr. Horwitz, a cruel-looking bachelor Mr. Caskill had brought in from town twice a week, he could usually be found with sheet music and a stand on the dining porch, seated or on his feet with the lacquered object tucked beneath his chin. And a strange thing occurred in Immanuel on his first few visits to the porch. Cross-legged on the cool, dusty floor, training his eyes on those ghostly footprints marching and disappearing into the jasmine, which, he'd decided, reeked specifically of male spoils, waiting for his young master, his old twin, to grow tired of craning his neck and drawing his hairy bow across the violin's strings, Immanuel experienced a lonesome impatience that turned quickly to anger. He suspected playing the violin was quite an easy thing to do, judging by Benjamin's sudden proficiency. Where at first he worried that the noises Benjamin produced would be tiresome, like the music the musicians had played on Christmas Eve, he found instead the songs Benjamin played—Continental, Benjamin called them—quite pleasant, or else mournful but in a soul-satisfying way. And so it wasn't a simple hatred of the violin, or fiddle, or whatever it was, he realized, that made these feelings of boredom and anger well up inside of him—on the contrary, he was quite entertained—but rather his odd positioning in the world again. His body aching but for want of labor, his mind racing after the wordless adventures the violin's strings spun, he understood, without ever knowing the words or their distinction, that what he'd felt on Christmas Eve was jealousy and that what he was feeling now was envy. Freed from the little master's lonely imagination, untwinned and welcome to wander wherever his unshared feet led him, he felt what his mother must've felt every time she'd arrived for the holidays to discover her own blood laughing beside the malarial pond atop the surface of which so many tired bodies bobbed on occasion the North Star optioned a more immediate, less harrowing release. The lonely passion of old hand tools, expended horseshoes, the bow hair Benjamin burned through and tossed into the fireplace. But yet another strange thing happened during these early visitations on the porch. Just when Immanuel didn't think he could take it any longer, and would just as soon head to the stables to beg Josiah to be his father, or drown himself in the malarial pond, or, even worse, march into the jasmine, Benjamin, who must've sensed the piling pressure in his twin, would suddenly stop playing, fold his sheet music, and look upon Immanuel with so much love and kindness, Immanuel would have to catch his breath on the male spoils of the jasmine wall and exhaust every unused muscle in his body to fight water from growing in his eyes. And eventually he came to anticipate this great shift. Benjamin, whose beautiful melodies could only be matched by his exquisite timing.

And so it was for a few years. In those interims between pieces and exercises, the two would return to their twinning and their dreaming. In dreams, Immanuel would follow Benjamin to military academy, to the Dakotas. After some uncertain service to his country, Benjamin would become a concert violinist, and Immanuel would travel the world with him as his valet, from Paris to Vienna to New York, carrying his violin and trunks. They would take wives and have children, who would await them at journey's end at the family home.

When the South seceded and the Confederacy was formed, New York was eschewed, but they'd be treated as kings in the new nation's capital in Richmond. And it was only when Benjamin, age sixteen, departed to train as a rifleman, that Immanuel's passioned loneliness returned.

In the wake of Benjamin's going-away celebration, Josiah discovered Immanuel sitting on the dining porch, distraught and drunk, having taken his first drink of alcohol from the stems of leftover champagne flutes. Josiah was drunk, too, having fraternized with Mr. Caskill when he caught the man weeping in the stables.

"Your mother's gone," Josiah told Immanuel gently, drink or tragedy bringing out an unaccustomed kindness in his voice.

"Been gone," was all Immanuel said.

"You don't understand. She crushed by a wagon wheel."

"Are you my daddy?"

"Half the mind to tell you Mr. Caskill your daddy, way you treated like the chosen one."

"Immanuel Caskill," Immanuel said.

Josiah started to laugh.

"What?" Immanuel asked.

Josiah extended his hand.

"Josiah Caskill, please to make your acquaintance. Might be your daddy after all."

"Did she feel pain?" Immanuel said, still shaking Josiah's hand.

"No more pain than she'd felt her whole life. The Lerners' was a real plantation. Surprised they didn't throw your mama out before life did. Know what a cat-o'-nine-tails is?"

"You a dictionary?"

"Know what it is?"

"It's a cat with nine tails!" Immanuel said, getting to his feet, exasperated.

Before Immanuel could fall over into the red open skull of a watermelon, Josiah caught him, and bringing him into his stink, he clutched Immanuel's cranium and pet it like old Randolph's, whom Josiah had buried and wept over the year prior.

"That's right. Never seen one but they say they real. Cat with nine tails," Josiah whispered.

It was announced that the soldiers in Benjamin's company were permitted to take one slave and one personal affect with them to war. And so, after his return from the military academy, Benjamin set off with Immanuel and his violin in search of glory.

They marched north and curried favor with God. In the camps, after the injured died or fell into dreams of missing limbs, Benjamin would pull out his violin and play. Often, the music was not the Continental sort Immanuel favored but rather the bawdry, festive kind he'd heard all those years ago on Christmas Eve. And just the same, the soldiers would laugh and dance as those captives had, while Immanuel and the other Black men they'd brought with them would clap along, in a bizarre mirror-pond reflection of Immanuel's memory. While battles were raging, Immanuel and the others would clean up after the festivities, prepare food, or tend to the injured. Hidden in stands of trees not unlike the magic copse of his childhood, or in open grasslands that brushed the chin of the sky, or caught in the crags of mountain terrain, breathing in a blue smoke the locals said seethed from the lungs of trees, however far his physical journey had taken him—from South Carolina, through North Carolina, to Virginia and Maryland—he took in more of the world through whispers than what he glimpsed with his own eyes. Cleaning the tobacco-colored dressings of wounded soldiers, heaving the gas sweat of a cauldron of soup, Immanuel listened to the other captives' stories. The joys or else the horrors they had known. Like him, many never knew their fathers, each had been torn from their mothers. One man could read. Immanuel heard tales of Africa, that motherland. The man who could read told them they were all free. Many men bore scars all over their bodies, inflicted on them by the very men who'd brought them to the battlefields. Many of the soldiers had forced these men to do ungodly things, and Immanuel stopped telling his stories of falling asleep in meadows with Benjamin. Some men spoke French and German and very little English. There were men with multiple wives and scores of children who said they were kings where they all came from. Most of the men had witnessed murders. Some of them were each other's wives. One man had killed his own wife. There were astronomers among them, each with a different interpretation of the night sky. One man handed out drawings of naked women he made in the dead of night. A few begged to join the fighting. One man ate dirt; another, a dog. On march, they would spy their kind hanging from trees. One man said he'd invented time travel but died from a mysterious illness before he could finish describing how it was done. One man had served the grand duke of Tuscany. A great number of men were boys, younger than

Immanuel, and they took turns getting drunk though none of them enjoyed it. The men buried each other and their captors. On their death beds, their captors bequeathed their captives to one another. Out of fear of ghostly retribution, the new captor and his new captive would take pains to honor the dead's wishes. The captives celebrated victories and mourned losses. They wiped the tears from soldiers' eyes. They prayed over the dead. One man, at each new encampment, claimed he'd already been there before and to prove it would close his eyes and describe the landscape in perfect detail, including hidden creeks and brooks from which freshwater could be drawn. Two men had no testicles. Many were long-lost brothers. There were two sets of long-lost twins. Together, they told each other stories to piece together a missing youth. Several men had had the hearing beaten out of them. Four men referred to their mothers as whores. One man said he would kill the whole lot of them, every white man, just as soon as God told him to. And every night, Immanuel would descend from the risen cloud of these men's voices and spoken lives and lay down next to Benjamin and sleep with one eye open awaiting the night God told that man it was time. Sometimes he would fall asleep thinking that he'd spring awake to save Benjamin while on other nights he'd fall asleep thinking that he'd roll over and kill Benjamin himself. Though it was also rumored that one of their ghosts had been following them since Virginia and that that mighty captive, now free, would release his brothers before they reached Canada, using the Union Minié ball with which he'd been killed when it flew through the camp, and with which he'd been buried, the soft lead having pressed to a stubborn, immovable sickle when it made contact with the base of his skull.

And so it was until Pennsylvania, which was a whole world of trees. Here, run out of strength, the Confederate army parted with their traveling slaves and any items that would not help them in battle. Handing Immanuel his beloved violin, Benjamin told Immanuel to leave with the others and return home, where the instrument would be safe and where he'd retrieve it after the war. Benjamin's father, Immanuel was told, would know what to do.

"And what about me, Benjamin?" Immanuel said, astonished by the sound of his own voice, so broad in comparison to the sorry-narrowed voice of his twin.

"Do you know what your name means, Immanuel?" Benjamin said when he finally spoke again. "It means *God is with us*. I'll ask that God return to my side when this war is over."

Led by injured soldiers on horseback, Immanuel and the other men marched southward, out of the trees, down through the mountain crags, into the fields and into the towns. In certain towns, white women came to meet them in the street and begged them to turn around. Every few nights men would splinter off to join family who lived nearby. The North Star at their backs, the astronomers shook their heads. They slept in fields or in plantations. They found starving whites and rich whites. Whether the plantation was abandoned or teeming with life, they slept in the slave quarters. In towns farther south, they found old men reading newspapers and smoking cigars or sullen women dragging their children through the dirt. Whole streets bloated with dead horses. Whole neighborhoods burned and burned. In an empty plantation, one of the men whose captor had made him his wife, took his own wife, though she died before the end of the week. And as Immanuel walked, in a burlap sack slashed across his back, he would feel the violin rubbing against him through the thinning fabric of his shirt, the skin beneath growing wet. He carried nothing else save for his rations and a cut of lead cloth, which he'd instructed his fellow travelers to wrap him in should his death require a hastened burial. The cloth would protect his earthly body in its shallow grave from animals.

In North Carolina, Immanuel asked a man if he'd ever seen a cat with nine tails.

"Nine tails? No. Though, I seen a cat with six toes."

On the border with South Carolina, the group broke out into separate factions. Thinner now, the group headed for Columbia fell asleep to the howling of wolves. Every morning, fewer and fewer remained for the remainder of the march. Immanuel saw men fall into the arms of women and children, Black and white. When he reached Columbia, he headed for Mr. Caskill's store and, reaching it shortly before nightfall, found it ransacked, the windows smashed through, the inside completely gutted. He went in and jumped up on the counter, withdrew the violin, and, for the first time in his life, tried to play it. After, he thought, rarely had anything sounded so frightful, and he started to laugh. Benjamin had made it sound so good, for so long Immanuel had thought for sure he'd have been able to produce something resembling a single note. He tried again and laughed again. They'd discussed so many things in those breaks between songs. Once, Benjamin had even brought up the smell of the jasmine.

"Don't you think—" he'd started.

And, after only a bit of stumbling and awkwardness, together, they'd talked the whole thing out, having watched horses and bovine and dogs and even cats. And Immanuel realized that he'd thought of everything in this life that way ever since. That nothing could be too complicated. That nothing could be so far from the path God had intended, just so long as everything had a role. That God was always with him.

"Yes, a role!" Benjamin had said. "That's exactly right. You're right! A role, of course."

Immanuel reassessed his roles. Unremarkable, they were. A partial son, a partial twin. A lady-in-waiting. A boy. A slave. He thought he'd use the violin to start a fire, to keep himself warm through the night, to burn down Mr. Caskill's shop, to engulf him and destroy him. Or were these roles given to him by an unremarkable God? he wondered. But how was it in the year of our Lord, 1863, that . . .

But then it was that he was sleeping. And then it was that he was walking to the family home some miles south still from Columbia, the violin still clinging to his back, because it was a beautiful violin, all the way from Italy, where Benjamin had promised to take him. He passed through the neighbor's plantation and found it deserted save for a handful of

Black men and women all sopping wet from head to toe. Not one of them spoke to him, only stared at him through eyes all watery and alight. It was dreadful, the wet ones and the abandoned plantation, the great house grown over with moss and vines, though it still didn't prepare him for what he saw when he reached home early that evening. Nothing but the stables were left standing. The rest comprised of a blighted and burned stretch of earth, a stand of useless trees, and a fallow field.

He wandered the acres in search of anyone, anything, and found nothing, no one. Nothing so much as a curtain thread. All emptiness, everywhere. In Mrs. Caskill's garden, uprooted and overturned, as if by the hand of a giant clumsy gardener, he fell to his knees and began scouring the dirt in search of bulbs, heritage bulbs, Mrs. Caskill called them, from Holland, from whence her people hailed. There was a cave around here somewhere. He found a bulb, a white mass the size of an infant's head, and clutched it in his hand. No cave, nothing remarkable. He went to where the Confederate jasmine had once stood and there was nothing, not even the footprints remained.

Curled up with the violin and the flower bulb in the horse stable, he thought of a wagon wheel and whispered to his mother. But nothing came of this dismal dream. And then he called out to Benjamin to deliver him.

"I've brought your violin home! Come and retrieve it!"

Through the open stable doors, he saw the world, a black painting arched in a blackened frame. From out of the blackness, a form stepped forward. A creation made from the cloven halves of an infant and a man. No.

"Josiah," Immanuel said, stumbling to his feet.

"Immanuel."

"Josiah."

Tired and limping.

"Immanuel. Immanuel, it's the end of the world."

On a morning like no other, the two crossed the fallow field to the neighbor's plantation, spotting a cat with no less and no more than nine tails as they advanced, though neither man remarked upon it, as dreams and spirits and hopes and regrets alike had begun walking the Earth in the light of day now. The drowned had swum out of the pond and requested burying. Josiah had grown weary of doing it and it was a good thing that Immanuel had returned when he did. Using old, discarded hand tools, they dug the graves and the drowned lowered themselves in. When it was over, Josiah turned to Immanuel, who was still carrying the violin on his back, and said, "This is no place for something like that."

Immanuel folded the violin within the lead cloth and buried it at the foot of a turkey oak. As with the drowned, they offered the violin no prayer, simply tossing the dirt on top and walking away.

"My mama, did she?" Immanuel asked as the two walked back across the fallow field.

"They'd already buried her," Josiah answered.

"Where are the others?"

"We're together. We got a little homestead together. I'm the only one who still comes back here. I work each day in the stables with my son."

Less than two years later, the war was over, and with the end of the war came the return of the soldiers. Every few days, Immanuel would travel into Columbia to try to catch sight of Benjamin but gave up after the returning men did not stop haranguing him for what had happened to their world while they were away. And so it was that Immanuel was shoeing an old and tired mare named Lucy when he received word that a Mr. Benjamin Caskill was demanding his presence at Town Hall.

A free man, Immanuel walked through the doors of the building and in one of its rooms found his old twin, weary and withered, seated behind a tall pine desk, the kind of haphazard furniture that glowed as white as ghosts in the all but vacant spaces of Columbia those days. With tears in his eyes, and refusing to stand, Benjamin, a man now, demanded to know where the violin was, seeing that Immanuel wasn't carrying it on his person.

"I should've known better than to entrust that priceless object with you."

"Benjamin, Mr. Caskill, as far as I know, that violin is safe," Immanuel said.

"Where is it then?"

"At home. I did as you'd instructed and took it home."

"In case you haven't noticed, home is no more."

"I took it home, Mr. Caskill."

Benjamin backed away from the desk strangely, angelic, gliding. When he rounded the desk, Immanuel saw that he was seated in a wooden wheelchair, his left leg a deflated slough of fine wool.

"Will you take me to where it is, Immanuel?" Benjamin said, the tears no longer in his eyes.

On the carriage ride home, Immanuel learned that Benjamin had been wounded at Gettysburg and been held prisoner until the treaty at Appomattox. He'd lost his left leg and the left side of his torso was atrophying, though he still had quite a bit of strength remaining in the arm and hand. His father and mother and brothers and sisters had all survived and were living in a new home in Columbia. The store had not been ransacked but bought up by the Confederate army and his father was busy converting its ruins into a store again. Benjamin didn't think he had much soldiering left in him, not that the South would be allowed a standing army, or that he'd have much luck traveling the world as a concert violinist, but he did have a few contacts in Washington, where he hoped to find work representing the new South.

"I've always been a dreamer, Immanuel," he said. "You know that better than anyone."

"Yes, sir," Immanuel said, the town turning to country through the window of the carriage.

"Now, what's this sudden formality all about, Immanuel? You don't think I'd soon forget we marched valiantly into war together, do you?"

"Not at all, Mr. Caskill."

When they reached the family home, there was much maneuvering to let Benjamin down for the buggy, into his wheelchair, and across the grounds to the foot of the tree where Immanuel had buried the violin. Benjamin paused at the sight of the tree, one of their boyhood turkey oaks but adorned with painted glass bottles. Before Benjamin could instruct him to do so, with no tools in sight, Immanuel got to his knees and began pulling at the earth with his hands. The grave was shallow enough, and he felt the hem of the lead cloth within minutes. Perspiring, he extracted the package from the Earth and presented it to Benjamin as Benjamin's father had all those years ago, with some surprise but little ceremony.

The object returned to his hands, Benjamin marveled at it for a moment.

"You don't suppose it . . ." he started. "It couldn't, but . . ."

And he gestured for Immanuel to hand him the bow. He kept the violin on his lap and tightened the bow, which crackled and emitted a gold dust as the hair lost its slack. It didn't sound the same as before but familiar enough in a distant way. Continental.

"My word," Benjamin said after a spell. "What do you say, Immanuel?"

Immanuel nodded.

"It sounds just fine," he said.

"Just fine, indeed, it's Lazarus risen from the dead!"

He fiddled with the tuning pegs, plucking at the strings.

"Yes, yes," he muttered.

And without further hesitation, he drove into a bawdry camp tune, a Christmas Eve song. He laughed and stomped his good foot.

"Inappropriate after losing the war?" he said, seeing a look on Immanuel's face that Immanuel could not see himself.

"I'll play one of those sullen tunes you liked so much," Benjamin continued, and began playing again, something Immanuel recognized but could no longer feel.

And without realizing it, Immanuel was walking away. He'd have already walked to the ends of the Earth had Benjamin not stopped playing and asked him to stay.

"There must be somewhere you can sit. Immanuel, I would very much like you to stay. It's all coming back to me. All of it. In that damned prison cell, this was all I could think of. I played violin in the air. It's all still here!"

Immanuel looked at his own hands and then the instrument. He was saddened imagining his half-whole body hidden in a cell. But his two feet were walking again, away from the carriage, away from the stables, away from the fallow field. Away from the copse of trees, the cats with nine tails, the malarial pond. He would not pass through the neighbor's plantation but take the road. Down the road, he'd left a horse shoeless. He'd left a remarkable thing.

WREN & RILEY

WREN WAS LEAVING NEW YORK to live in Wyoming with a white man named Riley. Yessenia and Junip, her friends and business partners, told her not to go. Not because Riley was white but because it was Wyoming.

"I mean, why *Wyoming*?" Yessenia asked in short.

"Why-*yo*-ming?" Junip stretched out into something resembling a caterwaul.

They grew up outside Tuba City, Arizona—second-generation Nahua transplants and non-tribal citizens—but four years in the city had turned them into New Yorkers, as Yessenia and Junip explained it. They did care that Riley was white but neither was quite willing to admit that to Wren.

"It's where Riley keeps his fortune," Wren said, and left.

She called Yessenia a month later to say Riley hadn't been lying. The house was huge. Three stages of the last ice age visible from the front porch, a little bit of the epoch before that one. She and Riley had begun living together in a bowl surrounded by some of the youngest mountains in the world. The silver noise of bull elk, bugling for love, kept Wren up most of the night. Black-footed trumpeter swans roosted in trees draped over a nearby lake Riley promised to dive into buck naked the first day of spring. As much as Wren looked forward to watching her stoic million-aire mountain man freeze his ass off, she admitted the idea of Riley's naked body slipping under the frigid glass of the waters, parting the steady reflection of those broken mountain peaks, turned her on. She said that Riley had his pilot's license, too. He'd fly them over Idaho to his beach house on the Oregon coast, where they'd take after the little oys-tercatchers dotting the shoreline and spit any pearls they found right back into the sea—they didn't need them, that's how rich they were, rich as birds. He'd already hired a contractor to convert the property's thousand-square-foot barn into a ceramics studio for her and was looking into buying a storefront in Jackson where she could sell her wares to tourists and collectors, just like in New York. Yessenia and Junip could come stay with them during the summers, hike and kayak through the Grand Teton National Park, attend intertribal powwows, if they wanted.

"That does sound nice," Yessenia was finally able to say, the fuzzy hum of the apartment's lousy phoneline tickling her inner ear in the little silence that followed. But maybe it was Wren's mountain line pro-ducing so much interference.

Yessenia rubbed her ear and stared into her water glass. Catching the light of a lamp, the water looked the color of olive oil. She pictured Wren marching contentedly through forest snow, the animals watching her without stirring as she passed.

Truthfully, Yessenia couldn't trust anyone with so much money, and Wren had broken their childhood promise never to go anywhere without each other. Now Wren was half a country away from the only two women who could keep her safe. Not that Yessenia thought she could say any of this to her friend. Wren insisted she'd been rescued from New York and the chokehold of the struggling artist, that she'd made the smartest choice she was ever going to make in her life. Instead, Yessenia tried to believe her. She tried very hard to be happy for her.

"We won't be having a wedding," Wren eventually clarified. "But you should visit, you really should. The two of you would make a killing in Jackson, I'm telling you."

For the second time that evening, Yessenia considered the invitation. There was no money for travel. Not visiting could be a punishment, at least for as long as they all still meant something to each another.

"Maybe next year," she said, and then, to get Wren off the phone, and because maybe it was true, "We're happy for you."

Four years straight, Yessenia made excuses for why she and Junip couldn't visit; each year she would listen for the disappointment in Wren's voice, the regret and hesitation in her own, and hang up.

JUNIP AND WREN were ceramicists. Growing up, they took lessons from their mothers, Navajo women from Tuba City, and a white woman from Lake Tahoe who lived like a lizard person in the desert between Tuba and Bitter Springs. They blended principles, techniques, systems, and meanings. They could make anything out of clay; they only kept making cups and plates and bowls and pitchers because people liked having things that helped them hold on to other things. Taking one of their saucers or butter dishes or bolo pendants into your hands, however, you sensed something beyond the object's purpose, some sort of indigenous Michelangelo genius, the way the items were as thin as bone tools, fell right into place anywhere, could double as body parts whenever you felt lonely.

Yessenia was a weaver and a loom artist, well versed in Nahua, Navajo, and modern techniques as well, and the three hid behind her shawls year-round. With every garment, she tried to make something to make a woman appear larger, the way a bird might when it feels threatened. It worked sometimes. Junip would come for Yessenia some nights, to yell at or hit her, and Yessenia would open her arms like a condor, her

shawl dropping and spreading at her sides, and send Junip stumbling
backward to the couch or bed to fall asleep. Afterward, Yessenia would
search for something else she'd woven, a blanket or even a towel, to
drape over Junip while she slept, to offer her the protection too. Sleep
was to be at sea, her mother had told her, a person couldn't be any more
vulnerable. Once, wrapping Junip in a tzalape, Yessenia heard Junip
begin to speak to her from her dreams, the sea.

"I hate you," Junip said, over and over. "I hate you, I hate you."

They could fight over anything, but those days Yessenia and Junip
mostly fought over whose idea it had been to leave Arizona in the first
place; whose fault it was Wren had left; how they were supposed to keep
on living in New York now that they'd lost a third of their income and a
fourth of the rent they shared with a Jamaican man named Steven.
Though, Junip had been violent with Yessenia before Wren left and long
before they'd ever made it to New York.

Standing over Junip's furious, sleeping body that night, Yessenia
thought of Arizona. A land of double-wides and LSD and long, droning
hours belonging to the Navajo old-timers who'd tell them to shut up and
listen to the world as it had been before the world they'd been born into.
And not just the one the young girls had been born into, but the one
everyone had, as far as memory could recall. Was it the same world her
people remembered? The Otomí? The Mazahua?

Stepping away from Junip, Yessenia recalled the Kaibab National
Forest. The time she, Junip, and Wren dragged a gas generator up a hill
through knee-high cliffrose to watch a scary movie with a bunch of pon-
derosa pine. Looking over her shoulder as she climbed, Yessenia was
dismayed by what she saw. Hummingbirds driving the clear-cut lane
they'd left behind, butter-colored petals flying off in the wind. It
stopped her where she stood, and Wren had to turn to her and say,
"There's plenty more where that came from. It'll grow back," to get her
moving again. When they reached the trees, they set up camp, passed a
joint around, and ate sandwiches they had packed while they waited for

it to get dark. After nightfall, they fired up the gas generator and climbed into their canvas tent, where they'd also positioned a miniature TV and a VHS player, both borrowed from the high school. Seated atop their blankets and sleeping bags, the girls lit another joint and pushed play. *The Amityville Horror.* Within minutes, Wren was asleep, snoring and farting long before the fake blood started to ooze. Glancing at Wren's sleeping figure, Junip asked Yessenia to please stay up with her.

"Are you scared?" Yessenia said.

"I just don't want to be left alone," Junip answered, and turned to look back at the tiny screen.

Like most of the movies they watched, *The Amityville Horror* made Junip laugh. People died horrible deaths in the movie and Junip laughed. Blood splattered and sprayed and Junip laughed.

Watching her friend watch the movie, Yessenia wondered how anyone could get so much pleasure out of violence. It wasn't like people didn't have violence in their own real lives. When the film ended, Junip caught Yessenia staring at her in confusion and said it was all the stuff about the Indian burial grounds that made her find the whole thing ridiculous.

"White people are so funny," she whispered, careful now not to wake Wren, though she hadn't seemed to care much at all while the movie was playing. "Losing their property is their biggest fear."

"That's what you got from the movie?" Yessenia said.

"Yessie, the whole movie is about a family trapped in a bad real estate investment. No harm would've come to them if they were just willing to cut their losses. And doesn't the white man know they're the ones haunting us?"

Yessenia kept staring at her friend, lit by the light of the credits, the soundtrack music warbling as they breathed, the generator roaring beside them through the tent's canvas wall. Wren had already stolen all of the blankets. Junip was the smartest person Yessenia knew. She simplified the world to a complex state of insignificance.

"Sometimes I think you're too smart to be hanging out with people like me and Wren," Yessenia said, hurting so bad but also amazed by her friend's insights and shaken still by the movie. Yessenia didn't know if she was haunted. Wasn't their little group just left all alone? Was it better to be haunted or alone?

"We're all too smart for this place," Junip said. "And someday we're all going to get out. And not because of my smarts, but Wren's looks."

They stared at the sleeping Wren again. Her even skin, her endless hair. Her even brows and thin nose. Junip was intelligent. Wren was beautiful. Yessenia didn't know what she was.

"And your talent," Junip said, reaching to touch Yessenia's hands. They'd worn her shawls up the hill, as the sun had set, and they were wearing them now. Wren got tangled in hers as she tossed and turned. Junip let go and instantly Yessenia felt brittle, incapable of moving her own fingers without losing them.

"It's too stuffy in here. I need some air," Junip said and unzipped the tent. "And I gotta turn off this damn generator. The squirrels are trying to sleep!"

Yessenia knew just the ones, with their tasseled ears and red spines and shocking, white tails. She followed Junip into the cold. For the squirrels, for Junip, for herself. The sky, an ice cave of gauzy constellations, beared down on them. Junip turned off the generator and, within seconds, took off all Yessenia's clothes. She left on her own. Within seconds, Yessenia lay down her hardening body on the tilting Earth and spread herself like she was about to have a baby. Brilliant Junip moved her hands all around. Hypothermic from the waist up, fevered from the navel down, Yessenia stared straight into the sky, her breath casting obscuring clouds in even streams beneath the starlight. She did nothing with her own hands. The stars were hers; her body, Junip's. She listened for the world as it had been but heard only the world as it was.

In the end, it was Wren's beauty that delivered them, the beauty of the objects she created. A shelf of bowls in a restaurant gift shop and an impassioned directive from a woman from New York on an artist's retreat.

"Move to Chelsea. Make some real money. I'll help you."

The girls rented two corners of a shop in Brooklyn that people rarely visited. Mainly, people came in looking for a bathroom. Twice, someone ODed on the toilet, and the staff had to put up a hand-painted sign. They subsisted on each other, living in a two-bedroom with Steven. Yessenia and Junip slept in one room, Steven the other, while Wren slept on the couch. The eighties crept on with glorious indifference toward them for forty-six months before Riley appeared in the shop.

Wren's arms, dipped in plaster, from her fingers to her elbows, were the color of milk when he found her. Her black, black hair fell over her shoulders, so long now she could tuck the ends into her shoes. Yessenia and Junip watched her fall in love and disappear. It took two months.

"Wren did this to us," Yessenia whispered to Junip. She knew Steven was already awake and listening. He'd want to talk in the morning. "This is all Wren's fault," she said again, louder this time.

FOUR GRUELING YEARS after Wren's first phone call from Wyoming, Riley was dead. Wren had killed him. Again, she called to speak with Yessenia on the phone. Again, Yessenia listened without saying much at all. The murder was totally legal, Wren explained. Self-defense. She'd gone before a judge and jury and emerged triumphant, as a kind of Rosie the Riveter of battered wives, a Take No Shit Sheila, she said. Women everywhere believed they could do it too! Shotgun blast in the living room, a ruined rug. Buckshot collecting in the arm and knee pits of the room, between frills and door hinges.

"He was beating me, Yessenia. He was going to kill me someday. But it's over now."

"I'm so sorry," Yessenia said.

Junip watched her from the other end of the apartment the night of the phone call, shifting, in her usual way, from curious to upset. She didn't like Yessenia talking on the phone too long. She didn't care to be left out of anything.

"I'm not," Wren said. "I'm just glad I had a gun and knew how to use it. Might not hurt to have one in the apartment the next time Junip goes on a rampage."

Yessenia didn't say anything, stared at Junip as she began angrily moving their few things around the kitchen.

Wren said, "I'm just kidding, Junip's not that bad."

Yessenia gagged into the receiver. She'd had no idea. AIDS was crawling through the walls in New York; a team of crafty youths was extracting stereos from every car on the block. They didn't own a car, but they could imagine the special kind of violation that must come from hearing your hi-fi play someone else's favorite radio station as they drove past your window. Her friend had been abused, had lost her husband, was a murderer no matter what a judge or jury said. She shouldn't have ignored her all these years, but when Yessenia tried to comfort her, Wren told her to give it a rest.

"All I need now is a hand moving my stuff out of the godforsaken state," she said.

"What is it?" Junip hissed.

"Wren needs our help," Yessenia said, cupping the receiver.

Three stages of the ice age. Part of another one. Wren could afford the movers but none of them would have the heart it'd take to really see it through properly. There were enough racks and points and antique Navajo rugs in it for Yessenia and Junip to pay their Brooklyn rent for a few years if they only came out and saw her, helped pack a U-Haul, and caravanned back to Arizona.

Off the phone, Yessenia told Junip everything.

"What's the weather like this time of year?" was all Junip could think to ask, simplifying the situation into a complex state of insignificance.

LANDING IN THE Jackson airport on a blue October afternoon, they were only a few minutes on the ground when they saw Wren drive up in an old mustard-colored Jeep. Her hair was short. The truck had belonged to Riley's father; like many things, it was Wren's in the end. The man had named the truck Mister. Wren called it Mister, too. An Alaskan huskie named Cheer Up sat in the back with Junip while Yessenia rode up front, choking Mister's dial for anything but country and bible babble, settling for Corinthians read in a twang before turning it off altogether.

The reunion didn't feel four years in the making, and the drive along the Grand Teton National Park was too beautiful to take death seriously. Sprawling stiff yellow prairie and purple sage. An endless stand of evergreen. Quaking aspen, dropping their yellow leaves and flashing their witch eyes, kept watch over everything. You could wear the aspen chalk as sunblock, drink the earth in a tea. The mountain peaks shined with something called alpenglow.

"Riley called them the tits. Used to bother me, but I guess that's what tetons means, in French. He'd say, 'Hey, Wren, ain't life the tits?' He had a lot of fun getting me worked up."

Yessenia listened for misery in her friend's voice, an openness to regret. She needed regret, she decided. Wren had looked so happy, waving at them from her mustard-colored truck, her hair shorn like the girls' in the punk clubs, a smiling dog by her side. Yessenia had been in rooms with men and women Junip had slept with, attended a birthday party and talked for twenty minutes with an uncle who used to feel her up when she was a kid, but being beside Wren contorted her, blurred her insides. She needed remorse.

"He wanted to put up a billboard," Wren said, "to remind people that all of this was worth fighting for. He had guns against animals and guns against men."

Yessenia imagined the billboard blocking the face of a mountain, a bullet hole tearing through the image or text the way bullet holes blew through the road signs back home in the desert.

"And you offed him with a shotgun like the beast he was," Junip said, and leaned forward, husky hair caught in her eyebrows when Yessenia turned to cut her a look.

Over the stick shift, Wren said, "Well, I wanted to get my point across."

"And you didn't even need a billboard," Junip said.

Silent, Yessenia stared at the back of her friend's ear. She'd never seen this part of Wren's body. What was it for? What could it help you hold? Michelangelo genius still throbbed inside, she tried to remember.

Yessenia saw the house and what a beautiful life it could've been, may have been for a little while. A massive cabin of blond, flaying timber with long windows encasing the sky like tall glasses of water. A house large enough for parties and guests but mostly to be alone. "Why Wyoming? Why so far?" she'd asked Wren. "Because Riley wants me for himself," Wren had said. "Wyoming is somewhere to belong to no one else." Yessenia was glad no children were involved, but her mother had said a woman without a heart for children was like a canteen filled with sand. In every home Yessenia had ever occupied—apartments, trailers, tents—she'd always imagined space for children, for the idea of them, the consummate. From Mister's front seat, she could see Wren and Riley's home in the Tetons was a basement excavated, propped on stilts, emptying. A ruin of selfishness at the end of the world, the beginning of another. She was glad children weren't involved, but how else was it supposed to have ended? How was Wren supposed to regret the inevitable?

At the foot of the icy Tetons, Yessenia gulped the hard, glacial air, watched herself approach the house with bags in hand, Junip's and her own, in the cabin windows' reflection. An unsteady Sherpa with stale apple on her breath, a childless woman with distended breasts sloshing across her broad chest. The Puerto Rican girls she knew called her Poca Tonta. The look made white men laugh at her and white women want to trample her into the gutter on the streets of New York. Junip and Wren, talking to one another behind her in the reflection, were like avian twins, sisters from the same egg, with necks to climb. The only difference between them was Junip's teeth were destroyed and

Wren's were not. If they never opened their mouths, they'd both be perfectly beautiful.

Inside the enormous cabin, Yessenia was taken aback by what eerily effective work Wren had done cleaning up after the murder. Not a trace of buckshot, no smell, no gore. A little island of blood on a Navajo rug, which Wren pointed out with a shrug. Some things go and they're gone. Yessenia remembered watching a man's body burn into the dry air when she was little. Different from the Navajo and Nahua customs, they'd gone to California for the funeral, a family friend. His spirit, she'd assumed, was probably that quaking heat-air gumming up the atmosphere just above the flames' tallest point. She didn't pay much attention to the metaphysics of most situations, so she was never sure, but she was almost certain all spirits had at least the power to congeal. She saw the tits from the kitchen windows, a woman laid on her back, tethered to the heavens by her nipples, a kind of religious torture.

"Know Southern women during the Civil War were jarring their pee to help make gunpowder for the troops?" Wren said. She was knocking around, putting together a snack.

Yessenia tried to see the antebellum ladies napping in their hot, cob-webbed parlors surrounded by glinting jars of golden urine. It was important for her to see the physical aspects of things people said. In New York, she'd almost painted Riley's murder to quit its lurching question in her mind. Now she could see she'd have been way off. A dead body in the home was like a dead body in the street; it'd most likely just have been lying there, for a while, at least. She'd seen a body in the street once. A boy napping in jeans and gym shoes, his shirt probably crumpled in his mom's apartment, on the couch—New York was sweltering. His face had a smoky opening in it the size and grimace of a swallowhole.

"Who told you that?" Junip said, asking about the pee.

"Read it in a letter some chick wrote me. Crazies from all over write me stuff like that every day," Wren said, and put fistfuls of pretzels into elliptical bowels, half-moons of ice into whiskey.

"Fan mail?" Yessenia asked.

"I guess that's what it's called," Wren said.

Then Junip shouted, "Bingo!"

She'd rolled a doobie one-handed, unnoticed, like a miracle.

"Oh, thank God," Wren said, and rushed for some matches in the stone and walnut kitchen. "Riley wasn't exactly a homeopath," she said over her shoulder. "More of a psychopath."

The oil was two generations family-owned and in Texas. Wren had seen the fields once, the tall crows going at it. "How I make the Earth move, let me name the ways," Riley had told her, and for a while it seemed like there wasn't a single object on planet Earth that wasn't connected to his field in some way. She'd asked *him* why Wyoming. He'd said because oil was dirty, he'd smelled it from the womb, it'd tanned the water he drank, and it was the war paint on his daddy's face when he beat his mother. When his brother and cousin died in a plane crash, up in oil flames, and it was all his, and he could afford to be away from it, he went to the cleanest place in America. Glacial-scrubbed. Wasn't there oil in Wyoming? Still, the rocks were so sharp they winnowed the air. For Yessenia, too thinly. In the kitchen, as she sucked at the canoeing joint, curled and gray brittle paper flecking to the timber rafters, she felt faint and had to find a stool. Outside, onyx colors were chasing after the pink setting sun. The chill in the house was a solid, and the women had circled close. Cheer Up had made himself into a neat pile in the middle of them.

"So, what was the last straw?" Junip asked.

Junip was capable of asking anyone anything. The ideas came from her ruined teeth, which had always been gray—a side effect of a antibiotic—and were blackening now. She was the one who got them rides when they were kids, scored them dope, collected spare change for beers; she was their pushy salesperson in Brooklyn. It was her brilliance, all grown-up. She'd directed Yessenia's life since that night in the Kaibab Forest. Junip, twenty-four now, the only one of them who'd grown up with a father. Yessenia remembered it taking Junip three months to finally take her clothes off in front of her, to show her the body she'd somehow hidden their whole lives. It was speckled with cigarette burns.

Wren pinched the remaining weed, soot, and paper to a ball and swallowed it like a pill.

"That's what the lawyer wanted to get straight. He said if we could tell a clear enough story, the jury would understand why I did it and believe that I'd done the right thing. He gave me this triangle diagram and was like, 'Okay, this corner is you marrying Riley, this opposite corner of the base is you shooting Riley, the peak's the worst thing that he ever did to you, you pick something extra bad for that one and two or three events scaling up from the marriage and two or three others scrambling down to the death.' What that guy didn't understand was being married to Riley wasn't like climbing a mountain and killing him certainly wasn't like coming off one either."

Then Wren's eyes were off like buoys, bobbing, blinking in the darkening room. Yessenia, high, wheezing, hoping her clutching lungs weren't actually making the sound she was hearing in her ears, caught sight of a dusky cylinder beside the fireplace. It wasn't a fire poker, but probably the murder weapon; she didn't look at it long enough at first. She'd been the one Wren had called, but Junip was the one who'd said they'd go. Upon second glance, the shotgun slanted against the stone wall like James Dean.

Breathe, she told herself. Hesitation had followed Yessenia like a sick dog her whole life. It would inflame and grow lethargic and keep her from herself and other important things. When Wren called, she was glad the old dog was still kicking around. Wren had killed her husband. The will designated her heir apparent to his wealth—the wells belonged to a board of trustees or a company, but some inexplicable amount of money was automatically hers. Breathe. Yessenia had watched enough TV to know the virtues and trappings of the black widow. Even if she believed Wren had had a right to kill Riley, which she didn't know if she had, there was the question of what Wren was owed in the end: her freedom, sure, but a fortune? Aware of her hair pushing through the skin atop her skull, her cuticles overwhelming her nails, Yessenia noticed Wren's white Keds skimming across the dark wood floor. Who wore white shoes to a murder scene?

"What will you do with all the money?" she asked Wren.

"Whatever I want," Wren said.

Breathe.

AROUND MIDNIGHT THEY were all high and drunk. Junip was using the unloaded shotgun like a cane. A gate outside swung open and shut, and Yessenia thought wind rarely exercised so much courtesy. Reagan's ghastly old face was on the TV. She wouldn't have noticed it then, but years later she'd reflect on how everything on TV in the eighties looked like a dream—it was the resolution.

"And you just keep sleeping in that bed?" Junip asked.

They'd talked of nothing else.

"It was my bed too. And now it's just mine. The movers are gonna kill themselves getting it into the truck. Solid mahogany," Wren said.

Yessenia, a distant planet, muttered, "I thought we were your movers."

"We'll move the little things," Wren said.

Yessenia couldn't take it anymore. The ambiguity. The indifference. The altitude, the alcohol, the weed.

"You don't feel any guilt?" Yessenia said.

She wasn't fearless, she just didn't drink often.

"About what?"

"Killing your husband."

"What part of he was beating me do you not understand?"

"You could've left. You could've come home."

"She is home," Junip said.

"You just didn't want to give this up," Yessenia said.

"Why don't you run away?" Wren asked Yessenia. "Why don't you go home?" she said, and somehow this made Junip smile.

"What did you think was going to happen?" Yessenia said. "You came out here knowing it was going to be a nightmare."

"It was heaven for a year, Yessenia. I had no idea what Riley was capable of."

"He was a man," Yessenia said.

"Steven is a man," Junip said.

"Riley was a straight white man," Yessenia said, toggling between Wren and Junip, uncertain with whom she was arguing, what she was arguing.

"Not all of us get off on women," Wren said.

Yessenia felt saliva readying her throat.

"And if you knew something back then, why didn't you say anything?" Wren said.

Yessenia hadn't said anything because she was scared. She didn't say anything now because she was scared.

"I'm not asking for anyone's forgiveness," Wren said, lowering her voice. "That's not why I asked you two to come. No forgiveness, no guilt. I asked you two to come get me the fuck out of here. To put an end to this. That's it."

"You weren't supposed to go without us," Yessenia said.

"You're right, Yessie," Wren said. "But we're together now, aren't we? And it's a miracle that we are. Not just me. All of us. It's not anything but a miracle."

Yessenia knew what she meant. Junip did too. They both knew Wren was right. They all knew sleep might've been a sea, but life aboveground, on dry land, in the desert, where everything else had a stinger or an armored face . . . Yessenia tried to remember how many girls. *How many girls?* Everyone talked about how the men had been picked up in buses and never came back. But only a few people ever brought up the girls. In Yessenia's mind, each of the disappeared, when she pictured them, were always walking, the last you saw of them were their elbows and the soles of their shoes. But then she knew they'd later been seen washing their faces in truck stop restrooms, holding a Budweiser in a dance hall in Perry or Cheyenne, answering an ad for an at-home nurse in Tulsa. She knew a stranger had seen the last of them before they disappeared forever.

Wren said, "And I'm glad we're together, even here. I need you, Yessenia. It's so important that you came."

She grabbed Yessenia by the hands, and for a moment, Yessenia did not feel so brittle.

"The kindest man I've ever met was a bear trainer," Wren said, weaving her head side to side to stay in Yessenia's sightline. "He was Riley's friend, he came to the house once, he didn't bring his bear. I told him all about you and Junip and our childhood and he listened and asked questions and didn't drink too much and told me all about his wife and kids. You've seen his bear in movies and commercials, I promise. He was sitting right where you are when I asked him, 'Let's say Debra Winger was acting in a scene with your bear and your bear starts to go haywire and tries to eat Debra Winger's face off, would you shoot it?' He didn't like this question, said he didn't like to imagine it, but if something like that did happen he'd let it happen. 'Can't blame a bear for being a bear,' is what he said at first, and then he told me a story about the first time he and the bear went to the southern hemisphere. They got off the plane in the middle of nowhere, someplace in South America, and the first thing the bear did was look up at the night sky and start crying. They had a police escort and the cop raised his gun to the animal and the trainer put his own body between them. The bear was only frightened, he said. Because the bear couldn't recognize any of the constellations in the night sky. He'd been all over Europe and the United States and never made a fuss because he knew exactly where home was. In South America, he was lost. The trainer said he couldn't kill a thing that read the stars or experienced the fear of getting lost. You're right, I should've known. Because that's what a man is. A person who forgives the animal. You've been right about everything forever."

WREN SHOWED YESSENIA and Junip to their room. Beside the bed was an Afghan loom on which the fine startings of a shawl were strung, stuck and dangling. Outside was a tallow moon. Moose, beleaguered with rut, horned in the woods, and when Wren left, Junip gave Yessenia a devilish look. Yessenia hated it when she didn't want to have sex because she always had to anyway. Getting turned on took courage first.

"I'm gonna pee," Yessenia said, and the way she said it made it sound like she was taking a stance, but she really wasn't.

In one of the upstairs bathrooms, from a few feet away, overlooking the toilet, a mounted doe watched you go. The taxidermist had given her a pulse in her throat, which he'd forced softly to the left. Her ears and nose were tuned to something, the hunter or her children, while her black eyes kept forward, dividing her captivation. What was the last thing the doe saw? Food? A skunk ambling through the litter? Or was the doe still seeing, watching now a stoned woman on a cold porcelain toilet, pretending to still be peeing? A male deer might gore a man during mating season. Female deer occasionally trample people when they think their young are in danger. Winding her hand with toilet paper, the expensive kind that left her feeling fuzzy and unclean, Yessenia remembered the month she'd worked as a janitor at an all-girls school when they first moved to New York and the smell of the rag traps she emptied every day. Waiting, she thought she could smell that rich and tarring scent in the room. She tucked down, but it wasn't coming from her. It was drifting off the doe's tongue. She'd only just located the clammy toilet handle under her armpit when she heard Junip shout her name and then "Wren!" Someone's feet running down the hall. Fists pounding at the bathroom door.

"Yessenia, Yessenia, Yessenia!" Junip's voice called from the other side.

She'd barely opened the bathroom door when Cheer Up came charging in, barking and circling, his whole body an electric fizz. He pointed to the doe and then went tearing around again.

"There's somebody in the house," Junip was saying, but Yessenia was after Cheer Up, smoothing his collar fur, telling him it was okay while she choked on that smell. She'd managed to pull her pants back up but hadn't buttoned them yet.

"Wren, is that you?" Junip called into the hall.

Cheer Up snapped and growled, let out a chirp.

"Goddamnit, shut that dog up," Junip said.

But Cheer Up wouldn't stop barking, outing the doe, drawing whoever Junip was talking about to them in the upstairs bathroom.

"What is that awful smell?" Junip said, and reached down to grab Cheer Up by the snout at a pass. He bit her, and she paused for a spell, looking at her blood on her hand before kicking the dog in its side. Bewildered, Cheer Up quit for a split second and then nearly knocked over both women racing back into the hallway.

"You hurt him!" Yessenia said, and Junip had to grab her to keep her from running after Cheer Up.

From the bathroom, in Junip's arms, Yessenia heard the animal's nails on the stairs, galloping down in the way she knew old dogs do, hip swiveled, front paws in quick succession, back paws in quick succession, tail a swinging side gate, the whole thing an unstoppable mess. And then she did hear him stop at the landing and could picture the dog looking onto the darkness, at something in the pooling shadows. The courteous wind. Their visitor. The man. Wren appeared in the doorway with a shotgun in her hands, a different one, more beautiful and polished, but she just as soon darted off too, down the stairs, leaving Cheer Up where he stood. "Argos, my ass!" Wren shouted, bursting out the front door.

From the landing, with Cheer Up by her side, Yessenia heard the report of buckshot on the field and its echo. The living room was lit up and there was nothing there but the stool on which she'd sat, greasy drained tumblers, the sleeping TV. Junip slinked past her and met Wren as she came back through the open front door.

"Think I scared him off," Wren said. There was a little bluing on the gun or some effect of night.

"What the hell is going on?" Yessenia said.

"There was someone in the house," Junip said.

"Don't know how, I set the alarm. Must've shut itself off, didn't go off when I ran through the front door," Wren said. "Shit."

"I don't understand," Yessenia said.

"I was lying in bed and Wren comes in and whispers that she hears someone downstairs, then I see someone running down the hall, Wren darts off to grab a shotgun and that's when I came after you," Junip said. "Thought he was going to get you."

"He's gone?" Yessenia said.

"On foot, he's still on the property for at least another thirty minutes in any direction, which means I ought to hunt him down while it's still considered trespassing," Wren said.

"No way," Junip said. "Just call the police."

"He's long gone by the time anyone gets out here," Wren said.

"It doesn't matter, he's out of the house," Yessenia said. "We should get out of the house too. We'll come back when the movers get here."

"I'm not leaving this house until I'm done with it," Wren said.

"Did you even see him?" Yessenia asked Wren.

"Just his shape," Wren said.

"You too?" she asked Junip.

"Just his shadow, yeah."

"Either each of you stays here or each of you takes a gun and flashlight," Wren said.

"What the hell, Wren?" Yessenia said.

"Those are your options. And if you see him and you can't shoot him, you aim at him anyways and you start screaming like hell," Wren said.

.   .   .

RILEY HAD THESE beautiful boots, and when they stepped into the studio in Crown Heights that first time, Wren asked him if she could put them in a shadow box for display. Rattlesnake. He'd killed and skinned each of the serpents himself. His friend crafted them into the size-fourteen masterpieces from which his giant body erupted. Stooped and slouching a bit at forty, he suffered from adventure, he was still beautiful in stone-wash jeans and a wrinkled oxford that Brooklyn spring day. There was ash in his brown hair and his glasses were circular and gold and he could take them off as he pleased and make it around the workshop no problem. Yessenia was working the register and Wren was working the slip. Wren's hair was long enough and her waist narrow enough that she could wear her hair as a belt, which she sometimes did at parties, much to the distress of her roots and ends, but the crowd usually loved it. Artisan textiles and wares, that was Riley's passion, and Wren said she didn't like big cities that much anyway. She never asked them what they thought about Riley. Had she, Yessenia would've said she liked him a lot. He'd checked himself out of his hotel in Manhattan and stayed with them in their dingy apartment for a time. He cooked and cleaned and stomped roaches but let mice carry on their way and he was easy and good to anyone who walked through the door no matter who they were or what they were on or who they'd slept with and he knew more Nahua history than they did and he once remarked to Yessenia and Junip that he knew love when he saw it and he wasn't at all the zealot he could've been, had every right to be, but was instead kind and gentle and smelled of cigars and cedar shavings. "He's like Teddy Roosevelt, or something," Junip had said. He reminded them of a time they'd never known. Before Yessenia's and Wren's fathers and half the other men were carted off to Vietnam never to return. A time immemorial and unimaginable, with separate plans for a different future. Maybe love had lived after all, Yessenia had thought, icing the olive marks Junip had left on her neck. Maybe this white man would rescue her too. But then

Riley must've sickened with some evil in Wyoming. Maybe it was those boots that bit him. He cut Wren's hair because he was finding it in his shit. He told her she wouldn't get a studio after all because her work was shit. He beat the shit out of her in that magic home of his beneath the mountains. Yessenia had had no idea and now she did, and Riley hadn't been bitten by anything but himself.

At some point in the night the moon had guttered, a totally different phase than the one Yessenia had seen from the bedroom window less than an hour earlier. Her flashlight caught the moisture on the black air. Wren had gone her own way, and Junip was hunched over her rifle like a plastic army man, even the way she stepped was reminiscent of their toy feet, bound in the mold. Ahead of them was a bristling wall of evergreen, colorless in the dark. Cheer Up, repaired from his spell on the staircase, went headlong into the underbrush. The Pluto of Wren's flashlight bobbed against some tall grass beside Yessenia.

"Cheer Up knows what's up," Junip whispered.

Junip walked enough paces to shrink to the size of Yessenia's thumbnail. The glacial air and marijuana turned Yessenia's thoughts thin and useless. Drained of adrenaline, she could hardly muster fear. Her greatest anxiety was an asthma attack, though she did not have asthma. Her every cell focused entirely on staying awake. But the trees were brushy and drowsy. She was looking at things or nothing changing shapes in a field of charcoal static. She looked for Junip, but Junip was buried in the dark. She listened for Wren, but heard only the rutting moose, the calls and the woodsy sound of their thrashing antlers. An elk bugle. Cheer Up did not bark or whine. The night swirled and swirled.

Then, from out of the dark scribbled wood came something like a sliver of soap. Milky like soap, slick and eroded to something smooth and tenuous like soap. In relief against the blackened wood, the white, soapen figure, as it drew closer, became not so small and not so tender, but more than six and a half feet tall, broad, stalking, and belonging to a man who was also stark naked in the gelid, open air. She could only see so much and so she composed the rest from memories. The truth was plain and awful. He had returned. He'd come back. There was no mistaking it. She'd seen the body before, swimming in a pool at the Y. While everyone else was busy staring at the black python streaking behind Wren's head as she swam, Yessenia had been watching Riley's body scale the green and generous length of the pool. She'd sat on those shoulders with that smoky head between her thighs to chicken fight Junip, who sat atop Steven's rickety frame. Nude Riley, back from the dead, paused midstride and turned to look directly at Yessenia. His ghost eyes were great and she knew he saw her perfectly without his glasses. He remembered this woman. The body beneath the body, the muscle-strapped skeleton, warped the surface of his skin, like a baby kicking inside. She'd seen a cat twitch like that. Why had she come to antagonize him at his home in the mountains? The gun in her hands, the last living thing he'd ever seen, he wouldn't let it have him again. He'd died ashamed of the shock and surprise. Never again. Riley. He'd cleaned himself of oil, she could see this now as he moved toward her, walking, running.

When he got to her, Riley would reach into her mouth and tear out her tongue, rip her hair from her skull, break her legs, and eat her for coming here, for seeing the shameful spot where he'd died. She saw her future yards away. Feet away. She saw it practically upon her, it was also her end, and then Riley's naked body tore off, dashed into a shadow, and left in its place the massive bloom of a moose charging out of the wood, the animal's broad, winged antlers. Cheer Up was dancing at its legs. Wren was shouting, "Shoot it, Yessenia! Shoot it!" Yessenia could feel it moving the ground. She could smell its yearning as it charged her, rearing its headpiece into the dying moon.

THE BEAST RAN for some time beyond her, rutting and dying before crashing like an aircraft, peeling up a curling dermis of earth in its final slide. The veins in the bull's antlers ebbed and winced with the last of it.

A reddened cave had opened up in its neck. Junip and Wren were panting with Cheer Up, and Yessenia could barely sip the air. She had no idea who'd taken it down. An elk kept bugling in the death silence.

"It was Riley in the house, wasn't it?" Yessenia said.

Wren bent over, panting.

"Riley's come back, hasn't he?"

"Did you see someone?" Wren said.

"I saw Riley."

"Did you shoot him?"

"I couldn't."

"Why didn't you shoot him?" Wren said.

Yessenia realized for the first time that Wren was wearing one of her shawls.

"He was naked and running toward me. I was scared," Yessenia said.

"Why didn't you shoot him, you idiot? Why didn't you shoot him?"

Junip pulled Cheer Up back from the moose. The husky was a bloody swab now.

"How could you be so stupid? Why didn't you shoot him?" Wren sobbed.

"You knew it was Riley. You knew he'd come back," Yessenia said, sobbing, too. "You've known all along, haven't you? That's why we're here."

But Wren tore back running, back into the wood. Junip looked up, holding the bloodied dog, her face bloody, too.

"You're so stupid," she said. "You've always been so fucking cowardly and stupid."

Yessenia saw Junip was also wearing one of her shawls. She looked away, toward the moose. Between its splayed legs, it had no testicles.

WREN, WHO PUT Yessenia and Junip on a plane back to New York that next day, moved to San Diego in the end and wrote letters to Junip but refused to speak to Yessenia for not having re-killed Riley. New York kept cleaning up its act and Junip took rent escalation as permission to return to the desert to do things that remain a mystery to Yessenia.

Steven passed away. Yessenia, carrying an urn of Steven's ashes, climbed his favorite mountain in the Catskills and scattered him in the wind as his will had dictated. Shortly thereafter, Yessenia left New York too, to teach looming at the Rhode Island School of Design. In Providence, she purchased a home, her first and only, on the Seekonk River. In the spring semester of 1998, she and two other staff members took a group of students to Uzbekistan as part of a study-abroad program hosted by an Uzbek artisan collective. It was a raining spring, a time of wet boughs, black soil, and the odor of roses. The government was cracking down on Islam that year, and she recalls having watched Muslim men being beaten in the streets. Over the course of her brief stay she met a man named Ablayar, fell in love, and married him. In the fall, once his papers were processed, he joined her in Providence. That winter she discovered she was infertile, which caused them both a great deal of suffering and nearly ended their marriage. Ablayar died of stomach cancer in 2005. "Forgive me," he'd said. She'd vowed never to cut her hair again, but he'd died anyway. As per his will, Yessenia traveled back to Uzbekistan with his cremains and scattered those along the Turkestan Range. The country was again rainy. At dinner with her father-in-law in his home, the old man, grief-stricken and stunned by his son's death, asked her about a story Ablayar had once told him. It involved a female moose with antlers. It was not fair that his son should have escaped the gruesome deaths of his generation, moved to America to be a husband, and still have died before his time. For her father-in-law's grief, she told him the story, in its entirety, not in any way she'd ever told Ablayar. After which, having opened a window a crack to wet his fingers to wipe his face, her father-in-law said, "Yes, that seems right. An unfortunate preservation, but sometimes it happens."

Dropping her off at the airport, her father-in-law offered her a suggestion for her hair, which she'd vowed not to cut when Ablayar first fell ill, but she was now burdened by. "You should weave something out of it," he said. "Something pretty."

She did as her father-in-law suggested and wove a short scarf out of her hair. From time to time she wears it for protection, as from the banks of the Seekonk she has seen men swimming, ferociously, in the nude shapes of Junip's father, Riley, Steven, and finally Ablayar, men of other places and times, and she can never be certain what kinds of pasts they want to build out of her future. And because she still cannot kill them or forgive them, she must live somehow safely with them. Beside the Seekonk, she is big, and no longer bruised, and so alive. And the men, dead, rutting in the waves, threaten and apologize. She wishes the old dog would quit her. And no longer does she listen for the way the world had been.

DEATH ON MARS

BEFORE HE DIED, STROM METTEL'S father, Cicero, disappeared into dreams about Mars. The idea of living on the planet swam his mind lobe to lobe, washing the gray matter in the same swampy froth as adolescent love. It wasn't such a wild idea. Unlike adolescence, Mars was no swamp. Unlike Earth, where large, foaming, groping bodies of water claimed more of the combed edges of the continents every day, there was no liquid water to speak of—which was no longer a problem, not really. Water was being manufactured on the Martian surface. Private trusts, venture capitalists, and a small cadre of the few remaining city states left on Earth were already fine-tuning mass industrial material transport to the Red Planet when the dreams emerged. A massive on-world extraction industry was underway, too. Cicero Mettel himself was invested in a solar company layering one Martian landscape with a bending skin of green glass that would soon capture enough energy to power a medium-sized city. Thirty humans were leading healthy, peaceful, productive, and exhibitionistic lives in a radiation-proof biodome at the foot of the Tharsis volcanoes. When Strom discovered eighty billion dollars secreted in a tax-free account titled Exodus shortly after his father's death in a house fire, he was not embarrassed at all. Rather, he was proud of the man for having had a plan, which most centenarians did not, having outlived their ambitions.

Ten years after Cicero's death, Strom moved to the alien planet himself, into a modestly sized condominium in the Port of Anglis, and hardly ever left the Red Planet at all. A father's dream had become a son's reality. As the son of one of the richest men in history, people asked after Strom's dreams. At first, he dreamed of making possible on Mars what his father had made possible on Earth, before the collapse. Or the folding, as it was referred to—like in the game of poker, like a paper crane, like an omelet. Infrastructure, mostly, civilization building. Strom saw opportunities everywhere, gifted the people of Mars (Martians, naturalized and natural-born) schools and swimming pools. He helped create new ways of living within corporate fiefdoms, a vulcanized-rubber-and-luminescent-glass way of living. He ordered ace pilots to race experimental crafts through canyons for the enjoyment of spectators. For a while, life was good.

But then Strom began to notice, over the years, an undiminishing gash between the life he'd known on Earth and the facsimile he provided himself on Mars. Mars was a startlingly original planet. A great northern expanse of sedimentary gooseflesh sprayed heavy follicles of carbon in the direction of the solar winds. What the hell was that about? And not a sound or echo existed outside anyone's sealed life. It was the double, or the hope of one, the echo, that had drawn Strom to the planet in the first place, the hope to reencounter the child he'd lost on Earth when he was a much younger man. The idea wasn't absurd, he didn't think so, not even all those years later, for what human had ventured anywhere if not in search of something lost? Hadn't the Martian colonies been founded on the dream of returning to modern existence, what hardly existed at all back on Earth? Eventually, the odds that he'd find his long-lost daughter on Mars seemed bleak enough, and he thought he'd give up. He quit looking for ghosts. He imagined returning to Earth, where his son, Otto, still lived, and reconvening with that fractured linear time, living and living and living, with no hope of ever getting anything back. His daughter's name was Mack.

However, desperate as he was, Strom did not depart from Mars then. The Exodus account was not the only secret Strom had discovered upon his father's death. In addition to the trillions in properties, investments, and cash savings Strom had already been promised, Cicero's last will and testament also entitled him to royalties from a series of books his father had evidently authored. They were nothing Strom had ever heard of. He thought: Probably strategic handbooks for entrepreneurs, a repressed memoir, maybe even some sort of espionage thing. And: Weird that he'd never bothered telling anyone about them, but books could be forgotten, even by those who'd written them. The books proved to be neither technical nor confessional in nature. It turned out, Cicero had been a prosaic BDSM novelist with a penchant for schmaltzy auto-erotic suicide endings. Skimming, reading, rereading the books, Strom discovered a man interested in the Icarian highs and lows of ecstasy. A complete stranger. Six in total, each novel was signed off with "Written by He Who Wrote It," in the tradition of anonymous Arab authors. At first, this revelation posed difficulties only personal in scope. Strom wondered who his father had been. But twenty years later, just when Strom could really picture himself back in that fractured linear time-line on Earth, falling into the demise—the folding—his father, from beyond the grave, released a new book, and under his own name this time, bringing Strom's plans—for exile, for return—to a standstill.

First, there was the scandal to deal with—minor; people didn't read and intercourse had come to feel quite punishing in general. Then there was the legal aspect. Strom predicted a shadow executor was sharing previously unpublished writing. For this Lincoln Abdelfattah, his father's lifelong personal attorney, promised to come out of retirement and take the Martian bar if it meant defending his old friend's honor. Ultimately, it never came to that. For reasons less tangible than Strom cared to admit, it became clear to him that it was his late father's residual AI bot, those pesky synthetic consciousnesses appearing more and more often after death these days, that was producing and publishing this newly devised work. So in the end, it was actually Strom's dead father's porn itself that kept him put on Mars. It was auspicious stuff, in need of divining, and this kind of work took time, something Earth didn't have.

This was a task made further difficult by the fact that the AI bot didn't stop with the one book: a month after the first novel's release, another one came out. A few months after that, another. Strom became an avid reader, if not a scholar, of the bot's novels. Neither enjoying nor despising them, but devouring each new release and hungrily awaiting the next, so much so he'd occasionally revisit one he'd already read in the interim, he discovered that his father had become a different kind of writer entirely in death. More philosophical, more anecdotal, less plotty and concupiscent. Born into a life without struggle, Cicero had been free to become an artist of no consequence; dead now, but also deeper—everywhere, in the sense that he was an AI bot pulsing through any network he pleased—he'd escaped actual termination, the last of life's living consequences. The lifetime of arbitrariness had taken a toll on the prose and left it body. The lack of flesh after death had its effects, too: the displeasure with which Cicero had finally died, the complete poverty of Icarian anything in the post-life, had produced writing Borgesian and brainy, full of familiar words but if spoken from a floating not-mouth. Still, these books were plenty pornographic, just not as much as the first six. Strom preferred his father's AI bot's books to his living father's. Strom was a prude. With every book, he became more convinced that this man, or this replica, through the comingling of raunchy sex scenes with unsubstantiated philosophical claims, was trying to teach him something, maybe a way to find Mack, whose AI bot had yet to materialize. Strom passed a year awaiting some sort of ta-da to come bursting forth from the texts until finally resolving that everything, the books, life in general, on Mars or on Earth, had no secrets at all, certainly none that pertained to Mack.

ON THE EVE of his 114th birthday, on a return flight from Earth (his first visit back in decades), Strom was halfway through his late father's bot's latest work (book six), an elegant little nothing entitled *Sculpture in the Dark*. He wasn't hating it. The trip to Earth had been unplanned, but everything else was going just as Strom had imagined it would. He'd finish the book before the simulated night's end and spend the second half of the two-week flight to the Martian Inner Colonies contemplating the piece, making amends, and writing his father's bot a letter, a fan letter of sorts, but also one of farewell, as Strom Mettel had resigned himself to dying as soon as he reached home. He would make history doing so, becoming the first colonist to die of natural causes in Martian history.

Devoid of want and need, the values of the powerful are different from the values of regular human beings, began the bot's latest. *Once one's love affair with hunger is over, there is one perfectly fine ode or elegy left and that's it, you can consider your artistic career finished. And this was why Kim Il-sung, in all his artistic power, had decided to make the Mansudae Art Studio a factory rather than a retreat or a colony or any other Eden, having chosen work—over painlessness—for all eternity.*

The book took place in the early twenty-first century and jumped between the Mansudae Art Studio in Pyongyang, North Korea; a Carraran marble quarry to which a colony of black yeast was laying siege in Tuscany, Italy; and the presidential residence in Harare, Zimbabwe. Concerning the lives of a North Korean master sculptor and his apprentice son, an eccentric young Italian who comes to manage the art studio in which they work, and the ailing African dictator who has commissioned the studio for a monumental sculpture of himself to commemorate his own death, the novel was the bot's most ambitious piece to date. A lateral epic. At its midway point, where Strom had stopped reading, the master sculptor, Kim Il-sung, had already died, leaving his thirty-year-old son to complete the dictator's sculpture, which was horribly behind schedule. A fact that doesn't go unnoticed in Zimbabwe, where the ruling leader has been watching an oppositional protest movement grow larger every day. In what proved to be an oddly heartfelt scene, threatening to cancel the commission, the President ponders out loud, "Why disturb the stone in the first place if it's destined to become rubble in two weeks? Why not let it sleep another twenty-five million years? A snowy, Tuscan, statuesque sleep. A famous sleep." Feeling the pressure, the North Korean government then began torturing the Italian studio manager in hopes it might inspire him to get the sculpture back on track. In the last scene Strom read, an electrical shock had just sent the Italian back to a repressed memory of witnessing an old man being crushed to death by a slab of marble in the village quarry.

The book's scrambled signs and symbols reminded Strom of being young, of taking auspices in an age of uncertainty. But this was what reading had been reduced or enlarged to in general: reminding. Several times while reading the book, Strom had to remind himself that his youth was a long time ago and that the questions and possibilities the book posed no longer existed for people like him. Mack's death was the last unforeseeable event Strom had ever witnessed—his father's home, built in the early 2000s, needing electrical work, had a sixty-seven percent chance of going up in flames eventually—and he had come to believe that the unprecedented events of his life all lived somewhere else amongst themselves, inaccessible behind a pay wall. This was why he had not found Mack: she lived in the world of mystery no longer reachable by conventional means, so far had convention drifted from the random atomic experiments that'd gotten this whole business (life, existence) started. He could live forever, but would have to do so without Mack, as science and money had beaten back mortality but failed to coerce those residing in the land of the dead to rejoin the living. If the AI bots were supposed to be ghosts, they were lousy ghosts. And Strom suspected death was somehow as rare and precious a currency in the underworld as it was aboveground. It was likely the cost of life; after all, life was the price one paid for death.

There'd been hundreds of deaths on Mars early on. Freak accidents and a rash of suicides. But since CIV-6, the colonial permutation that finally stuck, death had lost its negotiating powers. A deathless existence was part of the Martian package, a basic human right. You could die when you chose to, but no one had yet.

Death, for those who could afford to have it removed, had been successfully erased from human biology back on Earth too. There were deathless cities—biopolises—and the surrounding landscapes of death—bloating tropics littered with anarchic communes of hunter-gatherer-like peoples. But on Mars, death had been expurgated from the human psyche and its soul. Existential and financial arguments were made. Why leave a dying planet just so you can die elsewhere? A human life was worth billions upon atmospheric entry or birth. It'd been discussed in board meetings. Class systems had trained for centuries for what was happening on Mars, where the wealthy manufactured the air people breathed. Death would mean freedom and independence from oxygen. Give a man the right to die and he'll start living, as he had in the wilds of Earth. It was a matter of having the full range of motion. Strom wasn't repentant or revolutionary, but he was tired and he was alone. Death was the only place he hadn't looked for Mack.

Strom had recalled the last page of his father's bot's book and was wading into an unfamiliar sentence when his feed was suddenly overcome with news notifications. A thirty-four-year-old woman had been found dead in her Anglis apartment earlier that Martian afternoon. Murdered. Strom closed the book down and sank into his ergo-gel saddle, the report trickling across the pod's inner shield like glowing beads of condensate. The saddle eased bone degradation and the sealed pod improved respiratory health, but save for sleep and whenever Strom desired someplace quiet and private enough to read his father's bot's salacious book, Strom otherwise neglected his prescribed podtime, figuring he would have little use for his lungs and bones for very much longer. However, this news posed a problem. In all of Martian history, no one had ever been murdered. Surely, the return of murder would eclipse any sort of historical relevance Strom's death might've had.

Strom blamed Otto, his son, for this mishap. Not the murder, but the missed opportunity.

He had let himself believe that his death could function as a sort of gift to the Martian people. No one would confuse the act for something selfish, cowardly, or meaningless. He imagined them thinking, after he was gone, *Well, if a man with that much to lose can throw it all away, what's stopping me?* "My death can be the permission these people need," he'd tried explaining to Otto. Out of the blue, his son had requested his company back on Earth, and despite his better judgement, Strom had acquiesced. Otto was going through a divorce. He accused Strom of wanting to start a death cult.

"I won't be encouraging people to die for dying's sake. This isn't about worshipping death," Strom said.

Otto told Strom that he wouldn't have any control over how his death was interpreted. Then he called him egotistical, small, and entitled. Then the eighty-year-old began to cry and beg his father to never die. Strom extended his stay just to make him feel better.

You sonofabitch, Otto, Strom thought, who cares if you're going through a divorce? Alas, a son's doubt had crumbled a father's legacy. Whatever happened to *Saturn Devouring His Son*?

Strom was about to exit the pod, stalk and fume on the bridge, from which the former gold pinprick of Mars was now visible as a playful red ball, when a message notification hovered over his face. Another interruption. Thurston Morris, distant friend and former business partner. They'd gone to school together. Thurston Morris had had a mustache for sixty-seven years, which he trimmed religiously each day with blunt little scissors made of stainless-steel before going after his nose and ears with the same curious instrument. *My dear friend*, the note began, *I am so sorry. Contact me any time if you want to talk. It was your rightful legacy, but the poor girl was murdered, and so the equally bold honorific of first natural death can still be yours! Prematurely, Happy Birthday!*

Strom sighed, clouding the feed with actual condensate. The technicalities would blur his title into obscurity. The murder was already detailing the future course of history. A move back to self-predation, faith in scarcity, a cheap sort of existence that was expensive to maintain. In the end, Strom would be remembered for his swimming pools.

On the bridge, Strom thought of Otto and Thurston. They were not altogether different people, he was realizing now. They could both be characterized by their zeal, their zest for life. For as long as he could remember, they could both be caught having so much fun. And this zeal, this zest for life had done something to their idea of death. Thurston, since college, had wanted to live forever. At Strom's same age, immortality still seemed a pretty good idea to Thurston, and Strom thought the old maniac might actually go through with it. Otto might do the same. The two wanted nothing more than to escape their greatest fear. Sharing this fear and this desire with so many, they would never be left alone. Strom had felt left alone for a long time. Mack had been a prodigious swimmer, and yet she had drowned. What had I wanted that was so different from anybody else, he often wondered, that I should be left alone living this one nightmare? Everything else in this life, I have gotten, why not Mack? It struck him that life on Mars *was* mimicking life on Earth now, if only in the worst ways possible, and, like doubting a voice thrown down a cave, he had almost been too impatient to hear it come back to him.

Reaching under his collar, Strom yanked the chip patch his doctor had prescribed him for the flight. Though it was impossible, he thought he could feel its nanoweavers and service bacteria squiggle out of the quaggy clear slide, enter the air like sentient vapor, a soul-like thing, and himself beginning to die.

EVERY DETAIL REGARDING Rona Ibsen's death had been released by the time Strom's flight arrived at the port of Anglis. On 22.15 at 1143 Rona returned home from the velotrack—she was a pro cyclist—and charged a warm bath to her residential account. Judging by her latest living diagnostics upload, she'd soaked for a good forty minutes before drying off and starting in on a cup and a half of yogurt parfait, also charged to her account. Ostensibly pinkish, wicking into a sheer robe, she was surprised to receive an entry request from the southern gate of the apartment compound from her on-off boyfriend, Zane Rivers, but cleared him nonetheless. What transpired directly after he entered her entered her apartment is unclear, but it resulted in spilled parfait and Rona Ibsen eventually being killed. The actual murder was old-fashioned. Deep bludgeoning about the face after unsuccessful strangulation. There were no firearms on Mars. It was like that old bit of news that reached Europe from the New World way back in 1630 about John Billington, the *Mayflower* passenger and Plimoth-Patuxet resident who'd turned on his neighbor John Newcomen and shot him with a musket ball, killing him. The eternal return to that unfortunate exit, and fast, too, in hindsight. Shocking, but not unexpected.

Strom, dying, struggled with how to feel about the news of Ms. Ibsen's death. Tragedy-ed. Sensationalized. Disgusted. He chose dejected. Her bio, like so many on Mars, was exceptional. Wealthy, successful, she'd held a litany of Martian records. A reigning spelling bee champion with six wins under her belt. She'd been the fastest Martian female cyclist alive. All of it no longer mattered. She was now and forever the first to die.

Strom needed a friend, but would settle for much less, and so he took the shaft from the Port of Anglis to Nuermeer, an outer ring colony at the base of Mt. Olympus, where Thurston lived in a commune-like complex of rustic cabins with his extended family, many of them natural-born Martians. Strom's airsled was a little shaky, and he could feel the instruments in his ears unhinging, dropping their precious hairs as his body was ejaculated through the tube. After the shoot, he stood up, vertiginous. His head tined to certain frequencies on the air, including a few waves related to his own breathing, and he smiled. He was quite literally falling apart. The absence of the nanoweavers and service bacteria had already led to aggressive and advanced cell degradation. Light-headed, he pushed himself a little harder than usual just to see how his heart would react, and the muscle played in his chest like a trombone. Okay, he thought, mustn't tempt fate if I'm to will this into something spectacular still. But what was more spectacular than being bludgeoned to death in your own apartment? Okay, he thought then, must have more time to think then too, okay? So he strove in more sensible steps, trying on the tippy-tippy of musculo-nervous failure and the fried shuffle of a prion disease before settling on a simple suicidal lurch. In a sheet of metal, he thought his reflection looked philosophical, maybe a bit like his author father these days.

Thurston Morris had made his fortune on machine-language topographical translation. WORK WITH YOUR HANDS AGAIN was the slogan. He'd turned programming into manual labor. This was before the end of labor as anyone knew it. Now, the people of Earth, those living in the city-states, were finally retired, just in time to die off. Though Thurston owed most of his success to diminutive reform, it all started with a dream to revolutionize the labor market and mass education. At the center of the revolution was Thurston's patented putty-like material with which commands could be sculpted to build, modify, and repair programs, a system favored by foreign infrastructures (and their private subsidizers) still avoiding full-blown AI and staving off the massive unemployment figures that'd eventually come with it. No one had batted an eye when India's agricultural sector went full-automation, but when an international army of programmers started scripting UBI mandates of their own—these people could not just subsist and still be counted on to carry the IT weight of the world on their shoulders—well . . . But with Thurston's blessed invention, companies could suddenly tell employees to forget their UBI mandates, hell, they could forget their benefits, seeing that the common and chronically unemployed former factory worker was only a few night classes away from being a fully certified putty programmer. Their only other option was to try their luck in the wild. Stigma against smart self-generating code, international subsidies, and the protean price hikes on proprietary AI kept this scab labor (primarily foreign, deplorably compensated) in high demand, and after monopolizing programming methods, Thurston bought as many code farms anti-trust laws would allow and rode the wave to infamy. The labor exploitation extinction burst had been over more than fifty years now, but Thurston still couldn't make land on Earth without creating an uproar.

Mars understood Thurston better. Martian life, with its thirty-seven-minute-longer day, was fit for the entrepreneurial. It'd been cultivated by those who'd grown impatient with Earth, with its dwindling resources and mass regression to nearly Neolithic lifestyles. Thurston had personally lobbied for a straight tax, which drained him of impossible resources every time he drank a glass of water on the planet, but he found pleasure in defining the terms and conditions. When he'd spoken to the media in those early days of colonization and faced questions about labor-law violations and human travesty this, human travesty that, he'd point to the fact that he'd broken not a single law, he'd hardly even circumvented one, and this would often placate his critics despite their evidence of the contrary. But only on Earth, where nothing was new, were sad, broken things still all the rage. Martians came to mostly agree he'd only made use of what Earth had naturally provided: a massive population of unskilled laborers and the politico-economic incentive to use them. Even better, where others had used these same resources for the construction of fortresses of wealth, megalomaniacal political influence, or egotistical monuments to their own fledgling existence (the biopolises), people like Thurston had used his resources to help build a way for the human race to survive after its home planet gave up on them, which it would, soon, more every day. More than a man of the times, he was the man who'd created time, more time. Additionally, what he'd created on Mars was something careful, which was more than most people in history could say.

The domed grounds outside Thurston's cabin complex detected Strom's presence and an illuminated path directed him inside the compound to where Thurston was roaming the greenhouses.

"I know you have always hated how I repeat myself, but I'm just so sorry, my friend," Thurston said when Strom found him. He was admiring the white hollowed innards of a passion fruit. "I'd also forgotten I have an allergy of some sort to these. My lips feel full of needles. Did I wish you a happy birthday yet?"

"It's disgusting what that man did to her," Strom said.

"Oh, I know. Just a pure animal. He's out there alone in the desert, detached himself completely, entirely off-grid now. I wonder if he's praying, if he'll kill himself soon. He can't be too far away from where we stand right now, in fact."

"Are you going to issue a statement?"

"I don't believe I will. I'm not an elected official, I never was. Everything I say is misconstrued. If I condemn the murder, I inspire more murders somehow."

He petted his mustache. He was a man in silk robes. Strom wondered if this meant Thurston felt forced to condone the murder. What else was silence left to do?

"Don't make yourself the victim here," Strom said, choosing judgment over philosophy for the time being.

"On Mars?"

"In this situation."

"Hm. But you get to be the victim? With a dead girl in the morgue?"

"I'm not making myself a victim."

"They're using a shoehorn-like instrument as we speak, to . . ."

"Stop."

"I didn't ask you here so that I could teach you a lesson."

"You didn't ask me here. I came over."

"Did you now?"

Thurston's great-granddaughters were playing doubles under a violet scrim outside the greenhouses. Eighteen, sixteen, fourteen, and twelve, the eldest with the youngest against the second youngest and Piña, the only sister whose name Strom could remember. Piña was his daughter's age when she'd drowned—like a famous musician, swept away in the undertow—in the Pacific Ocean. Poor Mackie. Seventy years now. The girls kept the little lime going, the sound of their racquets as well-meaning as bones breaking are devastating. Strom tested his weight on his right leg, felt fissuring in his hip, an urgent heat about to tear away. The girls were born on Mars; they'd written essays on the colonization. They had the same cabbage complexion of those who'd descended from the *Mayflower*. They'd never know a revolution. There are no revolutions in air-sealed glass domes on oxygen-less planets. Even the underlings knew this was true. Piña played the line, slamming backhands like a woman steering a canoe. She'd shut her siblings out of the game when she noticed Strom watching.

"Uncle Strom!" she said, and let the racquet bounce across the court.

Piña, when Strom first told her of his long-lost daughter, experienced difficulty placing her feeling of loss. Her whole life she'd been involved against her will in a kind of worldwide surrogacy system or séance through which men were attempting to procure a false but vital sense of possibility, and therefore, she wasn't required to actively empathize with anything, being only a simple organic variable for their manipulation, like a houseplant, at most, a domesticated mammal. For her great-grandfather immortality was vital, for her own father (also Earth-born) it was vital to re-season the human spirit, to make it less bitter and embattled than the original recipe (he *was* an elected official), and for Uncle Strom it was simply vital that he be able to bring the dead back to life. But Mack meant something to Piña, which might've had something to do with why she dressed a little like her whenever she knew Strom was going to be around. To Strom, she'd have looked utterly unrecognizable in her thoughtless originality now had he not been able to spot the ghost sage tint of their matching hair anywhere.

"Lovely game you're playing out there," he said to her.

For Martians, there was nothing vital at all except water and oxygen and temperature regulation. They served at the honor of the despicable human race. Piña hoped someday soon the sea would swallow the final Earth cities whole and no one from that planet would ever come back to Mars. Yet she liked Strom.

"I wonder if there isn't something we can do to right this, Uncle Strom," she said.

Dust sifted from her sweatless body. She'd already heard about everything.

"I think there probably is," Thurston said from behind Strom.

They turned to look at him.

"An ironic death triangle out in the desert. On the day the first man wishing to die on Mars ventures out into the desert to die some brave pioneer death, he encounters the murderer of the first person killed on Mars. In a final heroic gesture, he kills the murderer, and then dies a peaceful, natural death of his own, all alone. The narrative is already set, you just have to cozy on in," Thurston said.

"If I could find him first," Strom said.

"I know exactly where he is. I have his beacon right here," Thurston said, and opened a light scrim from his pocket to reveal a map of the nearby mountains and a blinking green light. "This whole planet is mine. I'm free to comprehend it. *Mihi Cura Futuri*."

CHAPTER 6

The president let the satisfied woman from his chambers and watched his idle, revving body in a full-length mirror. Where have you been, old friend? he wondered. Born in a land that was no longer, having traversed a border that had been redrawn, he had been committing the rest of his animal existence to the dawning future of Africa. There is no Zimbabwe without me, he'd explained it a million times. Whenever the pro-democracy crowds gathered outside his palace, or the sentiment rose in the halls of parliament, whenever a confidante said, "Take it easy, old friend, retire," he would have to remind them: "There is no Zimbabwe without me." Knife scars and the burial mounds of vital organs that'd traded places after an explosion left his body with a most uncommon map. A map as uncommon and unknown as the map of his memory, the map of his country and his continent. Killing or fucking so hard he'd sometimes feel his gonads climb up into his cranium like hardboiled eggs . . .

"MY FATHER WAS a pornographer," Strom had to explain to Piña.

"Okay," she said.

The two were walking through a narrow canyon listening to a crystal-clear replication of his father's voice narrate the remainder of his latest novel, piped in through their helmets' speakers.

"His bot sprinkles these awkward erotic flourishes throughout. Try to ignore them," Strom said.

"Okay."

He knew it was inappropriate for Piña to be listening to such a text, but his time was limited. Under her spacesuit, Piña had donned an outfit like Mack's and was trying to be daughterly. A green light, like a cesarean scar, lay ahead of them, pointing the way to the murderer. The lack of life on Mars screamed. Listening to his father's voice, and the absence of animal voices on this planet, made Strom weepy. He was also in exponential pain, his body systems rocketing toward death as they moved closer to the killer.

"Can you pause it?" Piña said.

"Sure," Strom said, and paused the novel.

"What does *mihi cura futuri* mean?"

"The care of the future is mine," Strom said. "Your great-grandfather is an arrogant asshole and speaks beautifully."

CHAPTER 7

He dropped the case of the burr in his brain and sought Suk, whom he found sleeping with a note, written on cloth, pinned to his chest. Luigi's Korean was still not good, but he thought it read Not dead, but mourning. Kill me if you must, if you need this space to work. *Luigi cupped two palmfuls of plaster milk and splashed it on the young man's face, and the man awoke with comic fright. Right away, the chisel and hammer that'd slept beside him were in his fists, ready to kill.*

"Get back to work now," Luigi said. "Two great men must be remembered. Should we fail to meet the President's needs, both he and your father will be forgotten."

"I'm starving," Suk said, clearing the quick drying jism from his eyes.

The pretense made Luigi hard as the artist's stone. But there was no time to lose, and so he handed Suk his lunch, a sandwich weighted with plaster to give it the heft of something with sustenance. He longed for his mother's Tuscan kitchen. But few feasts catered heroes' lives.

"Now, you work," Luigi said, and Suk conceded.

STROM FAST-FORWARDED. THE book got graphic. Nasty in an alien and alienating way.

"He wasn't a pervert, not exactly," Strom said.

"Of course not," Piña said.

"It was a different time."

"Of course."

"What I think is strange is he never once went to an art museum, and yet, here he is, writing a book about art," Strom said.

"Maybe it's a metaphor."

Strom thought so.

"But what for?" he asked.

"Life and death. Power. Memory."

"You could write a report."

"Why *do* you want to die?" Piña asked.

"Yetzer lev ha'adam ra," Strom said.

"That doesn't sound like Latin."

"It's Hebrew."

"I didn't know you were Jewish."

"I don't think I am."

"And what does that phrase mean?"

"The imagination of the heart of man is evil."

"Hm."

"Man's heart was circumcised to quell its desires. And yet, throughout history, hunger, sexual desire, industry—what drives our will to survive—have always given way to gluttony, lust, and greed."

"But if you never die, you'll never have to answer for your sins."

"That's not exactly something Jews buy into."

Strom thought he saw a heron in the sky, in its lanky, swimming way. Impossible, though. His lungs flapped the air, achieved ankle-high lift-off.

"You're not afraid of becoming a bot?" Piña asked.

"I am a bot, Piña," Strom said.

This was something Piña seemed to understand.

"Mars is the afterlife. In the nineteenth century, we gave ourselves over to fate; in the twentieth, the market; in the twenty-first, both abandoned us. We had to give ourselves back over to the Earth, like pagans. We were supposed to die there, to be buried in it."

Piña stopped walking.

"Mars is the afterlife for you, Uncle Strom," she said, forcefully. "It's life for me."

He had clearly upset her and did not know what to say to make it better.

Quickly, though, because Martians were resilient or because Piña knew that Strom would be dead soon anyways, she started walking again in her Mack-ish way. She changed the subject and asked what Otto would do without him.

"Losing your parents used to be a rite of passage," Strom said. "If you were over the age of thirty, it was sad, but far from a travesty. Now it's all the same. You lose a houseplant and you write an elegy."

Strom stumbled at the sight of a snake that wasn't there. How long had it been since snakes?

"Why'd you wait so long?" Piña asked.

Strom steadied his eyes on the snake that wasn't there. What didn't sound ridiculous? To make Mackie proud? To wait for his dad to die? To see if Mackie hadn't died, but gone to Mars?

"We're almost there," he said.

CHAPTER 8

Suk had come to know the features of the man better than his own, better than his father's. He had an intimate understanding of his acne scars, which he pocked along his rigid, socialist cheeks. Weeping, wobbling with a chisel in his paw, atop the man's great crown, his tears became the leader's tears, rushing down his stony face. He'd slept with his head in the cuff of his outreaching arm.

In dreams, he saw the man whole, walking around. In dreams, this meant something like his father come back to life. The statue's sticker price would ensure his son could eat. The earnings would go toward the construction of a new missile silo, to protect the Republic from Imperial invaders. Condemned to work boots two sizes too small, Suk had taken pity on the president's marble feet, and had made him separate marble shoes to fit into, just in case he wanted to air his toes from time to time. When the statue was finally completed, the president's barefoot body had to be lifted by crane and eased into his shoes and fastened to them with bolts. But it was finished and Luigi smiled on Suk with the pride of a father, which filled Suk with a cocktail of accomplishment and irreparable loneliness. He wanted to don his own marble shoes and march into the sea. In celebration, Luigi unveiled a harem, and on the tacky floors of the art studio, a hundred men and women . . .

"**WHY HASN'T MACK'S** bot awakened yet?"

"It takes longer for kids."

"You don't want to wait to meet her?"

"Grief is a prison, Piña, I've known that for a long time. And yet, all these years, I thought I was the prisoner. Don't you see? I'm the jailer."

"What if your bot isn't interesting?"

"What are you, a journalist?"

The feed washed over to report that Rona Ibsen's bot had just come online. She was a virulent advocate for Martian labor rights. She was hosting a slave reunion in cyberdom. She'd started an organization called the Ladder. She threatened to infect the oxygen filtration system and kill off half of Anglis if Thurston Morris didn't come to the negotiation table and relinquish . . . And her bot was neutralized.

"Poor gal," Strom said.

CHAPTER 9

Chapter nine was silence. Breathing. Waiting. Then, out of the putty air, Strom and Piña saw them, a group of people, humans, of all ages and races and ethnicities witching around the figure of a man, the murderer, kind of a jock. In the crowd, Strom spotted his mother and his daughter, Mack. Mack levitated, swam with the veracity of a heron, and drowned, and repeated. His mother made her bed, sat at its edge, lay down, and was still, and repeated. A woman plied from an invisible noose. Another gripped her abdomen and sat down. They all repeated themselves. It looked amateurish, this ghost play. A group of women blew apart and returned to their places, blew apart and returned to their places. Strom took Mack's body like he was teaching her to swim and she slipped from his hands like a fish. Who misses fishes? he thought. I miss the fish. The murderer stood in amazement, tears running down the statue of his face.

Rona Ibsen appeared from behind a rock shelf with an army of sooty, mangled, and angry bodies. From cave-ins, and factory fires, and TB wards, the Ladder angled forward with the choreographed menace of a George A. Romero film. A petition went around to rename Mars Minerva—better yet, Athena, Athena was also the goddess of warfare. Strom's father's bot's reading voice was replaced with a woman's, booming like thunder. "Chapter ten," she said.

CHAPTER 10

Piña watched as her Uncle Strom crumpled to be a part of the bunch. He fell like a sack of something, anything, lay still a while, and repeated. He did it a dozen times before Rona Ibsen removed her murderer's head and placed it over her own head like a motorcycle helmet and rode her bicycle around the circle. When it was to be repeated, she handed back the head and her murderer placed it atop his shoulders before unfastening it again himself, placing it over her head as if in coronation and lowering to one knee. Rona rode and she rode. The sun set and Piña sat down to watch. She looked at Mack, so strangely herself, in her own clothes, drowning in plain air, no longer the wobbly reflection Piña wore around the Martian colonies like a skin condition. Mack didn't have acne, not even in HD, Piña noticed. "She's back, Uncle Strom!" she shouted. "Only because I'm leaving," Strom said and died. In the dark, the bodies committed the act of sculpture, accident or not. And all was well and good and beautiful and still ongoing in the morning when Piña finally walked home, intent on gathering her thoughts and writing them all down in a report for Otto, once she'd collected herself and washed the blood from her hair, beside her fingernails, and between her teeth. *There wasn't any life on Mars, so we put it there,* she repeated the proposed opening for the report in her head as she walked. *Though real life, as opposed to its ersatz, stolid equivalent on Mars, must certainly be something else entirely. In the next five paragraphs, I'll explain why.* She prepared an outline.

I. Death Looking at Life

    a. Looking at life from death is like looking at the Earth from the window of a spaceship: it's a vulnerable thing you might long for if it wasn't so perfectly suited for being left alone.

II. Life Looking at Death

    a. Looking at death from life is like reading a book written in Arabic and not realizing the text goes from right to left and it not mattering because you don't know Arabic anyway but can appreciate the calligraphy. You know not everything in the text is about God or something lofty. You know some of it just has to do with simple things, too.

III. Odes & Elegies

    a. An ode is basically written with enthusiasm and excitement about a person or thing. An elegy is generally sad and morose and is usually written to mourn the dead. Mars has moved on from both. We're not here to commemorate you or mourn you. And we're not you.

VI.

CONFESSIONS

RANSOMS

THE FIRST TIME DELFINO RAMIREZ was kidnapped and held for ransom by Los Zetas, he'd just come off a press tour celebrating his big win at the Premios TVyNovelas—his performance as a first-generation Mexican American border control agent grappling with the deportation of his father having finally elevated him into the upper echelons of Mexican television stardom at the age of thirty-five. The second time he was kidnapped and held for ransom by Los Zetas, he was busy studying for his comeback role as the lead in a telenovela about a Mexican drug lord grappling with his son's heroin addiction. Reality, I've realized, in both the world of la telenovela and our own, transcends irony, and none are more contrived than God's designs over our lives. Thankfully, most of us are simply too fortunate to notice—blessed are we the set dressers, members of hair and makeup, etc., the great off-screen masses the Lord spares the trials and contortions He reserves for His leading men and women.

Delfino was a leading man, you understand, and both aforementioned roles were exercises in ultra-empathy—an attempt to enter the mind of the enemy, public enemy number 1 and public enemy number 1a—and I recall many times during those grueling, breakneck runs when Delfino, or Big D, as anyone who's ever actually cared about Delfino will call him, thought he wouldn't be able to go on. But he was a method actor, and his method was madness, and he pushed through. As Big D's personal lawyer, and an avid fan of his telenovela work—his musical career as a rap artist, I never much cared for—I was endlessly astonished by his performances and the work that went into them. Big D was not by nature a very empathetic man, and I say this with respect, as a friend—I am also the godfather to his two sons. Had he gotten the chance to play that drug lord, I know for a fact his one Premio TVyNovela wouldn't have been lonely for long. It's a shame the show never materialized—I just don't think anyone deserves to be lonely like that, forever, not even a slender golden man barely the size of an adolescent iguana. Alas, what could have been is not what life is all about. Life is what is.

MY LIFE HAS always been about Big D. We grew up together in San Ángel in CDMX, both the sons of famous ranchera singers. As teenagers, we were sad dogs languishing in the pearl shadows of those men's white suits. Their mustaches, we marveled at—the way they lifted on TV like women bucking with pleasure whenever the two screamed like gitanos, accordions and string sections climaxing behind their voices. Amongst the four of us, and the nation, there was never any doubt that my father was the more talented of the two. Over the years, my singing has featured in hundreds of weddings, quinceañeras, mitzvahs, and karaoke sessions—it's still in demand—but I would never call myself an artist. To murder my own rich-kid blues, I studied law and translated the will of robber barons into digestible, semilegal endeavors. Second best or not, if you'd ever seen Big D's father perform live, you'd know what balls it took for my friend to enter showbiz himself. But that's what made Big D Big D, and maybe if my father had been the lesser artist of the two, Big D would be telling this story, and I would be living the life of a tragic Greek hero, as opposed to the tragic life of a mortal private citizen.

"Alvin, don't ever call yourself my wingman," Big D once told me as I vomited into a clean toilet. This was during his wedding reception. I had sung too hard, not drank too much. "You're my best friend, my lawyer, my guardian angel."

Angel or perpetual bachelor who, through the strongest years of my life, followed Big D around to clubs and held down the fort while he disappeared with the anonymous (adult) daughters of foreign leaders, my wings had suddenly been clipped, incapable of flight. I didn't know who I was going to be to him now that he was married, I'd been explaining. Big D took care of me, his little friend who grew up in the biggest house on our long street, and I owed him something in return, my counsel and all of my love. I'd had to make myself strong on occasion but was at a complete loss in the wedding venue's bathroom.

After he cleaned me up, washing my stinking, throbbing head in a sink like Jesus's stinking, throbbing feet, he told me to go dance with his bride, Sandra. I made myself strong to do so, I took flight. Sandra liked spending her parents' fitness chain's fortune on sewing cleft palates. A sinewy, wistful trail of facial scars prayed to her as far south as the Amazon River basin. And can you believe it wasn't until I was right on top of her, swinging her to the house band's cover of one of my father's most beautiful songs, that I realized she had one of those scars herself?

Up until that very moment I had felt that Sandra was taking Big D away from me. Pure jealous fear this was not—I worried most for what would happen to Big D after I'd been banished, not for myself. Big D was getting so big then, I imagined no woman in the world could possibly recognize how fragile he truly was. An addict and a spendthrift, he was fated to play the fool eventually. Any woman in her right mind would ride Big D for everything he was worth and save herself before his inevitable crash. If she took him away from me, he'd be completely alone in the end. A pauper in both purse and fellowship. But Sandra's scar suggested she was someone more than just another woman in her right mind. While we danced, from behind that suggestive scar, she said to me, "Maybe, with our powers combined, we can save him," and I realized Sandra was a woman safely out of her mind.

I gave her my blessing, post-nuptials, better late than never, right there on the dance floor, and I wasn't wrong in doing so. When we received the ransom note from Los Zetas that first time, she'd say something similar to what she whispered to me the night of her wedding. "Maybe this will save him."

It didn't, but God's will gave us a second chance. If only we'd have kept working as a team, Sandra and I. Alas.

I TRIED TO make the necessary corrections the first time Big D was kidnapped to turn the course of that horrific event in Big D's favor. This was three years ago. I was concerned not only for my friend's mortal safety, but the safety of his soul—I hope I can make this clear. My methods you may think a little extreme, but it is a tectonic existence we lead in Mexico—I was young, but I remember my father answering phones on live television after the 1985 earthquake, singing at a benefit concert— and meanwhile there is something in the Mexican spirit that is resistant to insurance. Perhaps we worry that being insured is a way of betting against God, that written in the fine print are subtle proclamations of hubris and humanist idolatry. More likely, the hesitancy has to do with Mexico's history of broken promises. Really, it's probably a matter of access, seeing that nearly sixty percent of Mexicans acquired health insurance once health care was universalized. Either way, when it came to Big D I needed something even more than insurance. I needed to be assured of his imminent salvation, as at least seventy percent of all promises made in the United Mexican States are still inevitably broken.

In the days that followed Big D's first kidnapping, his father came to blame himself for his son's demise. Big D had been snatched up while out whoring and doing drugs, his favorite pastime. I'll never forgive myself for not being with him that night. I was too busy protecting a client from allegations of wage theft. The coke dealer Big D met in an alley that night had taken one look at him, asked, "Hey, aren't you Delfino Ramirez?" and, when Big D answered in the affirmative, said, "One moment, I'm gonna grab you the good shit," only to return with Big D's fate. They asked for more money than Big D was worth, having read a *Forbes* article on how much his father was worth.

"It is my genes that gave him his talent, my neglect his incurable pain, and my guilt that prevented me from ever informing him that he was, in fact, very stupid, which could have occurred to him from time to time and made him more cautious," his father told me in the aftermath. "They want a fortune, fine, they can have mine."

The man had been diagnosed with stage-four prostate cancer the year before but still had a full head of hair, long and silver, which he often gripped at the roots with manicured but well-weathered hands, as if proofing a precious coin. His mustache, artfully trimmed, no longer the bucking bronco, had come to resemble the chromium handlebars of a classic Schwinn bicycle.

"I hear what you are saying, Francisco," I told the man, concocting my adjustments. "You are a loving father. But what will your son learn from such a . . . *New* Testament approach? What's to stop him from getting into the same sort of trouble if he gets off scot-free?"

At first his father dismissed me. The same little fat kid he'd seen flopping around his pool for decades, only now in a suit and tie. I was unmarried, I had no children of my own, he took me for a freak, probably. I am a freak. But what is most freakish about me is my devotion. There was a time when I belonged to three different cults. Big D was out of the country, in the Czech Republic. I was seeking assurance. When the cults found out about each other, instead of fighting over my mushy brain and flush bank account, each cult closed its doors to me. Before my exile, it had been the most exhilarating time of my life. Whether or not Big D's father knew about this, whether I was really a freak to him or not, as he made the arrangements for the release of his son, his anxiety turned to anger, an anger he usually reserved for making a cocktail with envy, the envy he usually reserved for my father, and said, "He's going to pay me back. Put it in writing, Alvin, send it to the bastards, and have them make him sign it: a document that says I take command of all of his finances. I've left everything to him in my will anyways, him and some half-siblings he's never heard about, but mainly to him. It won't be long now."

As per Big D's father's instructions, and my invisible manipulations, we made a boy of Big D again, beholden to his father's fortune and the allowance his wife received from her own parents, so that he could be reeducated. With no money of his own, two young boys to raise, and a supportive family behind him, he would be weaned off drugs and other women and find serious work and salvation. And the plan would have worked had a video of him resurfacing from captivity in urine-soaked pants and his face all covered in snot and tears not appeared on some tabloid website shortly after he was returned to us. It ruined his career and, thus, any monetary incentive for salvation. Again, the Mexican people, after so many failed promises, even if fully insured, must be given assurances. Post-nuanced-portrayal of an ambivalent villain— the telenovela's true protagonist was an intrepid but penniless female immigration lawyer named Lulu—the public and the Mexican media, having briefly celebrated his contributions by awarding him that Premio, turned their backs on their former hero for being a weakling, and he could barely stand on two legs most days.

From that day forward, every attempt we made to get his career back on track was a misstep. We put him on a daytime talk show to describe his experience, and he cried the whole episode. The term "ugly crying" was trending that year, and the episode's generous footage yielded a plethora of stills under which, in granular chyrons, were written dozens of nihilistic phrases, and though politicians were being beheaded left and right in our country, and the public lived in fear of the drug lords, they laughed at Big D, banishing their anxieties by making light of them, as Superman does when he traps those bad guys in a planar shard and slings them into outer space in *Superman II*.

To ease his pain, for this man I owe so much, I set up a little account for him to dip into. For trips, here and there, for inspiration, to get away from the tabloids. For leisure drugs—none of the hard stuff, I'd hoped. I never did believe in that gateway mumbo jumbo—the gates had already been swung wide open. A horrible idea this account was in the end, but I'll save my apologies.

TO CURE HIS son's washed-up telenovela star blues, to cure his own stage-four prostate cancer blues, Francisco took Big D, Sandra, the boys, and me on a trip to Paris. Two days we were in the city, dining finely and shopping like Mexicans, when Big D's father said, "I need to be out on the open sea. No, I need to see a mountain," and we were on a train to the Midi-Pyrénées to catch a cab to Cordes-sur-Ciel, a fortified medieval village in the foothills of the South of France.

Though mountains these hills were not, Big D's father was still in no shape to hike them, but he had a friend in the commune, a sculptor from Dubrovnik, whom he very much wanted to see one last time. Jakov was his name, and when he greeted us in the gutted wine bar he called home, a thirteenth-century fixer-upper off the town center, I took him for my Croatian counterpart. A small, round, clean-to-glistening man wrapped in a thin scarf dyed in the indigo this part of France was famous for. It was January and down in his wine cellar, which he had converted into his studio, a gelid membrane of cold air ebbed from the stone walls. He extracted very fine drinkware and we drank our fill while he showed us his work. These sculptures were figurative, socially real, made of stone, and resting on the icy floor.

"They're too tall to stand down here," he said in English. "But I must say, it was quite a shocker when I first came down to find them all on the ground. They're post–Socialist Republic, but they suddenly reminded me of all our toppled Titos. I realized this was no mistake. First, we topple dictators. Now, we topple men like you and me, Francisco."

"Will you display them this way?" I asked, watching Big D's father stare into the gaping ear cavity of a fallen statue.

"I would like to, but municipalities and museums say it is a tripping hazard," Jakov said.

The boys grew tired of art and wine talk and Big D sent them upstairs to admire Jakov's rats. The rats were large and menacing and had full freedom of expression in Jakov's former wine bar. It was something we all wanted to see, I think, but we continued drinking and listening to Jakov's stories instead. Village life, small town trifles, the best horse sausage in all the land. The cold, dark, dampness of the cellar had kept Big D small and glum the whole visit up to this point, but the wine and Jakov's tales, I could tell, were beginning to tip the scales.

He said, suddenly, "Maybe I'm not cut out for city life. Sandra, perhaps we should live in a place like this. I could make little French movies and the boys could go to a parochial school."

But before Sandra could answer—and who knows what she would've said then, there were no gyms here, the boys already attended a parochial school and hated it—Jakov shook his head and Francisco lifted a finger to the rafters.

"Have you not heard a word this man has said?" Francisco shouted. "The world is toppling its great men. Run out of dictators, they are trying to topple you. You, you must stand tall. You are a great man."

We heard a noise on the stairs and all turned to look. The boys were creeping down the uneven wooden steps, each of them balancing plump and stock-still rats on their extended forearms and giggling as they reentered the cellar.

"This is a good omen," Jakov whispered.

Sandra shook her head and Big D approached his boys.

"This is because you are gentle and good men," he said to his sons. "God's most untrusting inventions trust you."

And just as he said this, a rat walked slowly but confidently from one boy's arm onto to Big D's.

Big D, to everyone's perpetual surprise, had always been a devoted father. Our shock was purely logistical—none of us believed Big D incapable of love, he loved us all, if only inconsistently, unevenly; for some, Sandra especially, inconveniently. The unconditional being love's most challenging tense. What puzzled us was how Big D ever managed such meaningful relationships with his sons—biking the Hummingbird Highway in Belize, dropping them off at school whenever he was home, acting in their plays, caking them with sand like veal cutlets at the beach—while also maintaining so many extrafamilial engagements.

After giving Big D and his rat a thumbs-up, Francisco said, "I have to wee-wee," one of his favorite English expressions, and mounted the stairs.

While he was gone, and Jakov and the boys played with the rats, I listened as Sandra told Big D that he was a good and gentle man too, and that she'd live out the rest of her days in a rat-infested wine cellar in the South of France if it meant she could spend every last minute with her beautiful husband.

I found in this moment the birth of a divine possibility. I saw the future, narrow as a medieval porthole, beaming with the singular spotlight of the golden path. Big D would be resuscitated. Big D would rise. Big D would shine.

Francisco was whistling one of my father's songs and proofing his hair as he descended into the basement once again. Three steps from the bottom, he missed a step and entered gently the empty air. He made no attempt to catch himself as he fell and landed deftly on his head on the medieval stone floor.

FOR A TIME, there was a detention center in Brownsville, Texas, specifically designed for the children entering the United States in search of asylum. Greeting the children on the walls of their kennel-like accommodations was an illustration of President Donald J. Trump, the White House, and an inspirational quote written in both English and Spanish, taken from Mr. Trump's book *The Art of the Deal*. "Sometimes by losing the battle you find a new way to win the war," it read. A combination of *Sometimes, bad things happen for a reason* and *Better luck next time, kid*. The quote suggests learning from failure, and, therefore, its source is ironic—though Donald J. Trump is the poster boy of failure, he has never learned anything from his defeats: first, because he's never accepted the reality of defeat, and second, because he's never had to: as reality, acceptance, and life lessons hold absolutely no value for the rich.

Either the source of the message is ironic or the nature of the message is insincere. I have personal difficulty deciding which is the case, exactly, because a year before those words appeared in front of Latin America's lost children, a year before Walmarts along America's southern border were converted into detention centers, and a year before I reached chapter 10 of Trump's *Art of the Deal* myself, the chapter in which the quote appears, I spoke them, verbatim, to my friend Delfino "Big D" Ramirez, on the eve of his father's funeral. He had just learned of late changes made to the dead's will. Those assets being withheld from Big D—his own fortune and the portion of his father's he was to be allotted—were to continue being withheld until Big D appeared again in a major television show or movie. Already bereaved, Big D suddenly felt condemned.

"Sometimes by losing the battle you find a new way to win the war," I said, with his father gone and the money still so far away. We were riding first in line in the funeral procession to the Panteón Civil de Dolores, where Francisco would be interred in the Rotonda de las Personas Ilustres.

"You think so? What does that mean? You think so?" Big D asked.

"I do," I said. "I'm not sure what it means."

The frozen assets had become a chrysalis for my friend. It had been a year and a half since he was returned to us, and, though only partially, he had begun to transform. Big D was less a shell of the man he'd once been than the sleeping, gooey innards within. He and his family had adjusted somewhat to their new material standings—they still had the fitness fortune. But the money still meant everything, because the money had also come to symbolize Francisco's approval. He had called Big D great, yes, but his son had no way of knowing if he'd finally forgiven him.

My words, the ghostwriter's words, were of no matter, it would turn out, because around the same time I was realizing I had only ever been Big D's wingman, and never his guardian angel, three others of God's strangest creations, modern Mexican human beings, were being kept up at night by the itchy evolution of their own angelic wings. The Lord was already ghostwriting our future. And life, in its infinite possibilities, is about what *can* be, *too*, as you'll eventually see.

Roberta Dominguez, Big D's longtime agent, was about to call regarding a potential gig for an Arizona real estate company. At that same moment, a Mexican auteur, Sebastian Bolivar, an artist highly derivative of Alejandro González Iñárritu, was devising an ironic telenovela for the ages. Meanwhile, in Nuevo Laredo, a nobody named Pedro Arriaga was becoming the target of Zeta recruitment.

We had no idea. At the funeral, my father had not been able to stop weeping long enough to sing, and so Big D and I sang his father's songs instead, in perfect harmony.

IT WAS THE little things he missed the most. He recalled how at the apex of his career all of his hotel rooms came with complimentary Icelandic pumice stones. Champagne fridges, briefcases of assorted pharmaceuticals, the madonnas who would suddenly materialize at the foot of his bed were important to Mexico's hottest male actor—definitive markers so ubiquitous for success, his stardom could be seen from space—but it was these scratchy volcanic rocks piled zen-ly on a Japanese dish (wabi-sabi) beside the sink that had come to signify his ability to control every moment and inch of his fate. He could score any dinner with a quartet. He had been with so many women he could fall in and out of love at will. His life, like his roles, was his choosing. But somehow the ease with which he could scour the whole surface of his naked body, ridding it of unnecessary, tarnished, dead layers until he glowed with the raw, red light of his innermost organs meant the most to him. Then Big D found himself hovering over dented soap bars bound in tearing cardboard sleeves.

He woke up early one morning in Arizona to shave, sighed over the meager slipper of soap the Scottsdale Hilton's room service had left him, and decided he'd keep the beard. He left the hotel, skipping the complimentary continental breakfast, though he loved Belgian waffles and the florets of margarine that came in those little plastic cups.

The Arizona real estate developers had lent him a company Taurus for this trip, which he drove cautiously, glimpsing at the bleak GPS on his dash, through the slow streets of Scottsdale. The trunk was full of cardboard Fatheads of his likeness. It was a picture from the golden era. He'd had a beard back then too. He ruffled cheek dander from his facial hair and imagined he was bringing himself closer to that man by not shaving, if only he'd had the exfoliating Icelandic pumice stone. The GPS showed him passing one mall after another.

The development's ribbon cutting ceremony would begin at noon, but Big D liked to arrive early to be with his fans in a less official capacity. To give the people awaiting him the sense he could be their neighbor, a celebrity they'd bump into at the park by chance. Sometimes he'd arrive in running shoes and shorts. It was psychological marketing. It was a role. This morning he wore a thin, slate-colored Armani suit—the crotch was wearing dangerously thin, beaded with chafe bolls and spotted with holes exposing his hairless inner thighs underneath—tobacco-colored brogues by Tom Ford, and a pair of Persol 3260S sunglasses, which were women's sunglasses originally but also the very ones Marcello Mastroianni wore in *La Dolce Vita*. His luggage—Louis Vuitton, Monogram

Macassar, well-worn—was in the backseat. The promo gig was coming to an end for good, and he was going home that evening, where he'd throw himself into his new telenovela role as a high-ranking member of Los Zetas.

Like a strange rock formation, thirty ocher prefab micro-mansions blemished the eastern face of Camelback Mountain. "You have arrived," the GPS coolly alerted him. The homes' windows, shaded to the color of root beer, shot an awful reflective beam into the valley; in the xeriscaped backyards, bloated water moccasin mothers built dens in piles of dry leaf litter beside the green surfaces of underground pools. But every front yard was an eruption of spiny birds of paradise, each hooded driveway was perfect for at least two luxury SUVs, and maybe America's wealthy geriatric class was done investing in the God-enriched desert state, but Mexico's rising upper middle class was just beginning.

A crowd, decently sized, already festooned an empty white fountain outside the clubhouse. In the fountain, an alabaster Spanish-colonial horseman mounted toward the sun. Never expecting the former star of *La Frontera Mala* to be arriving in a 2000 Ford Taurus, they paid Big D no attention when he drove by.

He parked near a flash flood sewer. If he had nothing else left, he had his vanity. When his father performed in the seventies, he would appear from within the audience, dressed as a peasant, mumbling into a microphone hidden under a poncho, before drawing back the itchy garment and belting out a ballad, his back arching to a sea of applause, his rhinestone lapels burning with blinding icicle fire. These days, celebrity lacked such theater. Big D, rising from his compact chrysalis, would reclaim it, in Scottsdale, Arizona.

Along the street, a roadrunner tapped its claw feet onto the cement sidewalk, pecking woodroaches from the cracks as Big D passed carrying his own Fatheads tucked under his arm. His cardboard face swayed violently with his stride, as if this avatar of his past were being taken hostage by his present self. He stashed the cardboard cut-outs behind a utility bunker. Bunker because it was adorned in barbed wire, made entirely of brick, and locked with a heavy, tapioca-colored metal door. Facing the six-foot slabs of cardboard toward the building, maneuvering them carefully so that they wouldn't fall, he had nearly made it away unnoticed when a dust-covered Latino with a pencil mustache and a sun-bleached green cap appeared from within the bunker with a gasoline-powered weed whacker in his arms.

"Look," the man said to himself, and stepped out from behind the fence, brandishing his whacker.

It was ten minutes before Big D squawked a Sharpie across his own cardboard forehead and gently inserted his two-dimensional body into the back seat of the landscaper's company pickup. The man had been puzzled to find his favorite actor here in El Clubo de los Reyes. Bruised when, after a little explanation, he realized lesser fates await all those who crossed north of the border.

"Look at me," he told Big D. "I've got a degree in communications. But it's no use in a country that doesn't communicate in your language."

Big D dropped a fat blob of sweat onto the face of his sapphire dial Omega watch, flicked it from the glass surface with his index finger, and saw he had only thirty minutes before the song and dance routine. There was literally a song and dance. Cumbia. He said his goodbyes to the man, prepared his proverbial poncho hood to toss back, and ventured toward the crowd who were all staring into the quivering miasma of rising heat and blinding light surrounding the empty fountain. He'd go back later for the Fatheads, when people lined up for autographs.

Con swagger, as was instructed, he darted into the crowd, levering his arms in such a way to suggest reuniting with family and inviting their hugs. He did hug them, he kissed them. He offered knowing handshakes to the men, stepping back to point with mock accusation, flattering egos with garish assumptions about the previous night's nonexistent festivities. "What kind of trouble did you get yourself into?" "Have fun when the misses went to bed?" Then he looked at their wives like it was love at first sight. He kissed so many hands. People cheered, recited his lines, asked him about new roles. "Always working," he said. "It's one after another. Sometimes, I can't keep the parts separate." The interested buyers came from all over Mexico. Sonora, CDMX suburbs, Toluca. They varied also in age. Each one commented on the great shopping. They hadn't seen such luxury since the trip to La Jolla. But that was so close to Tijuana. They would like something farther from the border. Hence, Scottsdale.

Big D's spirit spiraled in the Catholic light of the fountain. High above, the desert birds, the zigzagging shapes he knew were hawks and the soft, draping shadows he knew were buzzards and vultures, caught the rising heat of the glowing horsemen and rode easy on the draft for a moment. A woman in a yellow dress so tight she looked dipped in it, an investor's daughter, spoke into his neck. "What is this scent you are wearing?"

"It's me," he said. Though she assumed he meant he had sprayed himself with his own designer scent that morning—a scent I had in fact created and that had failed at market—he'd actually run out of cologne and forgotten to apply deodorant before leaving the hotel.

AFTER THE EVENT and most of the crowd had departed, he lingered on for coffee in the staged living room of a deluxe model on Capitan Street with the excuse that he hated arriving too early for a flight.

"Airports," he told Melina, the woman in the yellow dress, "are swarming with too many fans."

Melina had wilted a bit, but she still looked fantastic. She was from Phoenix and had a condo downtown.

"It would be nice to spend some time in a real home whenever I'm up here," Big D said, though he had no plans of ever returning to Arizona.

He sat behind a brand-new Steinway and played one of his father's songs. Melina was so moved, she suggested they find a room upstairs. Lumbering over his groin, Big D told her, "In this house, there is only a living room. None of the upstairs even have floors yet."

"The couch is fine," Melina said.

After, he walked back to his car humming his father's tune, blocking Melina's number and then deleting her contact from his phone. He considered Sandra, mother of his children, momentarily. He promised himself that this time would be different. He'd reclaim his place in the world with honor and respect. He'd be faithful. He'd be good. He searched "how to retrieve deleted contacts" in Safari.

A reddish circle lassoed the desert sky. He had stayed longer than he should've, and he'd have to rush now. But he knew the airport well and wasn't anxious. He collected the Fatheads he'd neglected to bring in with him to the luncheon, popped the Taurus' trunk with his keys, and dropped them in. The company would grab the car from the airport and hold onto his likeness in perpetuity. Turning around, he discovered a young man standing behind him, ungainly and shaking a bit. He would've guessed it was another landscaper, but the kid, and he could tell he was only a teenager as the figure approached closer, was wearing street clothes.

"Hey, are you okay?" Big D asked, thinking now the kid was on drugs.

"I'm fine," he whimpered.

"I've got to get going."

"No, Big D."

It occurred to Big D that the kid might be some sort of deranged fan. A boy with fantasies he wanted enacted under the desert evening sky. But Big D could handle this.

"Listen, I don't have any head shots, but I've got these cut outs. They're better," Big D said, reopening his trunk and pulling out a Big D. "Bigger."

The kid stared at him.

"Who am I making this out to?" Big D asked, the Sharpie cap in his mouth, the cardboard pinned between his elbow and his lifted knee.

From behind him, he heard a voice say, "Los Zetas, homie."

He turned around to see a large man with tattoos on his face and dark, waxing moons of sweat under his swaying breasts.

Big D threw the cut out at the man and attempted to run, but the kid pulled out a gun and pushed it into his ribs. They put a rotting nylon bag over his head and threw him into his own trunk beside his cut outs. He felt them reach into his pockets and extract his phone and his wallet. In the dark, hyperventilating, he heard the trunk slam and felt the car pick up speed as it joined the main road. He had nearly calmed himself when, twenty minutes later, he heard the sudden popping of rocks that could only mean the car was going off-road, into the desert. The car stopped, the trunk lifted, letting in a gust of cold air. Transported into another vehicle's trunk, before it was closed, he was told he was going to die. Crying and spitting up, Big D felt as if he was waterboarding himself. Again? Really? Again?

THE KID WAS Pedro Arrigia of Nuevo Laredo. At thirteen, he'd lost his eighteen-year-old brother, his best friend, to the streets, and told Los Zetas so much three years later when they started applying pressure on him to join.

"Yeah, well, we could just kill you right now if you preferred," a middle-aged man said to Pedro as he tried to walk home from work one night. "This isn't *Saving Private Ryan*, you know."

Pedro slept in a baby-blue concrete room. Once every three months, he and his mother would take out all their furniture and affects onto the street and toss hot water and lye all over the house, scrub the walls and floors with a push broom, rinse the home with cold water, and wait for the house to airdry before putting everything back. The first wash that spring, Pedro left his brother's things outside to be picked off by the neighborhood. His dresser filled with notebooks filled with drawings of superheroes. His bed covered in stains. A pair of gym shoes, the ones he'd been wearing when he'd been shot down. The next day, finding all of the items gone, Pedro walked the neighborhood for hours in search of them. It was during this fruitless walk that Los Zetas approached him again, for what they said would be the last time. When they told him his first job would be to kidnap Delfino "Big D" Ramirez and hold him for ransom in the United States, he was shocked. He'd never been to the United States; he didn't have a visa. Hadn't they already kidnapped Big D and ransomed him for everything he was worth?

"Homie, we're Los Zetas, the Google of Mexico, we have our ways. And leave the logistics to our asset research department."

With an assumed alias and accompanying passport, Pedro boarded an airplane for the first time in his life and arrived in Phoenix Sky Harbor one day before the job. He spent that night being dragged from one strip club to the next by Coko, the enormous man with facial tattoos. He wanted desperately to call his mother, as all Mexicans do, or to run off and disappear into America, even turn himself in to the authorities and beg for asylum, but Los Zetas had told him they'd kill his mother if he did any of these things.

In the safe house in the desert, with the cargo in their possession, Coko started to laugh when the cargo started to squirm.

"Yo, bro, Big D is jonesin'," he said. "Yo, Big D, I knew your ass liked to party, but I didn't know you liked to get wet, motherfucker."

Pedro watched the man convulse.

"Last head that bag was put on got taken off, Big D," Coko said. "If you don't stop moving, the doctor's gonna have to alleviate some head pressure."

An indeterminate amount of time later, the room fell completely silent, and Big D tried and then pretended to sleep, hoping that by pretending he would eventually achieve his goal of leaving this hell, at least mentally. As he drifted between regrets, his nervous system screaming with the effects of opioid withdrawal, he heard Coko ask Pedro what his deal was, why he was so mopey, and listened to Pedro explain his predicament. When Pedro was finished, Coko laughed.

"That's the same shit we've all been through. That's what makes us family," Coko said.

"I have a family," Pedro said, lifting his voice.

"Chill, bro. You *had* a family."

"I had a family."

"I had a family too."

"What happened?"

Big D heard genuine interest in Pedro's voice.

"Where'd your dad go?"

No defensiveness in Coko's voice, genuine interest as well.

"I don't know."

Then Big D heard the unmistakable noise of Coko leaning back in a wooden chair, the sort of settling in for a long one gesture everyone from sea captains to famous ranchera singers used to signify that everyone should probably settle in, this was going to be a long one.

"My old man had this story he liked to tell me. See, my dad, in 1965, he became an orphan. He's living in some village in the middle of nowhere. He's nine and nobody wants to take care of him. Nobody can. So, his cousin takes him on this six-day journey to a monastery. They're riding on donkeys, sleeping on the side of the dirt road, eating these old ass tortillas and fruits from the trees. People come by and try to help them, because my dad's cousin is only like fifteen, or some shit, but his cousin says, 'No, no help. We gotta look poor as possible so nobody steals from us but we can't accept charity either.' My dad's got nothing but some Spanish coins his dad had. My dad said they saw ghosts during this journey. They came to this town that was all made of alabaster and completely empty. He thought they'd accidentally crossed over into heaven, but because it wasn't their time yet, all the dead, all the angels and Jesus and shit hid so that my dad and his cousin would keep going. There was this one guy they met on the road, he was carrying a pistol and his mouth was packed with gauze. He was looking for a traveling dentist who'd skipped town with his money before his appointment. And then there were just like hundreds of women with babies strapped to their backs. All of them were looking for their babies' fathers. Tricky thing was, my dad explained, when you're on the road—and I can relate to this—you meet so many people, and spend so little time with them, you never really know who's alive and who isn't. Anyway, when his cousin finally drops him off at the monastery, my dad realizes he's the only kid there, living or dead. It's just a bunch of old ass monks. They tell him, 'Don't worry, the other kids are on their way.' They teach him how to read and write better, about math, how to take care of animals. He keeps asking, 'When are the others kids coming?' They keep feeding him that same bullshit, 'They're coming, they're coming.' Years pass by. He reads nothing but Bible shit. No kids to play with, no stories to read, just farming and school and Bible shit. Guy can't even get his hands on a newspaper, because that stuff is like devil-worship or something. It corrupts the mind. He gets to thinking, Oh, I'll become a monk and maybe someday I'll get beheaded and become a saint. Like, that's his dream. Then, one day, he realizes some of the monks read newspapers. They leave them sitting in an office or something, and he sees one. He looks into a fireplace and sees little bits of burned newspaper. So, he plans and plans and one day, he steals a newspaper. You know what it says on the front page? 'Man has landed on the moon.' But before he can read the whole article, he hears a monk coming, so he runs away. Then he realizes that his hands are covered in ink stains. He panics. They're going to find out he read a newspaper! They'd never beat him before, but he knows these monks are actually mean. So, he runs to this creek and he claps his hands in the water, and he says the ink comes off his hands in clouds like schools of fish. That's what he said. When he got back, he knew everyone had read that newspaper, everyone knew people had gone to the moon, and he just waited for someone to say something, for something to be different, but no one did, nothing was. He was thirteen. He took those Spanish coins and walked to Mexico City. Got a job. Had me not too long after. And he said, 'Coko, I'm never gonna leave you. I'm never gonna hide the world from you. You're gonna know everything.' He went off to the US when I was eight. Left me with my mom. He sent money. Said we'd be able to join him soon. Then something happened. He said he didn't do anything wrong, but he got caught at the scene of a robbery, a store clerk had been shot and killed. He's still in prison here. People find a way of taking your people away from you. Then you find new people."

THIS IS HOW it was in Arizona. In CDMX, after receiving the ransom note, without her father-in-law around anymore, Sandra immediately called me over to begin working on a solution.

"You have to fix this, Alvin," she said. Having sent the children to her sister's and the maids home, the crumbs of life already accumulating and attracting ants in her kitchen, she stood amongst the ants all alone with me and wept on my shoulder.

In this moment of vulnerability, I shared with her a story I'd never told anyone before, to offer her my assurance. In secondary school, Big D and I had appeared in a play together, it was the one and only time we did, and the play was a Spanish version of Shakespeare's *Othello*. Big D played the role of Othello, of course; my role was and is immaterial. Rehearsals were slogging along. The play, our drama teacher told us, was destined for disaster, but we would face disaster with dignity, as Othello himself does. We rehearsed and rehearsed, performing scenes just shy of understanding, she assured us. Then, one night in rehearsal, Big D put on a British accent and a star was born. The director screamed, "Let's do the suicide scene," and we did. With that British accent, Big D delivered the famous line,

> And say, besides, that in Aleppo once,
> Where a malignant and a turbaned Turk
> Beat a Venetian, and traduced the state,
> I took by the throat the circumcisèd dog,
> And smote him—thus.

confessing to his wife's murder and killing himself by plunging an invisible dagger into his own heart, and it was nothing short of a revolution. When I tried on my best British accent, something Cockney to distinguish between the characters' places in the world, the director shouted, "Stop!"

"Don't you see?" she said. "The accent is Othello's illusion, and Othello's alone. It comes from the same inspired place as his paranoia and jealousy and, therefore, preordains his doom at his very first line. He's doomed as an outsider. An outsider because of his race but also his greatness. No other is as great or as doomed as Othello; therefore, no other shall speak as Delfino does."

She was a young woman, straight out of conservatory. Later that year, or the next, Big D slept with her (I didn't tell Sandra this), and she went on to direct many successful plays on all the world's stages. I did see.

"This world, our world, is not *Othello*," I told Sandra. "It is the world in which *Othello* was performed. Quite the opposite, in fact, it is a world in which we, the rest of the cast, might be doomed, but not Big D, and that is the reason no one speaks as he does, with the accent of the chosen the one. These people will not kill Big D, he is beloved, a national treasure."

Sandra touched her finger to the scar on her lip.

"What are you going to do?" she asked.

"I am going to broker a deal," I said.

"With what money?"

"My own."

COKO HAD GONE out for cocaine, leaving Big D alone with the quiet one who did not kick him in the ribs and who didn't smell like shit. In a brief respite from his opiate hunger pangs, he said, through the bag, "I know you're a good boy. Why are you doing this to me?"

"They'll kill me and my mother," Pedro reminded him, and Big D said nothing.

Then, as Big D lay there in that bitter, hopeless, but contemplative silence, the hope Sandra and I had for him began to take form, in the hardly existent space between his eyes and the rough folds of his hood. This is when it happened, when our Lear, our Othello, our King of Thebes realized God, the gods, had chosen him to be the root of all suffering so that he might be extracted to offer our society some relief. Because salvation is finding your role in your own damnation. Surely, you understand the Greek concept of catharsis. For years, I suffered backpain. Doctors, physical therapists, could offer me nothing. Finally, I was convinced to see a curandera. She put a gardening glove over my face, like those kerchiefs for the dead, and pulled a snake from my belly button. She removed the glove so that I could see it, the snake embracing her hands in the shapes of flyover highways as she held the creature over my head. She killed it by opening its face like a pistachio and made me drink its blood from its hyperextended mouth. After, she sewed its face back in place, cured it like jerky into a coiled medallion, and told me to carry it in my pocket for seven days, then bury it. For seven days, I shat blood; Big D helped me bury the snake at my father's ranch; and I've never experienced back pain since. I started doing gymnastics afterward. In the Arizona desert, Big D recognized in his twisted, sweat-soaked shape on the floor the coiled fetish object of the snake. If he were buried, headless in the desert, the world could finally have some relief.

Sandra, whom he brutalized with the shame of adultery, who touched her scar whenever she was afraid, could be given some relief. She'd spent so much time over the last fifteen years being afraid that she'd nearly rubbed the scar out, as one does the coat of arms from the backside of an unlucky nuevo peso. Their boys, whom I will not talk about because they are minors, could be offered some relief. My father, who loved him like a son—and maybe Big D was his son, and I Francisco's—could die in peace. What a relief. Pedro, the poor boy watching over his drug-thirsty body, could know peace, possibly for the first time in his life, and be relieved as well.

Suddenly, light, and not darkness, blinded Big D. He thought he was dead and, having passed some sort of moral exam, was being ushered into heaven, where he'd sing ballads with his father to God. His flaming eyes adjusted and looked painfully upon an open threshold, then Pedro, the boy leaning over him, pointing at the open door as he started to untie him.

"No!" Big D said. "Put the bag over my head before he gets back! Shut the door!"

Returned to darkness, he could hear Pedro weeping.

"This is my doing," he said to Pedro. "I was your father and I abandoned you."

SANDRA'S FITNESS MAGNATE father had grown tired of Big D and had been begging his daughter almost daily for years to leave the man and take the kids someplace safe, a house with a gym, the kids were miserable and getting soft. Regardless, when I told Sandra of my plan to empty my bank account for Big D's safe return, she insisted on calling the man first.

On the phone, he said, "I told you before, if this happened again, take it as a sign from God to move on. Do you want them to kidnap you too? Or the kids? No money."

Off the phone, before I could put my plan in action, Sandra said, "He's right, you know, my father. And if you think I haven't thought about it before, that if it ever happened again I'd just let him rot, you don't know me or the hell he's put me through, or you're just like him."

"Sandra, you're in shock, you don't know what you're saying," I said. "He was only doing his job."

"He's out there, fucking everything that moves, spending whatever money we have on drugs, and he asks me to send him pictures. He says, more, more, harder stuff. I think, at the front of my mind, for my husband, anything, drink of your wife as milk and honey, not even God would be ashamed. In the back of my mind, I think, but he's sleeping with other women, he wants this too still? He leaves his phone in a bar, a phone with no password; instead of calling the phone company to wipe it clean, he does nothing, and now my own sons can find pictures of the place they came from on the internet."

"A stupid mistake," I said. I'd reprimanded him myself. But what about my *Othello* speech?

"He says the cruelest things to me sometimes. Does he ever tell you that? Sometimes, when he's really messed up, he says I'm the worst thing that ever happened to him. That our children are all a part of my plan to hold him hostage."

I did know. Each time, he'd driven to my house afterward and asked me to beat him in my own home. Each time I told him no, on account of the bruises, how would he explain them? Once, and only once, to offer him relief, I smothered him with a couch cushion. He looked strange under the pillow, like the headless horseman. I gave up long before he gave the safety signal, the thumbs up, because I could feel him growing hard beneath me, and since feared I'd given him a new way to strip the paint from himself.

"The children," I said. "Do you want them to grow up with a headless father?"

To this Sandra conceded, and I arranged my own financial ruin in exchange for my best friend's life.

YOU MAY BE wondering, of course, What the heck is up with this guy? as in me, as in why would I go through so much trouble for this Big D, this scoundrel? To this, I say, more than one man was killed on the Ides of March. Every woman and man I have ever known, I have known through Big D. When in law school I was about to be exposed for cheating on an exam and kicked out of university, it was Big D, not my father, who loosened the itching noose from around my neck and paid off my instructor. When my own mother refused to buy me a puppy as a child, Big D asked for another of his own but told me it was mine and let me come over to his house whenever I wanted to play with it. What else is love?

He arrived from the Arizona desert. He had snacks, jugs of water, a sunhat. A caravan of travelers—Guatemalans, actually, almost all of them children—had discovered him on his journey and shared their supplies. Once my money went through, the Lord delivered Big D into our hands. At the same moment, He delivered Pedro into the hands of the American authorities. Some snafu, some delayed payoff, had resulted in Pedro's passport being flagged, and as he'd attempted to board the return flight home he was quietly escorted to his doom. I've tried to keep up, but I don't know where he is. Maybe in an American prison, maybe incarcerated somewhere in Mexico, maybe Gitmo. It turned out, Pedro was the sacrificial snake to Big D's healing ceremony. My own had been harmless too—non-toxic and even defanged. But Mexicans, even Mexican curanderas, even insured Mexican curanderas, must offer themselves assurances one way or another.

I have never been a fan of those Where Are They Now? shows. Gossipy investigations into the current whereabouts of had-beens. "Leave Britney alone," as they say is what I say. But Big D's story is not over yet, and I will never leave him alone. Though it was a fine enough ending, having him returned to us, I must continue. This is what my life is still about.

Because, to add insult to tragedy, it seemed Big D never drank the blood of his sacrificial snake, or perhaps the snake could have fallen from his pocket before he got the chance to bury it. Not long after his return, Sandra divorced him and took away the kids, and instead of being reborn, he disappeared into the couch on which I had once tried to kill him, and twice I have had to revive him by taking a needle out of one arm and putting another in the other, such that Pedro's unwilling sacrifice was actually for nothing. Pobrecito Pedro, lo siento.

My own path I've always considered a cleft left open; financial death only meant one extraction after another: cars, properties, my own stinking, throbbing body from my own home. But wherever I've gone, as I downgraded from mansion, to condo, to apartment, my friend followed me, carrying the couch on his back, like, well, you know, and this was too much. My own path I've always considered a cleft left open, wide with possibility—feast and/or famine—but to see my friend's life blown apart was the perched bird on the hood of the car teetering on the cliff's edge that finally sends the car over, except it wasn't funny or harrowing.

In his disillusionment, Big D told the derivative auteur hell-bent on rescuing his career to fuck off. I supported him one hundred percent in this, even if it meant leaving his family fortune in purgatory. I kept Big D fed and clothed, he was safe in my captivity, and he held himself for ransom. Things weren't fine, but we had until eternity, and I was ready to lift a Volkswagen over my head when he said when. We ate and watched movies; I tried some of his softer drugs. We lived. I lawyered. We survived. And this was enough until it wasn't. Crying in the tub as I washed his feet one night, he said to me, "If only my father could send me a sign that he still loved me, that he forgives me, even after all of this," and the look in his eye as he peered up at me from under the soap suds invading his face said everything I needed to know in order to do what I needed to do. I began by explaining some things to him. I revealed my designs. After, it was agreed that if I set things right, which I promised him I would, he'd forgive me.

To set things right, I called a private meeting with the studio execs who still held the rights to *Actores Malos*, the name of the proposed cartel telenovela. I stayed up late several nights before the meeting drafting a spec for an alternate show. In the meeting, the execs were impatient and distracted.

"It's fallen apart. The director's out because Delfino is out. He says the show's pointless without Delfino; the meta narrative, he insists, *is* the show. And we've moved on. We're just about done packing next year's lineup. So, we're not even sure why you're here," the senior exec said.

Having seen Big D in *Othello* and suffered through his horrible British accent, I said I agreed with the director. I also told the execs there was no way Big D was going to change his mind about giving up the role.

"But fuck meta-narrative, fuck that director, fuck art and innovation, what the Mexican people need now more than ever is the sweet relief that can only come with the truth," I said. "A true crime biographical telenovela, a tell-all that tells all, truly. *The Story of the Two Kidnappings of Delfino 'Big D' Ramirez*."

CDMX, the place of my youth, the distant memories of my future, played a movie through fifteenth-floor windows.

"We always knew you were an opportunist," one exec said.

"A kind of Donald Trump of the Mexican legal community," another said.

"So, you've come to exploit your friend? To sell his story?" the senior exec said.

I might've grown angry if I didn't already know how cynical these media types can be.

"I am a simple attorney," I explained. "Not an artist. My friend, however, is. And my friend has offered to executive produce and consult in the writing and filming of the telenovela."

This would be enough to unfreeze his assets.

"We already know the story from the tabloids," one of them said. "We're not interested anymore, and if we were, we could just write it and shoot it ourselves. Change some names, bye-bye legal problems. You know that."

I said, "The story in the tabloids has been touched by too many hands, it's been rubbed smooth, like a not-so-nuevo nuevo peso. What I offer is raw and untouched, as nuanced as God's green earth as it was in the beginning, and filled with startling new details nobody knows, not yet."

I resorted to the spec I'd prepared, which covered everything I've covered here. At times the execs seemed intrigued, at others bored. Again, I'm not an artist. In the end, they gathered their response rather quickly.

"We're not seeing it. Besides, we make classic telenovelas. Melodramas. Modern Mexican ancient Greek theatre. This isn't bad, but it's sadomasochism, Dickensian social plight porn. We don't do porn," the senior exec said, exasperated.

Seeing my glum face, I think it was glum, it might've been murderous, one of the younger ones said, "I don't know, maybe work on it some more, pass it around, something might come of it. I mean, the part about the late changes to his father's will seems interesting. There's some genre to that, a little mystery, some conspiracy stuff. But right now, it's kind of a red herring."

"Though, of course, if he did change that, if he added some sort of explanation, even if it made it more interesting, more palatable, marketable, it'd be pure speculation, fiction, he'd lose his whole tell-all angle, which is the only thing giving him a market edge," the wise senior exec said to the younger one.

"Can we be done now?" another man asked.

My moment had arrived. I had them exactly where I wanted them, as part of a narrative that would inevitably involve them too, and pull the writer/auteur back into the project with its meta quality. I told them then what I had told my naked friend from the humid edge of the tub earlier that same week.

"I made the late changes to the will," I said.

One exec chuckled.

"I guess the old man got the last laugh then. They're still frozen, and last I heard, you're broke too."

"I assure you, no one is laughing, in heaven or on Earth. This is what I wanted for Big D. Poverty is the price I've paid for what I've always wanted."

"What are you a lawyer by day and a sociopathic career coach by night?" the young exec asked.

"Should've protected him better," the senior exec said. "I'd have put a detail on him to make sure he didn't get into trouble again."

"You fail to recognize how much I want for my friend. After his father's death, he descended into a mixture of mediocrity and moral depravity. I did put a detail on him, but what is the point of protecting a simple slime ball? After the first kidnapping, I kept contacts within Los Zetas. I contacted one of them, and we worked out a deal for my guaranteed fortune and Big D's guaranteed safety."

"You had him kidnapped?"

The elder exec was incensed.

"Was Delfino in on this?" the young exec asked.

"Big D had no idea. I did it to jump-start his renaissance, both professional and personal. But I have failed again, you see. I misunderstood Sandra. I didn't think she would leave. No woman, not even a woman in a story, not even a woman in the story I am trying to tell, is going to exist solely for the sake of a man's revival. I misunderstood Big D. I didn't think her leaving would matter so much. But not even a man who spends his whole real life treating people like shit is incapable of reckoning with his own wrongdoings."

"He had a fucking show lined up already, why did you derail that?" said an exec who hadn't spoken yet, a woman.

"I wanted to rescue his soul! To bring him back to life. Career success and the return of his fortune with no adjustment of the terms was a bad deal. It was a bad deal!"

The senior exec started, "You understand you're implicating yourself in a very serious crime. This is a confession. We're obligated to—" but I interjected.

"You're under no obligations of any kind, certainly nothing legal and certainly nothing immediate. I'm going to leave this place and turn myself in to the authorities, and they will be obligated to determine my fate via a jury of my own peers."

The men and woman were quiet. I drank water.

Hydrated, I said, "A kid from Nuevo Laredo is incarcerated, Big D is addicted to heroin, and I will soon be going to prison—a small condolence for the awful things I've caused—and you, my friends, will be the last layer of human beings responsible for telling this story that may lead to my friend's redemption, who's currently in a rehab facility in La Jolla, which I have paid for with the last scraps of my money."

Poor now, I was learning a lesson. Big D was poor too, and, therefore, there was hope.

"You're in love with him, aren't you?" the young exec said.

"I'm a dealmaker. I lost a battle so that I could learn how to win a war. Two battles, but it's a big war. And say, besides, that in Aleppo once, where a malignant and a turbaned Turk beat a Venetian, and traduced the state, I took by the throat the circumcised dog, and smote him—thus," I said, opening my hands to the boardroom to suggest this moment was my dagger thrust into my chest.

The boardroom looked at me in disbelief.

"Is that Nabokov?" the young exec asked, astonished. I knew the short story he was referring to, "That in Aleppo Once . . ."

"It's Shakespeare," the woman said. "Shakespeare said it first."

But Big D had said it best.

THE PRIZE

I WAS ONLY A VOLUNTEER contributing remotely from Monterrey. La Fundación's office in Madrid, which had historically managed the annual international poetry competition itself, had been outsourcing editors ever since Mariano Rajoy was elected. Rajoy was out by the time I joined, those Spaniards having finally come to their senses after all those years of austerity. But the work of sorting through the competition's slush pile—that reeking heap of hope and tasteless resistance into which, for thirty euro, any poet working in the Spanish language could throw their own words—had yet to return home.

I had submitted to the contest every year since I was eighteen. Volunteering to help winnow the entries meant refraining from entering for the first time in almost a decade, as LF editors were barred from participating. It turned out to be a record-breaking year for submissions: an even ten thousand entries. I agreed to read two-hundred and fifty of those submissions over the course of two months and submit my top twenty-five. I imagined others, all over the world, doing the same. In an unexpected turn of events, however, I alone inherited all ten thousand and was given a year to read them. The poems arrived all at once, in a plastic-wrapped stack more than two meters tall, in my apartment courtyard. This beaming totem with my name and address written atop its otherwise bald pate, swirling with lizards attracted to the heat of its white, December reflection, was just so J. G. Ballard. I was being inexplicably fucked over by La Fundación, so Kafka.

In Madrid, in years past, there had been, like, forty paid readers—professors, editors, and other literary types. Together, they bailed writers out of political prisons, sent Susana Chávez lookalikes to the forgotten classrooms and community centers of the world, delivered a check of twenty-thousand euro to one obscure poet every February. In Monterrey, there was my girlfriend and me. Together, we read thirteen and a half poems a day in our underwear while we smoked too much pot, obscure poets in our own right. Those folks in Madrid would continue getting all the notoriety for their humanitarian contributions while we would remain obscure, despite our rights, despite our contributions, in spite of our humanity.

You might ask, "How did this happen?" My uncle who works for the city of Santa Fe, New Mexico, has a theory. He says nothing has ever changed between the Spanish and the indígenas anywhere. Old French and Spanish families get away with murder in New Mexico while the indígenas maintain riparian water rights to acequias whose sources are diminishing in our era of climate change and commodified water. "I don't know how those people sleep with themselves, how they live at night," my uncle says. I agree with him entirely. Ten thousand poems. I pictured my girlfriend and myself digging shallow acequias with our fingers, the poems evaporating or else being sucked up by global consumer culture. The twenty-thousand-euro prize at the end of it only added to the disillusionment. I was to pick ten poems for the celebrity judge, who was still unknown. I imagined an old Spanish professor awaiting the product of my labor, my maleficence, his body meat dripping over a leather chair like in a painting by Francis Bacon.

"How could you let this happen to us?" my girlfriend asked when the poems first arrived. Like mottled white doves settling in for the night but for the long haul, the LaserJet printouts molted on the countertops, our bed, the floor, windowsills, and toilet tank, sucked to the airducts. "One day," I said aloud, "I'm going to step on one of these pages and the world beneath it will have eroded and I'll fall right through the center of the Earth, wind up standing on my head somewhere in China."

I thought of the poor poet Susana Chávez. Susana, murdered in her hometown of Ciudad Juárez, who said, *Ni una muerte más* and became *una muerte más*. How, indeed.

"They must've found out my grandma was indigenous," I said, recalling my uncle's theory.

"I thought your grandma was Dutch?"

"That too."

Much of the work in the slush pile was bad. In one poem the speaker would be a male member of the Israeli Defense Force professing his love to a male member of Hamas. In another, a male member of Hamas would profess his love to a male member of the Israeli Defense Force. From what we could tell, none of the poets who'd entered were Israeli or Palestinian. I'm not opposed to interreligious nonheteronormative love poems, radical love, radical empathy, radical hope, radical anything, I want justice and freedom for all people, but when a poem is engineered to be a rhetorical bomb . . . After a while, though, I could no longer blame the poets. For twenty thousand euros, one suspects the world expects only the outlandish: something personal, universal, timely, timeless, and, ultimately, sexy. Loyal to relevancy. I searched foreign obituaries to see if some of the poets were dead. I awaited poems sent by the family or close friends of dead poets. The days crawled, thirteen and a half poems a day, all of the poems supposedly written by the living. At times it felt as if my girlfriend and I were the last people on Earth who could read. Eventually, my girlfriend stopped reading. Eventually, she left.

Deadline after deadline was missed, for nearly a year. One love poem after another, liberating or damning humanity. What was happening in Mexico, the world, my own life, during this time, I had no idea. There were refugees in tents on our side of the northern border, children in cages on the other side, I know this now. But because none of this appeared in the poems, the poems having been written the year or years before, this truth had not come into full relief yet, the way Olivia's leaving did not come into full relief until just right now. Because now, I am looking at the poems she'd enjoyed and set aside for me to consider but never did.

Because I came across Zha Yuanming's "Untitled" first.

Joining La Fundación's volunteer legion of readers (mercenaries) had been Olivia's idea, an attempt to remedy the cynical malaise I'd been suffering. Year after year, I'd read the prize-winning poem and think, My God, the judge picked this out of spite! Winners received news about their achievements from behind bars, in burn wards, in exile. The judges' choices were made to spite the horrors of the world, a courageous act, but back then, I thought, this is empathy in extremis! It was envy.

"Have a say, then," Olivia had said. "Here's your chance."

So, I volunteered.

However, the story of a white male librarian from Fort Wayne, Indiana, earning a spot in *Best American Poetry* under a Chinese pseudonym was already well known. Reality, filled with decapitated heads, was already cast in horror genre ennui. Pickled with the same conditions under which the judges strained to celebrate empathy, before Olivia convinced me to sign up, I had already found Zha Yuanming online, a Chinese factory worker dying from liver cancer. And in that temporary lapse of sanity, between denial of my own mediocrity and acceptance of La Fundación's rejection of my mediocrity, I wrote "Untitled" and submitted the poem in his name. Worst-case scenario, a poor man received a sudden windfall of money and my words lived on in almost infamy, I reasoned, unaware of the batshit responsibilities and opportunities that awaited me.

Olivia's plan could've cured me, you understand. Like flossing, literature can do wonders when you open up to it. And the infinite slush pile did teach me that clever thing about suspicions and expectations around literary prizes: that we're often our worst when trying to be the best, that people (poets) can be forgiven for coming on a little strong. So, I can safely say that I'd have discarded "Zha Yuanming's" poem as soon as it appeared at the top of the stack had the Kafka thing not happened. But the poems took over. Olivia left. I'd wanted access to the Ivory Tower and now I was the only one home. My uncle's postcolonial theory throbbed in my head.

"Untitled" sat on my table, a genuine sin, a real lie, a true coopting of another race and culture, for a whole day without me reading it.

"Olivia!" I called into the paper-white void. (There were still so many poems left). (Between poetry and my graphic design job, I didn't have time to clean up, to find another way of being).

But no one answered back. No one came to sit beside me and talk. I pictured a professor in Spain, who wore greasy rings for some reason. I pictured the enormity of the secret, irrelevant fuck-you of sabotaging an international poetry competition. I reread the poem.

The speaker works in a microchip factory. One of his coworkers is a lady who's always complaining about her love life. The speaker finds her annoying but endearing. In the third stanza, the lady says her boyfriend won't marry her because of the mole on her face. The speaker wishes he could tell her about their boss, who moans her name in the bathroom while rubbing one out each day. Suddenly, the lady disappears; the woman who replaces her says mole-face jumped out a window. Heartbroken, the speaker finishes by saying he's about to crap his pants—he's been avoiding the bathroom all day, fearful he might hear his boss weeping in there.

Can one really ever reduce 1.351 billion lives to a literary device? I wondered. I'd worked in a factory once. I have possessed love for people for whom that love could mean nothing. I have loved people I could not possibly save. When had poetry become so *nonfictional*?

I submitted "Untitled" and nine other poems to the office in Madrid. The following day I received an email stating that the judge, who was a woman, had requested I choose the winner. Tragedy had befallen her family, and this was her relinquishing control, her saying, "Okay, Universe." The person writing the email on the judge's behalf, her assistant, said, "You can do this! You've gotten us this far!" This may sound odd, disingenuous, but I was quite surprised when I awarded Zha first place. Much more surprised than I was a week later when the assistant emailed me again to say Zha was dead.

"Perhaps a relative would accept the prize?? We'll pay to send you out there!"

A friend and former coworker named Lan was the only person I could reach, though she said she'd be happy to accept the prize on Zha's behalf. "I'd like to set up a foundation," she said. In Shanghai, LF set me up in a tiny hotel room with too much furniture. Lan agreed to meet at another hotel, one where her brother worked.

Lan turned out to be a very hip-looking young woman. She wore tall white gym shoes and boxy stonewashed jeans and a big silver mylar coat. In her brother's hotel lobby, still wearing her puffy coat, she handed me a perforated shoebox, pages shifting inside.

"I didn't even know Yuanming wrote poetry," she said in English. "Much less in Spanish."

"Maybe he hired a translator?" I said.

"But then I found those," she said, pointing to the box. "It turns out he was a regular Su Shi."

I opened the shoebox. The poems, typed or handwritten, were in Mandarin.

Lan said, "Setting up foundations is very difficult here, we should take this money and translate and publish the rest of his work."

The irony was as rich as a tarpit.

"Do you still work at the factory?" I asked Lan.

"No," she said.

Then she explained that two years ago, a dozen of her coworkers had marched to the roof of the factory and leapt into the lot below. For months, ghosts rode the elevators to the top in order to jump again. Finally, the facility was razed. Two architects designed something made entirely of safety nets to replace it. Returning to work, Lan had been mystified to find out exactly what that meant. In architecture, even metaphors are material. The floors were nets, she said. The walls were nets; every door and hallway: a narrow separating of two nets. Beneath every window, which was really only a looser knit net, there was the cantilevered crawl of another net, such that if one were to cut or wiggle their way out they wouldn't fall.

"Today, the building appears as a faint, graphite sketch in the sky— the presence of people woven inside incidental," she said. "During breaks the whole place fills with phone chatter. Come winter, when it snows, everything disappears. In the spring, the woven-in people began to hang themselves with the nets. But you don't believe me. Yuanming would've corroborated . . ."

Finger smudge, ink, pulp, and mold rose from the box, the silicified smell of the former shoes. A cardboard heart. The heart, a strange library.

I did not believe her. And suddenly I knew the poems I held in my hands were hers, that if we published them under Zha Yuanming's name, this woman and I would somehow manage to get the same thing out of the same miserable death.

Her brother appeared. A concierge.

"Jacuzzi to celebrate!" he said. "For Yuanming! I'm off in ten minutes!"

LATER, WITH MY body rested inside the gurgling pool, I noticed a mole beside Lan's nose. Her brother was pouring flutes of champagne, and Lan and I were discussing what other poems I could contribute to the collection.

"We only get this one chance?" I asked.

Both she and I had spent years being rejected by publishers. Zha Yuanming's sudden notoriety alone would change that. We'd each be ten thousand euros richer, plus half the advance and royalties of the collection, if we indeed found a publisher. If we couldn't, we'd use the prize money to self-publish his posthumous book.

"Unfortunately," she said, accepting a flute from her brother.

I took one too.

"But there were so many things I wanted to say," I said.

"You can't. For example, he'd have had no way of knowing about Susana Chávez. So, you can't mention her."

"The refugee tents, the children in cages, the looks on all these people's faces?"

"He was already dead," Lan said.

Soaking, drinking my champagne, celebrating, I felt everything fizz up, evaporate in fumes. Ten thousand poems dried their feathers and left. Then I left, came back to Monterrey, wrote poems from Zha Yuanming's perspective for months, mostly about reeducation camps, helped Lan translate, and found a popular press willing to publish Zha's book. When I wrote to see if they needed my assistance again, La Fundación told me the slush pile would be returning to Madrid, where forty salaried readers hungrily awaited the literary challenge. "Good job, though! Poetry owes you one!" I graphic designed. I reread the original ten thousand poems and picked one hundred to appear in an anthology using my notoriety as a celebrity citizen judge, but every publisher I wrote to about my concept replied by saying, "I'm sorry, who are you again?" When I wrote the poets with my idea to publish them myself (using my half of the prize money, since no publisher was willing to bite), they replied, "I'm sorry, who are you again?" I gave up. Lan and I talked on the phone. Sometimes she sounded as miserable as I was, sometimes less.

But that was a while ago.

Now, I sit here rereading the poems Olivia set aside, good poems. I'm also tracking a package currently out for delivery somewhere in the city of Monterrey. A book by Zha Yuanming will arrive in my courtyard by end of day. A stack a few centimeters thick. Advance reviews have been positive. About half the collection's poems are mine. Do they say what I meant to say? I wonder.

On the phone with Lan, I say I want to tell people I'm sorry.

ACKNOWLEDGMENTS

Again, thank you to Linda Swanson-Davies and Susan Burmeister-Brown at *Glimmer Train* for publishing "The Box"—you started my career. Marya Spence, lover of ghost stories, thank you for taking such great care of these stories and of me. Danny Vazquez and everyone else at Astra House, thank you for bringing these stories into the world. Nicole Chung and Mallory Soto at *Catapult*, Stephanie Goehring at and beyond *Conflict of Interest*, Benjamin Schaefer and Kate Bernheimer at *Fairy Tale Review*, Sean Redmond of *fields*, and Fernando A. Flores and Kelly Link—thank you for seeing something in these stories and being the first to introduce them to readers.

Thank you, Rebecca Markovits, Adeena Reitberger, Nate Brown, Amanda Faraone, and everyone else at *American Short Fiction*.

Monica Berlin, Nick Regiacorte, and Greg Gilbert, my Knox family.

Thank you to my family for your continuing love and support. Maggie and Sal Soto, my parents, and Richard and Ginger, my parents-in-law.

My mishpocha, Robin and Eric—*salud!*

David, Frank, Matti, and Zack, thank you, brothers.

Jared Bartman and Abbigail N. Rosewood—thank you for your support.

Napoleon the cat, thanks for your continued flexibility and positive attitude.

RG, I love you. I wrote this book for you.

ABOUT THE AUTHOR

Adam Soto is the author of *This Weightless World*. The web editor of *American Short Fiction*, he holds an MFA from the Iowa Writers' Workshop and is a former Michener-Copernicus Foundation Fellow. He lives with his wife in Austin, Texas, where he is a teacher and a musician.